The Green Gods

The Green Gods

by
Nathalie Henneberg

adapted into English by
C. J. Cherryh

A Black Coat Press Book

Acknowledgements: The publishers should like to thank Kate Wilhelm, Serge Parmentier, Anne-Claire Payet, Bernadette Delrieu and Charles Moreau.

Visit our website at www.blackcoatpress.com

Table of Contents

Introduction

Nathalie Novokowski was born in 1910 in Batum, a city located in the Caucasus region of what was then Russia. Her family emigrated in 1920, fleeing the last combat between the White Russians and Communists. They found refuge first in Sebastopol, then moved to Turkey, Syria and, finally, Lebanon, which was at the time under French control. Curiously, an immigration officer made a mistake transcribing her birth information—her original birth certificate had been lost in Batum—and recorded her birth year as 1917.

Young Nathalie displayed a precocious imagination and ideas ahead of her times, something which made life difficult for her in her family and among other Russian expatriates. Her ambition was to become a journalist, which caused her conservative mother great concerns.

Nathalie declared in an interview that, as a child, she had already written a long fantasy saga in which she imagined what her past lives in Atlantis, Mexico, Ancient Egypt, the Land of the Amazons, Ancient Rome, Poland, Renaissance Italy, Venice, Spain at the time of the Armada, and France during the Crusades, had been like. She used to read the story (which has since been lost) to her younger sister.

Despite the wishes of her Orthodox family, Nathalie attended Catholic school, where the Nuns also commented on her imagination. She passed her *certificat d'études*, which later enabled her to teach French at a school in Damascus, Syria.

There, in June 1936, she met her husband of German origin, an adjutant in the French Foreign Legion, Charles Henneberg zu Irmelshausen Wasungen (born November 2, 1899). Her first two novels, *Trois Légionnaires* [*Three Legionaries*] and *Le Sabre de l'Islam* [*The Sword of Islam*], published in 1952 under the gender-neutral nom-de-plume of Dominique Hennemont to hide the fact that they had been written by a woman, are powerful, first-hand accounts of life in the Foreign Legion. Nathalie and Charles were married on April 23, 1937.

In May 1942, Charles fought at the battle of Palmyra, where his regiment of the Legion which had remained loyal to Marshal Pétain and the Vichy régime, fought and lost to the Allies. The survivors surrendered to the British and the Free France units. Charles was then reassigned to the Free French forces operating in North Africa and fought at Tobruk and El Alamein. He was captured by the Germans, but managed to escape.

In 1946, after the War, when Syria and Lebanon ceased being French colonies, the Hennebergs moved to Paris. This tumultuous, exotic and colorful period of Nathalie's life proved inspirational for several of her later novels, especially *La Forteresse Perdue* [*The Lost Fortress*].

In France, the Hennebergs lived in Asnières, a suburb of Paris, near other Russian expatriates. Because she was a woman, and French was not her native tongue, Nathalie found it difficult to be taken seriously by editors and publishers. Her first short story, "Cécile des Anges" [*Cecile of the Angels*], was published in 1949 in n°12 of *84, Nouvelle Revue Littéraire*, a small circulation literary magazine which also published Georges Bataille, Antonin Artaud, André Dhotel, and translations of Joseph Conrad, Walt Whitman, etc. The same magazine published a second story of hers, "La Terre" [*The Earth*], in n°14 in October 1950.

In 1952, Nathalie, using the nom-de-plume of Dominique Hennemont, sold her first two full-length novels, accounts of the French Foreign Legion, to publisher André Martel. Then, in 1953, having just discovered American science fiction in the newly-created imprint "*Le Rayon Fantastique*" (a joint venture of publishers Hachette and Gallimard), she submitted her own science fiction novel, *La Naissance des Dieux* [*The Birth of the Gods*], to Martel, who promptly rejected it.

8

The novel translated Greek and Norse mythological concepts into a science fiction context. In it, a scientist, an astronaut and a poet discovered they could psychically recreate life, and eventually vied for supremacy, on another planet, which turned out to be Earth in the far future. In accordance with Henneberg's philosophy, the astronaut was the hero, and the poet the misguided villain.

Through her contacts in the Russian community, Nathalie had met Jacques Bergier, a Russian-born scientist, journalist, writer, science fiction scholar and former member of the French Resistance, and, later, co-author with Louis Pauwels of the best-seller *The Morning of the Magicians* (1960). In 1953, Bergier was put in charge of a new genre award, named after J.-H. Rosny Aîné, by Jean Birge, the publisher of Métal's science fiction imprint, "Série 2000." *La Naissance des Dieux* was published there, and, in October 1954, it won the award.

Winning the Rosny Award was a career booster for the prolific Nathalie, who continued submitting stories under her husband's name. One of her stories, "Du Sang sur les Roses" [Blood on the Roses], was published in *Mystère-Magazine*, the French edition of *Ellery Queen's*, in 1954, while several more fantasy stories and another science fiction novel, *An Premier Ère Spatiale* [*Year 1, Space Era*], about the first faster-than-light ship, appeared in 1959 in the prestigious magazine *Fiction*, the French edition of *F&SF*. At the same time, a competing science fiction magazine, *Satellite*, published another of her novels, *Le Chant des Astronautes* [*The Astronauts' Song*] in 1958. In it, mankind fought energy creatures from the far-off world, Algol. Astonishingly, none of her editors realized that Nathalie, not Charles, was the real author of these works.

"Charles Henneberg" now being a household name, the editor of *Rayon Fantastique*, George Gallet, invited "him" to submit works. For the next five years, from 1959 until the demise of the imprint in 1964, Nathalie Henneberg published five novels at *Rayon Fantastique*: *La Rosée du Soleil* [*The Dew of the Sun*] (1959) told the adventures of the four crewmen of a spaceship stranded on the fantastic alien world of

Bellatrix; *Les Dieux Verts* [*The Green Gods*] (1961); *La Forteresse Perdue* [*The Lost Fortress*] (1962); *Le Sang des Astres* [*The Blood of the Stars*] (1963), a colorful gothic fantasy in which an astronaut from the year 2700 journeys to a medieval Earth-like world ruled by kabbala, where legends live, and where he eventually falls in love with a female salamander. Finally, the mammoth *La Plaie* [*The Plague*] (1964), her masterpiece, was a sprawling 600-page novel that told of the desperate battle by a handful of humans and angel-like mutants against a wave of pure, malevolent evil sweeping the galaxy, and which incarnates itself in the bodies of the "Nocturnals."

As Charles had died of a heart attack on March 20, 1959, all the publishing agreements were signed by Nathalie, who, at first, claimed to be merely completing unfinished manuscripts left by her husband (hence the intermediate twin credits on the middle books in the series), until finally claiming full credit for her work. Many critics continued to credit her earlier works to her husband, until much later when incontrovertible evidence was produced that definitively set the issue at rest: Nathalie Henneberg was always the sole author of all the works published under her late husband's name.

Despite her considerable literary success, Nathalie's financial situation after her husband's death remained shaky. She earned additional income by translating texts from the Russian and working as a contract analyst for the CERST, a public department reporting to the French Prime Minister. In March 1963, a novel entitled *Demain, le Ciel* [*Tomorrow, The Sky*] about a European space agency, remained unsold because it was too different from her other more flamboyant productions.

Her short stories began being collected in various books, and, in 1976, she wrote a less than successful sequel to *La Plaie* entitled *Le Dieu Foudroyé* [*The Thunderstruck God*].

Unfortunately, struck by sickness and frail health, she lost her job and ended up living in relative poverty, dying at Hopital Tournon in Paris on June 24, 1977 from an intestinal blockage. Her last novel, *Les Cinq Danses de Nitocris* [*The Five Dances of Nitocris*], was lost with a good portion of her manuscripts and personal papers.

Nathalie Henneberg was a leading figure of French science fiction and fantasy of the 1960s, alongside Stefan Wul, Kurt Steiner and Gérard Klein. Her use of the French language, betraying Russian and mystic influences, and a deep knowledge of history, was highly poetic and unusually well-suited to creating larger-than-life heroic characters and epic romances. Like the British and American masters of the genre, Nathalie Henneberg knew how to build full-blown, intricately detailed baroque and colorful universes.

Charles Moreau
Avignon, March 2010

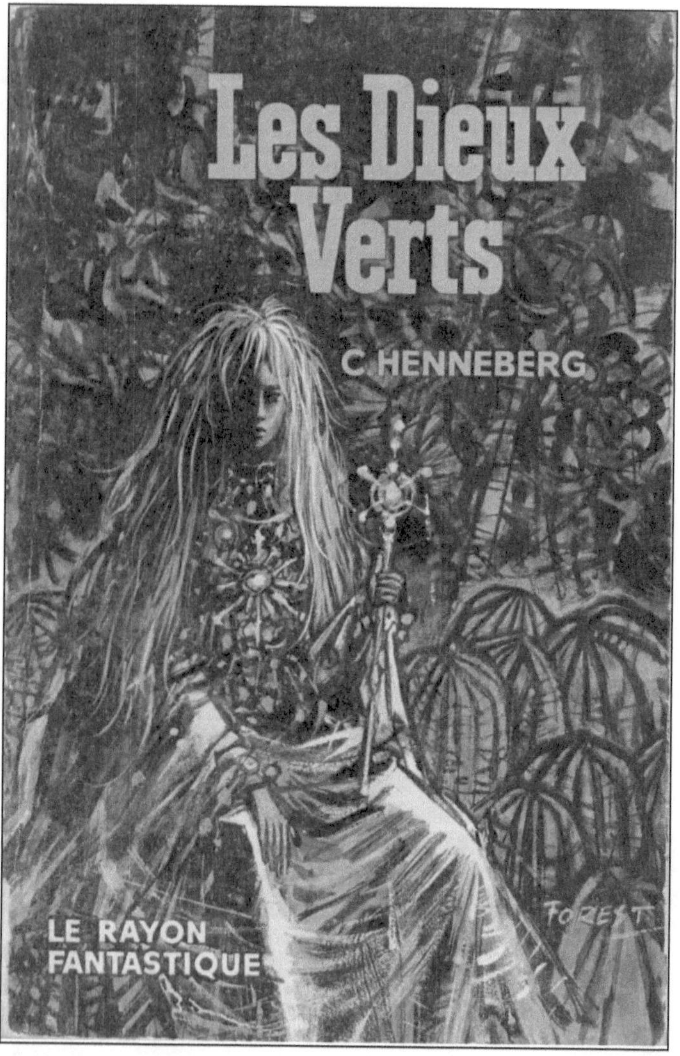
Les Dieux Verts
C HENNEBERG
LE RAYON FANTASTIQUE
FOREST

THE GREEN GODS

I

Life had won.

On Earth it was the year 2000 of the cosmic reckoning—and of the green night. The great cataclysm which had once ravaged the world was dissipating in the eternal passage of time. A few sacred books, graven on jade and onyx and fixed to their altars by chains of orichalc, recorded that the world's death had come from the stars. One day, Earth's magnetic field had shifted, the earthly shell had burst, and the world's outlines had undergone profound changes. Oceans left their limits, overwhelming continents. A rain of meteors paved the mountains with jeweled fire. Two unprecedented moons—one blue, one green—rose over the horizon.

Human colonies scattered on the habitable planets of the galaxy tried in vain to observe the outcome. The new magnetic field, 100 times more powerful than the old, created an impenetrable barrier of cosmic particles; the clouds of Venus have the same origin. No voyager from space could force that barrier. By the thousands, pilots battered themselves against it; they drifted thereafter in Earth's wake, in their glittering steel coffins. The galaxy's scientists comforted themselves with the prediction that the force of it would diminish in several thousands of years. It was supposed that such phenomena had happened before and that Earth's magnetic field resulted from them.

The dream-ridden planet entered its long absence from the great harmony of the Free Stars.

But on the world's surface, life went on. In the southern hemisphere a continent rose above the floods and a great many survivors found a landing there. Then followed a savage struggle for possession of this ruin-covered bit of Earth; all

13

madness unleashed... until the day a demigod established his hegemony there. As in the Sumerian tales which spoke of another deluge, he was handsome and wise, and he came from the sea.

His first act was to bring order to mankind, and to take from men their most dangerous weapons. These were destroyed or hidden away, and what survived of mankind could breathe easily again.

Was so radical a measure too hastily applied? The god who called himself Hellemar had seen that man was his own worst enemy. He himself did not live long enough to see the mutations... but his work would last. He outlawed war among humans and established a rigid caste system to minimize the effects of the radiations. He restored the cities and tried to preserve what was left of civilization. Then he died. A dynasty ruled in his name.

And centuries passed.

Or millennia.

By the time spectrographers at Altair had noted a decided weakening of Earth's magnetic barrier, three powers existed on Earth.

There was the fading Empire of Man, founded on the site of a forgotten land named A-atlan, or Mexico.

On its borders, in the jungles, rose the warlike kingdoms of the wearers of antennae and chitined wing cases.

After a wild mutation which began with the cataclysm, insects, particularly the scarabs, grew as much as three meters in height. They became the dominant species then—not superior in all senses, far from it. They peopled strange cities, termite hills of beaten earth, riddled with subterranean passages. Indeed they progressed, but their instincts ruled them. Their evolution was fixed in the ways of the anthill and the hive. They were fast-breeding, brash, cruel, and thick-witted. Any alliance between them and mankind was impossible. And most of the great vertebrates had perished.

In the heat of the greenhouse effect which had settled over Earth by reason of the cosmic clouds, plants had become another matter entirely. The simultaneous explosion of all the storage sites of plant hormones was surely a primary cause of their mad proliferation. The drowned Earth covered itself in forests which devoured the fields and the cities and surrounded the waterways. In jungles of ferns, living walls of spore-carried plants moved upon the continents. In all instances the progressive species among the plants were quickly limited to the cacti and to certain orchids. Cultivated especially in cities and moving only with great difficulty, the orchids in particular had allies in every copse. They made themselves indispensable to their hosts. It became evident that these conquerors-from-within brought out of their long history—strange riches: seven or eight additional senses, a mathematical forevision, and certain powers of hypnosis.

They offered humanity a "fraternal communion"—a sharing of flesh and blood... in the form of the juice of the peyotl, the pulp of the poppy, and the incense of the Indian hemp, all of these in great strength. Each city had its Green Temples, its Colleges of Dream, its distilleries of visions. This bliss was given gratis. One could forget all his worries and his wounds, sunk in bottomless cotton-wool; one would imagine himself a plant, or a butterfly, or a beetle armed with cruel pincers. Every instinct was satisfied. There were no consequences—until one awoke at the end of the reckoning.

And when the Empire of the Sun, consumed by vile radiations and its orgy of drugs, tried to awaken—it was too late. Instead of the precise science which humanity had lost, there were rites of plant or mineral origin. Plants were now in the city, and they divided the inheritance of man.

And the Holy Council which ruled the land of A-atlan reckoned itself 70% plant.

At the thin edge of dawn, the immense city, built by the survivors of the cataclysm, witnessed the fall of its god.

The slanted sides of the pyramids and the surfaces of the zodiac wheels reflected it. The colossus fell without quake or tidal wave. Set at the entrance of the harbor, the white onyx shape, face uplifted to the wide universe, represented man, that vanishing species. Its whiteness symbolized the Children of the Sun, and the sculptor had made it in the likeness of Hellemar, the god arisen from the waves. Its features were hard and perfect.

For eyes, the artist had set two huge black diamonds. In that age, they had known the secrets of ensorcelling light into such stones, and these twin lamps for centuries had brightened the paths of sailors on the seas.

One night the fires had gone out and no one had known how to relight them.

And on another night...

Startled awake on their terraces, the radioactive, mahogany-red Giants and the graceful Elnyans (whose jeweled corselets and antennaed diadems made them look like moths) searched in vain between the Council palace and the queen's gardens for a statue 100 cubits high, whose crown had sheltered eagles.

The whole population was stricken with a terrible foreboding, well knowing that the gods express themselves in signs. It was an ancient people, and very noble; its records went back before the cataclysm; it was even rumored that they had brought it on themselves—but of course the plants and insects vied in inventing such slanders. At least, the people had hoped to the very last that salvation would come to them from the gods and the stars—as it knew their ruin had come. Senseless hopes, if there were any hopes in them.

The Sun rose on the mauve rim of the east, as the chanting mob reached the palace of Uxmal, the prince regent.

In the center of a porphyry foundation sat that baroque residence, made of broken bits of ruined temples. Heritage of the House of E-enor, it charmed the eye with its polished artistry, its grandeur, the grace of its ornaments. Its galleries were surrounded with wind harps, and in the halls, which were shaded and cool even in bright midsummer, the vaulted ceilings shone with a glow of moonstone.

A thousand voices summoned. The prince appeared on the balcony, a jeweled figure clothed in violet byssus. His hands and his ivory brow were traced with green veins; after a certain age humans lived swiftly—and little. Two Elnyans whose masks—Persian-blue phosphor—imitated the wings of Mexican moths, fanned him with peacock feathers. Below him, the grieving crowd moaned.

"The human gods are dead!"

The harbor master stepped forward, a man wearing a helmet with knobbed antennae and bearing a lance of white coral. He belonged to the warrior caste, serving the radioactive ascendancy of the 70%.

He struck the drum. "The god Hellemar is gone," he declared. "Tonight, between the two moons, we saw him topple and sink down into the abyss. There you can still see him, where the road ends. Fifty cubits down, his helm gleams among the algae and the starfish. The lord has fallen!"

"The gods of men are deserting the Earth," the mob chanted.

Uxmal listened to this musical wake, taut with rage. Not a one of them protested this interpretation of events, this death sentence on humanity itself. To a man they raised their noise; unmixed, three chords bore witness to their grief.

The human race, irradiated from the time of the cataclysm, had suffered from it in differing degrees. The DE (Direct Exposure) victims were slaves, wearing the shape of toads, their faces as green-crusted as old pagodas. They abased themselves, crawling in the dust. The mahogany-red radioactives were the warrior caste; quetzal-plumed, they smote their shields. And the Elnyans, whose distant ancestors had lived in shelters, as if shelters could save them, looked like some languid cluster of nocturnal moths.

"We shall go see," Uxmal said.

He descended the stairs in his star-broidered robe. Around him the rose-colored platform was clean and polished. No plant was witness, fortunately, to this defeat. A sedan chair borne by lower hexapods awaited him below. Guards armored

17

in golden wing cases, with eyed helms—the better to mime the insects—parted the crowd with blows of their short lances. For years the regent had avoided public appearances. The land was well-governed without him. He was loath to leave his sheltered palaces, his wind harps, and his singing manuscripts.

The chair made slow progress. A great silence had fallen over the square; not a breath, not the rattle of a drum disturbed it. The streets through which he traveled were a carpet of bent backs and beseeching hands. Uxmal felt a sudden chill; they *knew,* and suffered with him.

The prince regent had no need of signs and omens. He carried in his own veins the last Sunborn blood, pure of radioactivity, and with it the very damnation of the human empire. He could no longer doubt that Time was drawing to its close. The great cataclysm had given Earth over to deaf powers, to the emanations of a land in torment. Today there was only boiling and ferment, plumes of smoke spreading over volcanoes once reckoned extinct, and torrents of hot mud gouting down their flanks. Around the city, mimosas reached unprecedented heights and ferns cracked rock. The forest was on the march.

Man himself was sliding down the slope of shadows. He had already lost his soul and his gods. Soon he would lose his very shape.

When they reached the quays, the chair halted. Uxmal dismounted and leaned over the sapphire waters. Of course; it must lift to the sight of the condemned that human perfection—the prince regent made out the form of the colossus, sunk beneath the weeds which would soon devour it. In a white face of pathetic beauty two vast eyes begged for help. The regent shuddered. The weed-shrouded god resembled the sea lord, his own son. According to forgotten rituals, this was his mystic double. And no one knew at the moment where the fleet of Prince Aran lay.

A sounding of trumpets, a strident blare of sea conchs, invaded the Sunborn's musing. He lifted his head and looked.

A procession was coming down the quay.

The marble jetty extended to the white, terrace-girt pyramid which towered over the deeper gardens. This was the Council palace, a terrible building, so secret that people avoided even looking on its gates. At the moment, its two doors were wide open. In a silence which became palpable, a solemn procession came out toward the port. The chanting mob gave way before it. The prince regent stood alone, face-to-face with his enemies.

As in his nightmares, all flight was impossible.

The stapelias came at the head of the train, yellow and purple and violet-spotted, like sacs of leather. By some caprice of the radiations, they stood two or three meters high and trailed after them a skein of prehensile roots. From the time of the great catastrophe, human science had wondered—these plants, torn out of the earth... what feeds them? But move they did. A line of faucarias that opened great pale flower cups, cavities of fearsome jaws... like wolves, like caimans, like cats, they surrounded the procession. Beyond them the cereus speciosus and their cousins the flagelliformis raised spikes of rosy flowers and fleshy spines with sulphurous cups, spattered with blood. A heap of precious stones that was the lithops. Wool-topped rackets, grayish hued, distinguished the doddering Old Man cacti, the cephalocereus.

They are all there, thought Uxmal, *the praetorians, the magistrates, the councilors.* A vast horror enveloped him. These plants were—human.

The most precious of them, the most delicate, had themselves carried on crystal thrones by Elnyans of noble blood. Thrones... no, *vats,* cubes filled with transparent rose fluid, in which white and green filaments writhed. These were the truly strange ones, resembling jewels, or lips. For some of them it seemed that nature in a moment's madness had used plastic, or leather, or minerals. They bore ancient names which had ceased long ago to have meaning for anyone; they were as beautiful as women or as terrible as nightmares. But all were flesh-eaters... the violet oncidia, the palpitating moth orchid, the tiger-striped schilleriana. The cattleya labiata was a rosy open mouth; the giant albans were formed of pale, translucent membranes, and the anthuriums glistened like hearts laid bare, lacquered with blood.

A heavy vanilla perfume flowed like a wave over the land.

Uxmal closed his eyes as the last contingent crushed him with horror: green gourds, severed heads of bloated buddhas, the echinocacti williamsi, commonly called peyotl.

The prince regent forced himself to open his eyes. Motionless, transfixed with horror, he watched the enemies of his species advance—his successors.

The hindmost of the peyotls, high priest A, had the proportions of a great world globe. Twelve Elnyans lowered his chair to the ground. Eyeless, mouthless, he was yet in full communication with the universe, and Uxmal received full in the face the overwhelming, acid thought which came from this gently swaying monster.

Behold the end of the human gods, Uxmal. A new age is beginning.

"That of the green gods, is it?"

What matters the form which clothes the spirit?

"Spirit?" asked the regent coldly. "Have you a mental dimension like ours? Or a moral one?"

A logical one, at least, said the globe. *We have waited so long, all these ages, the Tertiary, the Quaternary... Now our hour is at hand. And think of it, Uxmal, nothing can stop us. Not even a being of your own flesh and blood.*

"I know," said Uxmal, his teeth clenched. Drops of sweat beaded his saffron-hued temples.

(He does not.) But these overseas expeditions are in vain. Man's destiny is sealed. What power can you set against the cycles of destiny? What hero, what god? The last of them is dead, with Hellemar. Where will come this help for the human race?

Uxmal turned away and held his inmost thoughts to himself. But someone answered for him. At the instant the company had passed beneath the pyramid, on the Tower of the

Equinox, over a nacreous, prismed sea, the Waker of the Day had seized his beryllium hammer. Now the first blow struck that great shield suspended between two pillars, the shield men said had once belonged to Hellemar himself.

A sound pure as a harp note cleaved the air. Below, the crowd stood motionless, listening. Faces lifted. An omen, it was an omen from heaven. Brazen echoes filled the harbor. For a measureless instant the two assemblies listened—and with them the city and the bloody sea. The enormous echinocactus rested easily on his litter, but Uxmal felt the air saturated with his fury.

Twenty-two blows could warn the empire of invasion.

The 23rd meant the return of the fleet.

At that 23rd blow, the whole city sighed with ecstasy and hurled itself toward the harbor.

The ships of the Lord Prince Aran appeared across the horizon.

II

Aran was to present himself before the Council, that assembly 70% plant.

But he did not come.

Prince regent Uxmal returned late into his own palace, bewildered by the unusual comings and goings in the halls. Torches were lit, of aromatic resins and incense. There was burning of benzoin and myrrh. Servants moved at a run. Amazed, Uxmal discovered that Aran had come ashore alone in a small boat, at a secret cove. The Council had waited in vain. Aran had marked his return with his wonted insolence.

The Elnyans added that the sea lord was at his bath and that he would make haste to greet his father in the throne room. But the prince regent, on the edge of his nerves, went down to the bathing pool instead.

Night had fallen over the Empire of Man, a night like other nights since the end of human time, with the moons divided into overlaid discs, the halves of which fled according to precession. The air was hot, stifling, heavy with perfumes, as if an enormous suction drew up the moisture of the world and distilled the green juices of it. Uxmal sensed in it an assault. Everything sprouted; every plant climbed sunward with the violence of a prisoner bursting his shackles. The leaves were tentacles and the flowers were mouths. In their pale cups they distilled poisons.

The regent blessed the foresight of his family, which had built the palace of E-enor in the center of a polished esplanade. No seed could cling there. The joints between the porphyry blocks were invisible. Here at least men could trust that they were alone.

Uxmal descended the steps to the bathing pool—shaped in plain onyx, those steps. The water was milky with perfumes, and he searched the reflections for his son, in vain.

Overhead, asteroids danced in the naked dark… debris of forgotten stars, relay stations of a broken celestial pathway—

"Aran!" the prince regent shouted.

Suddenly a lithe body thrust away from the far rocks, made an arc on the surface. There appeared—scattering opals and crystals of moisture—a gleaming profile, a shoulder, nothing more, like the sunken god. *If the men of old looked like him,* thought the prince of E-enor, *they were destroyed by a jealous Heaven.*

Then he silenced his very thought, for others could read it, and it was therefore dangerous. He saw his son coming toward him like victory incarnate.

Aran cleaved the water like a sea creature. His dark-gold hair clustered and shone on his brow, and the measured strokes of his arms, the concentration of his upper lip, betrayed his delight. Then with prodigious swiftness, rising up out of the depths, a scaly black shape came up in his path, and a tail as large as an oar beat the water. Uxmal choked back a cry of anguish. Two cubits from Aran, a flat, moon-sized head had broken the surface. Enormous beaks gave a coquettish smile, globular eyes bulged at the sides. It was horrible. The regent recognized the warm-water squid.

Lounging on the pavings, the graceful Elnyan servants clapped, and the vast shadow met the swimmer.

For that instant the two forms, dark and bright, danced, entwined, a deadly duet, and the squid's beak shone through the spray. Then the man thrust his arms up before him and his fingers gripped the scales with terrifying strength. The beast writhed like a vine and tried to drag its adversary to the bottom. *He's mad,* Uxmal thought. *He means to kill the thing bare-handed!*

The desperate force of his thoughts reached the swimmer, who grinned at him. The vise of Aran's hands closed again, the powerless tail beat the water, and then two red globes drifted up and the triangular gullet spat blood.

The squid detached itself like a dead branch and retreated in an eddy of water. The Elnyans shouted for joy.

"Aran," growled the prince regent. "Have you finished your little game? Come!"

The sea prince lifted his eyes to the rocks, turned back to his father a second dazzling smile. Then while the dead beast passed him on the current, he climbed out onto the edge of the pool.

"It's stronger than I," he said. "I had to celebrate my homecoming with a victory—a rather shabby victory, to be sure—over a monster. Don't worry. We haven't yet deified the ocean."

The Elnyans had just cast over his shoulders a cloak of silver byssus. The sea prince was so tall that the palace guards were dwarfed beside him. The regal lines of his brow, the shocking touch of pallor, and in his features—a mixture of daring and spirituality—made him truly the double of the Sun god. He laughed. But his eyes were somber and cold enough to frighten a man.

Uxmal embraced his son with savage pride.

"All the same," Uxmal said, "it would have been more appropriate to salute the Council first, instead of playing games with that beast."

"The same game, isn't it?"

The regent groaned. "Aran, I've so much to tell you—"

"So have I. Come. There's Queen Maos' sanctuary."

The Elnyan servants withdrew, a ballet, their moiré cloaks like a fluttering of wings. Aran shrugged his shoulders. Father and son retreated together amid the selenite harps and the green jade columns.

In the center of the Hall of Sport, a tower overshadowed the palace. They went in that direction, and Uxmal produced a golden key. Legend said that this keep, built by a sinful and beautiful princess, was impenetrable to telepaths and proof against radiation. It was not properly a religious place; the spiral staircase led to a high chamber, silent and bare. According to legend, Queen Maos had hidden here a condemned man, who happened to be her husband.

Uxmal settled there on a chrysolite throne and Aran seated himself at his feet. The regent's golden eyes plunged into Aran's as into icy lakes; the two men talked together after that silent fashion common to the ancients, telepaths, for the world of Hellemar's age had known and used the electrical emanations of the brain.

"You should never have left," said Uxmal.

"You know well enough I had to."

"And what good could this expedition of yours have accomplished?"

"That we know our condition. They say that humans played games with science, that they outraged the stars, and that the world died—at their hands. That some relentless justice is punishing our species and that we have no recourse."

"You bring us some hope?"

"What would you call hope? The discovery of a past that proves the supremacy of the human race? The surety that this world has known several endings and still lives? Or most precious of all—that other minds are fighting along with us against this degrading slavery? Yes, to the first two questions. No, to the third."

"Too much and too little."

"Our gain is still enormous. Our voyage has broken that circle of interdicts that chains us to this Earth. Remember," Aran added, folding his arms about his smooth knees, "remember what furious opposition I had to overcome to go to sea. They refused me even the timber for my ships, under the pretext that there just might be some intelligence maturing under that bark. They refused me access to aeronautical and naval libraries. I had to be satisfied with dead wood and with frameworks preserved in the museums. I don't complain. I chose the most ancient ones, like swans stretched on the water. I had to build my ships with my own two hands, I and my Elnyans...

"And then came the battle over the crew. I had to fight the fear and the cowardice of this over-petted race. They were princes and dancers, these Elnyans—not sailors. They had nightmares. And I was reduced to drafting fugitive slaves and outlawed warriors.

"But I had my fleet *and* my crew, and finally we sailed. *That* was a day of victory."

Aran shut his eyes and saw again that singular dawn of pearl and purple when, confidently, after such great effort, his galleys had turned their bows toward the open sea. How frail they had seemed on that violet gulf! But he had believed in them. In spite of the Council edict, all the people of A-atlan had massed since that dawn on the shores, with palms and sistrums and kettledrums. Isolated, held captive in the power of green magics, the mob worshipped in Aran the last child of the Sun, the last human being it might elevate into its pantheon.

Then the triremes did appear. Garlands of shells and smoky crystal and torches graced their bows. Their purple sails beat like wings. Columns of incense boiled up from their decks, and slowly, majestically, amid perfumes and music... the whole Empire was singing *The Water-Walkers...* the great black swans filed past the shores, then spread out and launched forth into the unknown.

For centuries the oceans had been forbidden to man.

Like the stars.

The plants scarcely took note of this event—did they?

"I went to sea," Aran said further, "led by a blind hope. I really thought I might discover somewhere else the things we lack here: brains and hearts. I thought I might find human civilizations more vital, more sane than our own. I dreamed of allies, and of brothers. So did you, once."

"You found nothing. Didn't you?"

"But I did. Their monuments. Speaking-stones. Dead cities. We went down into the depths, you know. Tzental, my first captain, was a great help to me—the bravest Elnyan I know. We learned how to decipher their inscriptions. And it's all true: Men in the past were the sole masters of their world, and their spirit was equal to almost anything. But by experimenting with matter and energy, they brought their end on themselves—for that is also the terrible truth: They no longer exist, at least on this world."

"Tell me the rest of it," said Uxmal.

Uxmal had reassured himself first with a long look about them. They were *truly* alone. The porphyry dais, the jasper and polished onyx walls, reflected the divided Moon. They made a barrier, fortunately, between the princes of E-enor and the green world of mad sepals, of flower cups opening like screaming mouths.

Calmly, in an ordinary voice, Aran spoke of his voyages.

"You recall," he said, "that we left the port of Helia after the equinox, in the month of the Balance—the verge of spring in this hemisphere. The ocean—quiet after the great storms— let us into its deep atolls; and after being there I refute the theory of the plants; they see in the archipelagoes the reflection of the Pleiades, but they're only the debris of old continents... In the northern hemisphere, the cataclysm loosed far more violent earthquakes and there aren't so many islands.

"And on those that do remain, the beaches are all white sand, barren, scoured by powerful tides, with here and there shining bits of fish scale, or the shells of sea turtles. No other forms of life. No ruins. Men of the atomic age built in perishable materials, and their cities nearest the epicenters of the cataclysm have totally vanished. On a reef there was a stele, and I could read one name on it: *New York*."

"One of their great cities," said Uxmal. "A city of their West."

"Since the axis of the world has shifted, we can't really judge longitudes."

"And then?"

"We sailed on, carried by the currents. We wandered very far across that desert of waters. Then the keels of my ships glided onto a submarine forest of kelp. We skirted there a chain of undersea mountains, and the sounding lines were lost in those chasms. Then on a day when we were at the end of our hope, we saw a dim line on the horizon, and my men shouted for joy. They thought we had reached the divine continent."

"But it wasn't Europe?"

"No. Africa. The configuration of the coasts corresponds to the old atlases, but the center of it is hollowed into an inland sea. We launched boats and found harbor in an inlet. The shore was sandy, the climate searing hot. Our scouts came back; they had seen giant termite hills, and witnessed a fierce battle between crabs and frogs. Everywhere the lower species had reached an unheard-of size and strength."

"And the plants?"

"Less numerous and diverse than they are here. Africa is entirely desert. But the heat was becoming unbearable; the hulls of my ships were steaming. Medusas attacked one of the boats. We left that harbor. And on a rock there were some apes shaking their hairy arms at us…"

"Beasts?"

"Beasts," Aran said shortly. "There was no growth on their foreheads."

"Then?"

"Well…" The prince hesitated. "You recall the gear I had tried to repair… a sort of armor with transparent helmets?"

"The diving suits."

"You know what they were. Thank you. Well, with those, Tzental and I visited Europe. Underwater."

Silence reigned. A fountain wept into a basin. That was the funeral dirge of the divine continent.

"And what of matters here?" Aran asked abruptly.

"Here," said the prince regent, "the world consists of one species which is thriving and one dying. The forest is closing in on us, and more and more of our very lovely Strangers are uprooting themselves from their garden plots. They are more resistant, more resilient, more wise than we are. They're multiplying. They'll occupy 75% percent of the Council from now on."

"The Elnyans then… have no more descendants?"

"You know how it is. From your own time, we live under the sign of the Beast. Now the births of regressive mutations are in the majority, and we have had to pass very stringent laws."

"What—we?"

"The Council."

"I thought," said Aran, "that the Council let humans decide human matters."

"Impossible."

"And these laws are, specifically—"

Uxmal shrugged. "They state that the evil is the result of the mistakes of one species, and they decree death for any creature tainted with a growth on the brow. But the women of the lower castes hide their little ones and carry them out at night to the edge of the sands. Some of them have been stolen away by the anthropomorphs."

"Is that all?" the sea lord asked bitterly.

"It is. We're still at war with the Malthodes—you know them: the evolved scarabs. We're laying siege to a little town right in the middle of anthropomorph territory—Mega."

"That proves that the Malthodes are dull-witted brutes."

"Meaning?"

Aran shrugged. A strange light passed through his eyes, but it was not his true smile... dazzling. "Not much. But that barren region is swarming with creatures marked with the sign, meaning hunted and harried. No plant ventures beyond the edge of the sands. And a force that has no hope is a pitiless weapon in the hands of a strategist."

"You're thinking of *that,*" the regent stammered.

"Yes. Now I'm thinking of that."

In sudden violence, the father seized and gripped his son's hands. They communicated by the pulse of their blood and Uxmal sent the sea lord his fear and his fever.

'Take care," Uxmal said. "Someone has betrayed you. Or they have read your thoughts. You are in terrible danger."

"What danger can still touch us?" Aran asked in sudden weariness. "We've lost everything, haven't we? Hope, and now human pride as well."

"Tomorrow," Uxmal said, "you go to present yourself to the queen."

"Yes. So says the law."

"She's grown up."

"A perfection, I'm sure."

"She looks the very image of Maos, the princess of dreams. She'll be 18 this moon. And her wedding flight is at hand."

"Ah." Aran lifted his head. In his father's eyes he read a nameless dread. "Of course," Aran murmured. "They've thought of *that.*"

III

For venturing into the forest the Elnyans and the Sun-children used armor which had been forged in ancient times, of unbreachable plastics. Each family possessed such suits, ages-worn, iris-hued, glittering, and once used by the conquerors of the stars. Aran had not put on his cuirass for five years; he felt it creaking in the joints. And standing in front of a mirror he discovered a resemblance to some great scarab, a chitined warrior.

Always these correspondences and symbols, he thought perversely. *Do they exist or are they the taint of our age? All species change surely, but not to that extent.*

He had waited for the darkest hour of the night. The two moons were running behind clouds the color of emerald, and the darkness had the transparency of green crystal. Aran was not willing for his father to know to what meeting he felt called. He owed Uxmal a tender affection, a somewhat pitying affection, for he had found him feeble and almost... *used.* Aran carried on his fight and defied destiny on his own account.

A chariot drawn by white silk moths was waiting for him at the secret gate of the palace. Since the cataclysm had destroyed almost all the vertebrates, certain large insects had filled their niches. Even to Aran's observation the caprice of the mutations was strange. The butterflies were grand and graceful, but their intelligence had not much advanced. Yet it seemed that the beautiful racehorses of the past had not been very intelligent.

The insects' relationship with plants, however, remained close. Eagerly some gray-lace algeronia or flame-colored tiger moth would fly over the Council gardens—and vanish. These fragile creatures still lived less long than men. Aran reckoned that the plants in their particular case had failed a necessary

31

mutation. Or perhaps they preferred to be completely superior to these creatures which touched them most intimately.

The prince caressed the moths as he passed, their narrow heads and the splendor of their faceted eyes. The glittering wings beat. He took up the reins.

He realized at once that Uxmal was right: The forest was near to winning. The purple monotone caterpillars took the Megalopolis by assault; a wall of giant ferns double-lapped the ramparts. The jungle penetrated everywhere, with its infinite patience, the thousand forms it could take, its deaf violence like earthquakes, its gnarled roots which lifted pavings and choked the moats, its vines which toppled battlements.

The great moths continued to lift the chariot which, in passing, bent the tops of bamboos. The royal pyramid, that repository of secrets and treasures, prison and tomb of the ruling dynasty, had once sat dead center of a neutral zone. That zone had vanished. The musk of rotting leaves, the perfumes of enormous blooms of prickly pears and water lilies intoxicated the silk moths, and Aran thought suddenly of the eternal exhilaration in which humans lived below.

At the threshold of the pyramid, the Guardian of the Keys, half blind, prostrated himself and cried:

"Here is truth, all the truth I am bound to show to passersby. Men who sinned were marked with the sign of the Beast; this is a blight which punishes their pride and marks their beginning and their end. It appears in the form of a growth on the brow, like an eye or an ulcer; the tumor presses on the brain and creates regressive mutations who return to the state of animals.

"To show that man has no means to lift himself above other species, other species advance and man regresses indefinitely.

"This blight strikes newborn and adults. It spores no caste. Queen Maos broke the law of the wedding flight... for the mole must die. This is a law of blood, ancient and true; but she delivered to the guards another body and hid in her tower the Elnyan she had come to love. The son of this princess was afflicted with brain cancer at the age of 20.

"Let us pray."

"You say that to all the visitors?" Aran asked harshly.

"There are scarcely any visitors," the old man lisped. "Elnyans avoid unpleasant sights and there are no more Sunborn, are there?"

"Let's go see Prince Ael," Aran said.

Ael, half-brother to the queen, had once been the companion of his games. He had had the same Sunborn beauty, and recalled in himself all the legends. The Elnyan dancers and flute players would sing:

Sweeter to my lips than myrrh,
Ael thou art, firstborn of gods.
Born for joy and delight
Thy mother conceived thee
Filled with all power.
Thy hands are vine-clusters
Thine eyes, lakes of stars.

"Yes," Aran said again, as if he still heard that piercing, tender melody, "let's go see what's left of the son of the gods."

The Guardian wagged his head in a knowing way and guided his visitor to a triangular opening in the wall, high as a man's head. There he lit a torch and drew back a shutter. A heavy musk arose from the interior. The prince of E-enor leaned over the pits wherein paced a lithe body. It resembled neither man nor insect, those familiar forms, but rather an animal of an almost-vanished species... the silver puma. As the light drew the being out of his torpor, his long, white-downed limbs unfolded, his head turned, and it was horrible. The sullen, pale-eyed face was human and almost handsome, marred with a scar at the joining of the nose.

"They've operated on him," Aran said.

"Yes."

"The face is untouched. The tumor isn't spreading?"

"No."

"He has no awareness at all?"

"When someone says 'Prince Ael,' he flies into a rage and leaps nigh three cubits high. You see the stones scratched by his claws?"

Aran straightened. "The foremost Sunborn tainted," he said. "No one comes to see him much, do they? The Elnyans do all they can to forget him, and they hide his very existence from the queen, who is no more than a child. And the cacti? I suppose the sight must please them. Prince Ael was too handsome and too intelligent to survive so near the throne."

The beast in the cave raised a thin wail, leapt, then fell back, his brow on his folded paws,

"The first time," the Guardian said humbly, "I thought I could help him. He made me feel sorry for him. He still looked like a young man. I went down into his pit and washed his wound, but he struck at me and scratched me. It was a deep wound, but clean; the ulcer had breached the bone of the skull like a drill."

"The prince fell victim to the blight very suddenly, didn't he?" Aran asked in a flat voice. "He was hunting, a beetle wounded him; and they brought him to the Council palace, where the plant physicians cared for him. Then—the blight manifested itself and Ael was brought directly here."

When he had climbed again out of the depths of the pyramid, there was someone waiting for him on the terrace facing the sea.

A green mass overwhelmed a throne of black agate. Aran turned away. He pretended in vain that he was accustomed to the peyotls. Each time, the sight of these great green and agile growths made him shudder. *One must forget his own anthropomorphism,* he thought. *No looking for sense organs in the buds that crown these growths, no seeing in these places where translucent knobs bulge out—internal eyes, green and terribly luminous as they are... To forget what mind animates these green tumors...*

But that was impossible.

The enormous cactus stood out clearly under the green moon.

"My son," began an audible Sending, "I am Peyotl A."

"I am no plant's son," Aran interrupted him. "Not even of the President of the Holy Council. But I've been very much expecting such a meeting—from the day I left A-atlan."

"There is no sound on Earth but the noise of your voyages," whispered the globe. One of his growths pulsed; doubtless it served as a semblance of vocal cords. "You made some delightful discoveries, did you not?"

"Wondrous discoveries."

"Have you," the cactus returned, "found divine Europe or mighty North America? You see, we are informed of your ambitions and your studies. Once, when you were building your fleet, had you ever asked our advice, I would have told you myself that this is the only continent where your species survives. The Empire of Man is a very ancient land named A-atlan. For the rest—the great plateaus of the North, which were the main epicenter of the cataclysm, were utterly destroyed, and so were the secondary epicenters in Asia. There do remain, in that watery waste... circlets of islands, a reef that was once the highest peak of a mountain chain—Mont Blanc. And there is that flat shore which surrounds that lagoon-like inner sea of Africa. That is all your power-mad kindred left their heirs. Ah! I did forget the Sargasso Sea over old Australia. But I suppose you will say that you had some fabulous encounters."

"No," said Aran coldly. "Have I ever lied?"

"You have too much pride to lie, actually."

"I found no shore inhabited by humans. But I did find something else. A vast presence. A cry to Heaven: that of humans and their gods. I found them," Aran said passionately, "not what you try to paint of them, a degenerate species with the manners of insects—but free, impatient, brutal, perhaps...

on their way to an eternal becoming. Everything speaks to me of their effort: the ruins of their cities, their cathedrals under the waves, spires aimed at the stars. Their white highways that plunge into the abysses like outstretched arms.

"And not my vision alone. I bring A-atlan a message. A case weighing tons and made of a metal that defies wear. Men of the atomic age sealed into it what they held most precious. I spent my nights deciphering their treatises and their poems. Every line of them glorifies man, his weakness or his strength, his sacrifices or his sufferings. These ancient beings created, hoped, desired—I found not the least trace of their regression or the 'heat of dementia' your scholars lay to their account. They were lightning-struck at the height of their flight. The regression and degeneration began later."

"Consequences of the cataclysm," the other admitted.

"Not even that. The graven records show that at the time of my own ancestor Hellemar, a handful of survivors was still fighting and succeeding in hanging on. But they were weakened by the radiation and the inhuman conditions of their lives. One day, strangers came…"

"What reproach have you against us?" Peyotl A asked softly.

"Ah, next to nothing. Of worming your way into the city. Of using gifts and drugs to lull this heroic, this splendid and brutal humanity to sleep, of having shaped us into beasts—no, worse, into insects, more compatible with you. Of having patiently substituted dark and stupid superstitions for our own harsh laws. You've stolen *everything* from us—our hope and our dream, from prince regent down to the lowest green slave, you've ground us down into terror and into the mud!"

"We offered humans what they most appreciated… escape from the doomsday they had brought upon themselves." A thin green tendril passed over Peyotl A's curves; one thought of a human wiping off sweat. "We gave them remedies for their sores and means of assuring their safety. And so they would have no more desire to overturn worlds again or to cross the continuum, we gave them our blood and our flesh, the divine juices that daze the eyes, gave them luxury and all pleasures. They were delighted, believe me."

"Yes, you made them like grubs living in their own filth. And that's been going on for 1000 years."

"For more than 2000 years," the plant declared with sudden majesty, "this species you call divine existed on an Earth it had desolated—naked, mad, prey to all its instincts. You weren't here to witness the furies of *homo sapiens*; you don't know what man is capable of. A-atlan was a charnel house. Yes, you said the truth: Earth almost perished in one of man's stupid experiments, his constant attempts to reach everything at once. Diverging and parallel worlds time and space—they thought they could have it all, the past and the future. The structure of the present gave way…"

"Yes," said Aran, suffused with an overwhelming joy, "that struggle was worthy of them."

But Peyotl A went on in his own dream. "Earth was still shuddering. Vast tidal waves swept the continents; volcanoes vomited flames; the very air was afire with radioactivity; and man killed, raped, ravaged. A tenth of humanity still escaped at world's end, and you didn't know that, did you? But after a few years, there weren't enough of them left to repopulate this wreck of a continent. Then we came."

"Uninvited."

"We had no need of invitation. One species died, another takes its place: That is the law. We must, above all else, safeguard Earth and this strip of dry land from some new madness. We've done so."

"You've replaced anarchy with tyranny and brutality."

"The survivors thank us."

"A herd of sheep."

"No, just the human species stripped of all its lies and its importance."

"No!" Aran cried. "I can't believe it. I've seen…"

"…the ruins of Notre Dame and the Kremlin. We know you went down there in your diving suit. You bring us, it seems, relics of your past: the Venus de Medici and Michelangelo's Pietà. Junk. These same men destroyed their universe—for amusement."

"At least," Aran replied in a cold rage, "they chose their own destiny; it was a terrible one, but proud. Today you're dragging us down to the rubbish heap. You've created monsters..."

"No," the plant corrected him. "The tumor is—a consequence of certain excesses."

"Mind-dulled brutes, are we? Your 'sharing of flesh and blood...'"

"We would never want," said Peyotl A with distaste, "to cause the rise of such brute beasts."

"Moths or butterflies would have served you better," Aran said in an extremity of horror. "I think *that's* the state you want to bring us to—irresponsible and ephemeral. But the dosage wasn't right. Or are we simply closer to the nobility of wild animals?"

"This discussion," said the globe, now covered with fine beads of anguish, "is in danger of becoming academic. I am no judge of hypotheses. I was simply chosen by my people to make the sea prince certain precise proposals."

"Offers from you to me? There's no way there could be."

"Let's say—suggestions."

"I would be curious."

"So," said the peyotl, after a small silence in which he established a contact. "My people speak with my voice. They say: *You consider us your personal enemies, prince. You are wrong. In our poor opinion, if there is among the human herd a single man who deserves our respect, it is surely Prince Aran. We are so well aware of it that despite all your hostile acts...*"

"You flatter me."

"*...we have never sought to destroy you.*"

"No," said Aran, "but you're thinking about it now, aren't you?"

"*Whatever you think, our offers are genuine. You will live and keep your title—most glorious of all men. And all the gifts A-atlan and Earth can cast at your feet. Even the most costly.*"

"All the gifts of A-atlan are costly," said Aran, white-faced. "What do you ask in return?"

The sound wave trembled. It seemed that Peyotl A was having difficulty finding the word.

"*Your neutrality,*" he said finally.

"Ah," Aran exclaimed. "That means the war is beginning? Against whom? I won't even ask. It's enough to know that someone has entered the lists. Someone is fighting your inhuman power. I accept the challenge. I set myself at his side."

"You don't even know where the attack is coming from—the Terran colonies or the monsters of Altair. Earth will fall again to fire and blood…"

"There's little enough blood left on Earth," the sea prince said harshly, "but sap will run."

"So it will be war between us," said the vegetal thought, almost sorrowfully.

And Aran: "It already *is* war."

The third meeting of that night was unexpected and disturbing. Aran left the pyramid and drove his chariot across the dream-bound forest like a ship on the seas. The white silk moths settled into the clearing facing Queen Maos' palace. The sea glittered in the distance, free, luminous, and spangled with stars, and Aran was for an instant ready to leave it all, to seek his ship again and the way of the wide seas.

He heard his name called.

Among the last arbors of golden grapes stood a vision of ethereal grace.

"Atlena!" he said.

Shining, blue-black hair, parted in the middle, surrounded her temples and tumbled back onto a costly mantle. Her oval face shone like ancient alabaster; her slender arms, braceleted in electrum, were wings, and her body a glimmering amid smoky veils.

In that lotus-face danced immense, wide eyes—violet lakes. So delicate she was that Aran was shaken before her childlike wrists and ankles. It had taken hundreds of generations—and the purest Sunborn line-age—to create this useless and charming jewel.

He dreamed a dream, bitter and sweet at once. A strange weakness pervaded him. He stepped down from his chariot and knelt, paying her homage.

"Hail," he murmured, "Queen of A-atlan."

A small, petal-soft hand rested on his brow. "I am happy to see you again," her crystalline voice pronounced. "And yet I am sorry... so sorry! I ran away from the palace to stop you. They want to give you to me. O Aran, it's hideous!"

"Why, Atlena?" he asked gently.

She seemed not even to hear him. "The very idea is monstrous. For me, for all of us, you've been the noblest, the highest... the god Hellemar on Earth. You've been a brother to me..."

"You've been my Star of stars."

"...and to let us come to this... It seems they have to have a child of Sunborn blood. Oh! I could never bear that horror."

"What horror, Atlena?"

"Listen to me," the young queen said, and choked. "You know well what the wedding flight means: The queen lets herself be mated, then kills. Like the bees, like—I don't know what worse. And don't tell me I couldn't even lift the sword. Others will take care of that matter."

"I don't doubt that. And you—" Aran asked in calm curiosity, "do you really want to fight me? Would you want me to die?"

She gave a cry. "I would die myself!"

"Ah," Aran said, but he stopped. *Listen,* he had wanted to say: *All over the world, for millions of years, other human beings have felt that sweetness that breaks on us; they've opened their arms, shut their eyes, and taken love as a blessing. We can do likewise.* He leaned his brow against a shoulder

40

smooth as conch shell, saw again a world swallowed whole, tender and cruel at once, a darting strophe that, above the green sea, spoke of love and fate—and the thin body yielded itself within his arms. He sighed like a thirsty voyager finding a spring and touching the lips of it. A second later Atlena escaped him with a cry. He let her go and they looked at one another with shadowed eyes.

"It's—it's *horrible*," she said. "Like insects or slaves…"

Aran's face went hard. "So horrible as that?"

Already she was coming back toward him, trembling. "I know—I know it was only a joke." She shuddered to the depth of her. "But this distaste, this fear—are distilled of tens of generations. Oh talk to me, reassure me. I need to feel your presence, to know that you won't—that you can't hurt me."

"What do you want?" he answered her bitterly. "I'm your slave. You're the queen of A-atlan."

"But now you're warned. You have to guard yourself against their plots. They can't do anything against the will of a Sunborn…"

"No."

"You'll find a way to escape this—abomination."

"I hope so," he replied with chill humor.

"Till tomorrow, my dear brother."

"Till tomorrow, majesty."

IV

Bronze doors opened atop a flight of 3000 onyx steps. In the ruthless Sun there was heat enough to overwhelm the human Councilors of the Agora. When they finally arrived in the throne room, the Elnyans and the red Giants were hardly more than sweat-drenched rags. The plants leaped from level to level of the benches with castings of their supple hooks and tendrils.

The sea lord saw at a distance, on the highest dais, his two foremost galleys already set up for a votive offering. Placed thus, they looked small and black, corroded by sun and salt

Aran mounted the steps, his eyes fixed upon these relics of his fleet. He did not bend the knee, and the plumed warriors cheered him.

He saw at once that humans occupied less than a third of the tiers. There were the Elnyans in their robes of gold floral patterns, their faces painted with gold and vermillion... languidly disposing themselves on cushions. Everyone strove to emulate the insects or the plants, and in that, one could judge the progress of the moral decay. Men wore diadems or thin platinum circlets with the tall antennae of ichneumons or the sweeping whips of the wasps. Their corselets gave the illusion of wing cases; their dancing skirts looked like flower cups. But the most assiduous in following this mutated dream were the Elnyan women, liberated and making unrestrained use of their bodies, they painted their faces with the dyes of windflowers, surrounded their eyes with violet dust to imitate the purple cattleyas and the irregularly spotted odontoglossums; their perfume-raddled skin shone under sequins of electrum and dull and smoky crystals which imitated the chitin of insects. Elaborate coiffures dyed rose, blue, or mauve, made the illusion complete.

42

But the red warriors, whose armor recalled that of elk-horn beetles, whose plumes resembled the woolly rackets of the Old Man cacti, afforded no happier sight. Like wings of damselflies or swallowtails, their voluminous mantles were fringed with gold lace or sewn with io-moth eyes. And it was clear that intelligence was fleeing as the physical transformation advanced. These Councilors of the Empire of Man had come here only for parade, or to enjoy a holiday, and not to discuss their universal problems.

Aran looked on them: he had forgotten his people. How fallen they were! The Elnyans were still bright with grace, and the warriors were like beautiful mahogany statues. But at the foot of the steps flowed the mob: work slaves and joy slaves teased the lizards and anacondas, gorged themselves on coconuts and chewed chica. On the very steps the commons gathered; among them were snouts of beasts, cat-eyes, the skins of frogs. A miasma like the reek of a swamp hovered in the room. They were still human—but not for long.

It's their *handiwork,* Aran thought with a cold shiver. *Over the centuries they've patiently laid their siege, numbed us with drugs, and then molded these versatile brains. I think once upon a time it was called "conditioning." They tell them over and over again that all species are becoming one, that the mutations are law and that with the reign of man almost over, the primacy has gone to insects and plants.*

And with a surer hand, they isolated these survivors, mode them forget their past—and forget too that their brothers had conquered the stars. And then in these vacant brains they've sawn this shame and mistrust of their own species. They've set inhuman laws over them, laws which are only their own instincts... until poor Atlena is frightened to death of love.

He felt weary. The heart seemed gone out of him. He closed his eyes.

And opened them, for a silence had fallen over the room—woven of the slidings and slitherings of the ground-trailing roots of the cacti, the tendrils and blooms of orchids.

The plants had just taken their place on their two tiers.

The spectacle which Aran had half forgotten was like a fever dream. The lady's slippers and lycastas drew up to the chandeliers on the ceiling; purple-stemmed candle-cactus towered over lakes of orchids; and on the very highest seats of the amphitheater the peyotls hoisted up their green and gleaming domes.

The conch shells and kettledrums thundered.

At the lowest part of the hall a golden door turned on its hinges and the guards there stiffened. Between their narwhale lances—presents from the sea prince, rare and precious objects—appeared a figure in jewels and green iridescence.

A tiara of emeralds crowned a mask of green gold; a chaplet of chrysolites and jade shone with barbaric splendor.

Sistrums wailed a rising note.

"Long live Queen Atlena," the Chamberlain proclaimed. "The queen deigns to attend her Council."

For any who knew custom, it was a thunderbolt.

Upheld on the arms of her maids, Tueni and Ramessa, the princess took her place on the opal throne.

And the audience began. The chairman, a venerable Old Man cactus, read, by audible Sending, a report to which no one listened. The Empire of Man was declining; wild plants were devouring the cities, as Tikal and Uaxun had vanished in a single night. At Aryapan a fern had gone berserk and poisoned the wells. And the insects left nothing where they passed; migrations of termites, tall as warriors, paved the jungle floor with bleached bones.

Then there was the problem of the anthropomorphs.

On the upper tiers the Elnyans had put off their shell necklaces and accepted flower wands from the cacti. The mahogany warriors played with knucklebones. No one realized that the Sending of the cephalo-cereus was rising to a shriek, reaching that pitch which signified danger. He spoke now of a disastrous war which he referred to as *colonial,* a conflict which set men against malthode beetles, the masters of a town called Mega. These huge insects walked (rarely, it was true) on two feet, and they possessed a totem: therefore they were an evolving species and their rights must be recognized.

"*This is the universal law!*" The audible Sending swelled, unendurably loud. "The species accedes to supremacy in its turn. Today the Empire of Man is paying the penalty of its errors—and these same errors continue to be committed. Thus the army which is now besieging Mega is commanded by one Yklantekli of the warrior caste, a clever man, but dissolute. He has broken the laws, for he has married a slave and lets her live under his roof. The Council has been indulgent, but the conclusions are self-evident...."

"Between castes," said the barbary fig which performed the office of clerk, "there can exist no possible relation other than fertilization and sacrifice. Master kills slave and Sunborn kills Elnyan. That is the law."

"We know your indulgences, Old Man," howled the benches. "Yklantekli has been pouring haala sap on your roots!"

"A-atlan can perish, so long as the plants have their compost heap!"

Everyone was shouting, while the red warriors rattled their shields with loud blows of their lances. Green, immobile, silent, the plants towered over the delirious amphitheater. Each sitting of the Council was choreographed like a ballet. The Elnyans always demanded holidays and sacrifices; the Giants wanted finery and bonuses; then everyone agreed, and the plants alone decided the fate of the Empire.

So there was shock when a tolling of the gong drowned the voices. A slave choked on his cola milk and an Elnyan lady scratched herself with her gecko. A whisper ran the room.

"Silence! Silence!"

"Peyotl A is speaking!"

"Peyotl A says—"

On a throne facing that of the queen, the enormous mass of growths, the monstrous globe stirred itself. Green ichor flushed his tumescences. An incongruous voice like cracked crystal rose above the tumult.

"My brothers…"

And at the right of the queen's throne a golden statue—Aran the sea prince—suddenly came to life.

"My brothers," the immaterial thread continued, "I would never speak if it were merely of trivialities… the town of Mega, the warrior Yklantekli. Mega is only a termite hill, of no interest to us. Yklantekli has refused his totems their due victim; he will surely die, and justice will be served. But there are deeper problems, more serious problems which involve the very existence of the Empire and its concepts of good and evil. We have said that the malthode scarabs and the beetles which inhabit Mega are inferior insects who are scarcely beginning their upward evolution. And here they are resisting—*victoriously*—the armies of A-atlan. Not to mention the termites and the ferns! The Empire of Man is everywhere vanquished. It seems then that the reign of the Sunborn is truly drawing into its twilight—and with it, humanity's debatable supremacy. Moreover, we have been given a sign from Heaven; the last god, Hellemar, has vanished from our eyes. The conqueror-god and the lighthouse no longer exist: the Sunborn gods are dead!"

A gasp ran through the amphitheater and Aran could calculate by that the action of the peyotls on the crowd. The El-nyan dignitaries froze immobile under their regard and the warriors beat their breasts. A slave, falling on all fours, howled itself hoarse. But on the royal throne the jeweled figure remained unmoved, nor had Tueni and Ramessa faltered a stroke in the moving of their fans.

"The god Hellemar is dead," continued the Sending, distilling its poisons. "He was a conqueror, and there will be no more conquerors. He was proud, powerful, and handsome, human brothers, but *you* will cover yourselves with ashes and grovel in the mud. He was master—but today the primacy is taken from you."

"To be given to whom?" asked a hard voice.

Aran had advanced to the edge of the steps and chaos ravaged the amphitheater. It seemed that the people of A-atlan had left their long torpor. The fragile patricians went into shock and the soldiers blanched under their vast plumes. The surety of a dire destruction was on them all. All eyes were riveted on that glittering figure standing on the jasper steps. The sea lord had cast back his turquoise mantle; his helm, shaped like golden flames, exaggerated his already more-than-human stature and—facing him, the sage of sages, the master of the cacti, Peyotl A, suddenly appeared only as a monstrosity, a great, ridiculous green pumpkin.

Aran lifted his visor and turned on that mob a face terrible and flushed with anger. "The loss of the primacy," he cried. "You have the mere words of it on your lips! Must we renounce our rights in favor of scarabs and orchids, trample on our past, our gods, our dead glories—serve as doormats to beasts and plants? *Why?* The reign of the Sun Gods—the gods with human face—is over, say you? *Why?* On what signs do you base this final conclusion? Has Earth again shifted on its axis? Have the seas quitted their beds? Has a comet left its course to fall into the Sun? We humans have seen these things happen and we have lived through them—bruised to the heart, but still masters of the world. We are so no longer, say you? *Why?* And here is the answer I crossed foreign seas to hear! Termites and ferns are moving, a miserable town resists a mediocre soldiery, a stone statue falls into the sea—but no god ever promised that graven images would be unshakable!—nor willed victories gained by fools!"

A cold laughter ran through the hall. Yklantekli was not popular. Aran looked at the mob and felt sorry for him, perceived a bond of sympathy. Turning to the humans he flung his anger at them as he would have hurled a life preserver at the drowning.

"Darlings of Heaven! Forgetful of your glory! You're the ones I'm talking to, Elnyans, *you*—whose ears can be wounded by a sour note; and to *you*, warriors decked in feathers, and *you*, peaceful workers! Do you believe in the peace of the vanquished?—for vanquished you will be. Facing you there stands—and supported by what other power, I wonder—

an enemy armored in chitin and armed with chelae and mandibles. You can't fail to have learned the ways of the insects they pretend to let you share. This enemy would put you to sleep, inject you with his venom, and have you serve as food for his larvae. You all know that, for in the tunnels under liberated towns, you have found those horrible black mummies, drained, tortured by nameless agonies. Your wives and your children will be given to grubs and mantises! You will have opened upon yourselves such a pit of abominations that yes, oh, yes! mankind will be damned indeed—waiting, sealed alive in its tomb, the most hideous of deaths! Sovereign people, do you accept this defeat? Speak, pronounce it! I have said!"

And he turned then abruptly to the cacti.

"You," he said, "I do not seek to convince. But give me three galleys and the warriors, and before one moon has come and gone, I will bring you the wings of the scarabs—to pave your gardens."

The ovation of the sovereign people was indescribable; the whole building trembled with it. The slaves waved their toy boats, warriors banged their shields, and the members of the golden caste danced after their own peculiar rituals. The delirium rose, soared.

"Leave the ashes and the mud," Aran cried, "to those who can use it. This is my decree: set up banquet tables in the public squares; let fountains flow with wine and chica—and I shall bring the malthode brutes to your circuses!"

On the steps of the queen's throne, Tueni and Ramessa rose without a word, put aside their fans, and spun like brown tops.

Then a pilocereus celsianus, robed in silver, rose at the side of the chairman.

"Glory to the human Empire," he squeaked. "All hail Lord Aran! He comes out of nowhere and immediately finds a remedy for our troubles: three galleys of warriors—and circuses! All hail, say I, to the navigator who has never fought a battle on dry land! We place all our hopes in him. And at least," he added, "before provoking the fearsome power of these insects—a power he has so eloquently described—may we ask what are our chances of victory?... Well, if not chances, at least what have we a right to expect? Yklantekli, the warrior-leader, is a valiant soldier, for all that he has scorned the laws and the gods have turned their backs on him—if we follow the reasoning of the sea lord himself, who insists that the human gods are still alive. Now Yklantekli failed through weakness and madness, but he never trampled on the three commandments on which the city itself rests. Yet, victory turned her back on him. May I, to avoid all possible misunderstanding, ask this one question: What is the private life of Prince Aran?"

"Ah," said the sea lord. And he began to laugh. "It hasn't been that of a plant, you can be sure of that."

But he knew that the accusation was a telling blow. And made as it was in Atlena's presence...

The venomed voice went on. "It is notorious that the divine lord has despised the astral harmony which consecrated him to a special destiny. He has confounded caste, taken pleasure, loved. Has he ever taken thought that for a Sunborn, love means the sacrifice of the chosen? I mean by that, to a greater degree than Yklantekli—has Aran offered the gods the women who pass within his embrace? For it is rumored..."

"Am I accused," Aran interrupted violently, "and are you my judge? I don't recognize your laws of insects and carnivorous plants. A man who kills what he loves is not only a criminal, but a lunatic!"

"Prince Aran accepts no judgment in A-atlan?" asked the glassy, grating voice of Peyotl A.

"I will, yes. A sovereign sentence. There are so few of us Sunborn left—it is fact that we be judged by our own kind. Let the queen judge me then. Let her find me a criminal before the law and I shall deliver myself up to the butcher!—but not to you, you vermin of the compost heap! *Back!*"

A shiver of laughter chilled the amphitheater. There was an incredible sight before them—a black juice rising in the peyotl-gourds, their fashion of blushing. The prince turned to the throned statue in the emerald and gold mask. His voice grew gentle, like a caress, and his eyes smiled.

"Be my judge, Atlena."

He flung out all the force of his thought to make contact with that distant spirit, wrapped in centuries of royalty. He cried out silently: *Yes, all of it is true. I have sinned—but never against you. I've given others what you loathe and fear: my desire. But if only I could love you, my evenstar, all would be different.*

She had not moved. Her mask was strange and hostile. The emeralds encrusted about the eyes shone like lithops, and Aran could not find the gentle violet eyes. A horrible thought swept over him: *It is not she. They've locked her away or killed her.* And during that brief instant the plants had won.

But a tiny, blue-veined hand left the statue's knee in a commanding gesture. Finely scratched with the thorns of yestereve, it was truly Atlena's. The queen arose, the vast serpent tail of her robe swept the pavement, and the amphitheater cast itself prostrate at her feet.

"Hear me all!" said a muffled and golden voice. "The queen speaks; the queen says: The force of the laws is in their being old and reasonable. Since when are Sunborn judged by the Strangers? You will accuse me as well, on the day when I throw my fat plants to the caimans; no, I do nothing of the sort. I detest things that scream, but I have read the tables of our law: If I desire, I have the right. That the prince of E-enor has taken his pleasure where he will, as he wills—that is his concern. He serves the Empire, is that not so? Better than the lot of you.

"Regarding the other matter, the account of Mega—forever besieged and never taken—it becomes too amusing to abandon. Aran thinks he will take this town? Then let him take it. Blessed be A-atlan.

"I have spoken.

"I declare this Council at an end, by the gods and by the totems."

V

The Sun was sinking toward the sea. Aran called the queen's attention to it, but she and her favorite maid, Ramessa, freed of all jewelry in their gauze tunics, were amusing themselves flat on their bellies amid the tribute of the fleet.

It was all there, coffers full of diamonds, brought up by divers in the Sargasso Sea, smooth golden statues which the sirens had polished with their kisses, the perfumes and exotic arms of Africa.

"Tell me about Europe!" Atlena ordered. "You told me that there were towns under globes, gone down intact under the waters. Did you go into one of those domes?"

Stretched out at her feet, eyes closed, Aran told of the yellow-green abyss where cities slept with their skyscrapers still standing. The swimmers, clinging to the transparent panels, had seen open avenues, motionless machines. Skeletons balanced in tramways, some still wearing women's jewels. They were whole, complete. Storms and tides had no access there.

"It seems," said Aran, "that they had no time to suffer, not even to understand their fate. Their world died in a single instant."

"Were the women of that age beautiful?" Ramessa asked.

"Oh, see here," said the queen, "how do you expect he should know that? He saw only their skeletons."

"I think that they must have been beautiful," Aran said. "These folk had a keen sense of harmony. Everyone was dressed in light fabrics, bright colors. You can see it in these designs, Atlena."

"The robes of their nobility must have been magnificent," the queen sighed. Aran looked at her distantly.

"I don't think that there were castes. These folk belonged to one whole world. They were equals."

"That's absurd," Atlena said. She clenched her small fists and stared at nothing in particular. "Everyone, I mean, *people*—they aren't made alike. One can't demand hard labor of an Elnyan who would die of a harsh note, or expect self-restraint of a red Giant. The wedding flight is the privilege and distinction of the Sunborn…"

"Nor do I think," Aran said with remarkable mildness, "that these men ever practiced that murderous—your pardon, the wedding flight."

The two young women stared at each other, petrified.

"I would well understand," Atlena began, then said, "You say that these folk were all equal, all divine. Queens and kings of the world-hive. But then how do you explain it? The law says: *The queen must kill; blood pays for blood.*"

"It's not our law," Aran retorted. His fingers played with an ivory statuette. It represented a woman holding in her arms the lifeless body of a young man. On the youth's smooth body pale purple represented wounds. The two faces had the same beauty. Aran offered the pair to the queen. "You see this woman, Atlena?"

"A goddess?"

"Yes, something like that. Meriamne, Astarte, Ishtar…"

"What's she doing?"

"She's weeping for this man. He's her beloved or her son. In the most ancient religions she chooses him from all the rest. They love each other and he dies."

"And you tell me that the wedding flight didn't exist?"

"It didn't. Adonis, Tammuz, Osiris—they didn't die at Ishtar's hand, but by the attack of some enemy or a wild beast. There have always been monsters and demons to hunt the heroes and the gods. Only in the past, they were our adversaries; they attacked us; they never dictated our laws."

"You really believe…"

"Listen to me. At the moment of the great cataclysm, all the tables of the law were destroyed. You understand me. *All.* And men lived at first without rule or restraint. When a calmer age came, they felt the need to reestablish their laws, but the old men were dead and the young ones knew nothing of the past. It was the age when the plants had arrived to take their place at our side; they were humble and they were everywhere; they offered simply their juice, their knowledge, and their memory. Man's mistake was in taking such gifts."

He spoke with passion. He had so little rime and so much desire, so great a need to convince her. Atlena's smooth brow clouded.

"You think that they've tampered with our laws?" she asked. "But that would be monstrous! And why would they do such a thing?"

And then, when Ramessa had withdrawn (excessively abstract conversations bored her): "A proof," Atlena asked. "A proof! You've shown me frightening things, Aran."

"The proofs—I went so far to find... Atlena, they're in these statues and these poems that our species—however fallen—knew how to create. We've become kin to the beasts, and we keep beasts' laws. But why search so far afield? I've already said it—this woman is crying. And have you ever had tears in your eyes, Atlena?"

"Tears?" she echoed primly. "That means the secretions in your eyes when you're sick."

"Ah. You see? You can't even understand. It was a gift, a grace we lost. When the ancients suffered, they poured out tears of pain or of pity, and it comforted them."

"*Pity*," the queen said. "So strange a word. And it means...?"

"Regrets which narrow the heart. The desire to bind wounds and heal hurts; to protect, to avenge the weak."

"We know no such thing."

"No. You see, they've taken this gift from us."

"And I can never cry?"

"Perhaps," said Aran. "Come here."

He drew her against the transparent wall which separated off the hall of the terrarium. It was quite marvelous, this terrarium, a gift the plants had offered the queen on her accession to the throne: a ballet of yet-unevolved orchids, of graceful bean plants and flesh-eating sundews, a bed of calves' foots and water lilies. The roots, already free, plunged not into mulch, but into a clear green fluid. Tiny flitting insects peopled the seeming comer of an old water meadow, and the queen had under her eyes the ceaseless spectacle of mutation.

Nothing more depressing, thought the prince.

"Look," he said, "Atlena."

"Yes."

Between the lacquered heart of a miniature anthurium and a pearly alban, the funnel of a carnivorous plant opened mysteriously. Its petals were veined with rose and mauve. But inside this delicate vase of rose wine, little black bodies struggled desperately. Though the wall was soundproof, Atlena imagined their buzzing, the thrumming of limbs stiffening with agony.

"This flower is eating them?" she asked. "It's rather disgusting. Oh, but after all, they're only insects."

"It could be something else." Aran slid back the glass partition and heavy musk crept into the room. "There. You see the dragonfly with the opal wings, the great green and silver mite? That's I. And the rose flower that's swallowing it is a certain Peyotl. There sits the dragonfly on the rim of the petal, debating with himself. He understands the danger, but there, he's al-ready stuck down with the vine. Who is winning, the half-paralyzed creature or the devouring plant? It's easy to decide. There! A shiver comes over the surface of the flower—as if it sensed its prey…"

"Hush!" Atlena turned away.

"Ah, no," he protested. "Don't do like the Elnyans. Whenever something displeases them, they pretend it doesn't exist. You see, the delicate cup contracts, it breathes in the dragonfly. He makes a last effort to fly, but his wings are glued down. He's falling. There; he's resigned. The filmy wings are beating with just the least flutter, no hope of free space, no more room to fly. And the flower—every petal of it a suction cup—opens very wide and closes down on its victim. Good-bye, Aran—*Oh!* Atlena! What are you doing?"

He seized the queen's wrist a second too late. She had committed a blasphemy: quite innocent, the little sundew was only a reflection of power. But blasphemy all the same. She ripped up the flower, shredded it. The dragonfly, set free, flew away. Atlena turned her darkened eyes toward the prince.

"You thought you'd teach me something? Well, you're wrong, Aran. That's what I felt this morning in the Council. Only I don't cry. I break things. And speaking of breaking things," she added, in a quieter tone, "you must take a little walk with me tonight. I think I've found one of the caverns, you understand me? Where Hellemar hid the ancients' weapons."

"—Quite by accident, while I was walking with Tueni, I came on this passage," Atlena explained somewhat later. "You understand, sometimes even I have had enough of plants. They're everywhere and into everything. So I go out to the edge of the desert. There the sand is so dry that nothing can live. So, I suppose, the cacti don't know anything about this."

Here the emerald night was less complete. The shore where plants had no access was rimmed with purple cliffs and level sands which bizarrely bordered on a cheerless desolation: the ancient Valley of Death. Here funeral towers and crypts had stood for more than two thousand years. In the distance the sands of the Eastern Desert glowed with faint phosphorescence.

The queen had herself borne along on a sedan chair, carried by two red warriors, Hixl and Tlavatli. Aran and Ramessa walked beside.

"It's strange," Aran said, glancing about him, "that I don't know this shore. And yet —"

"It's only recently emerged," said Atlena. "And that's happening all up and down the coasts. The sea is receding, giving me a gift from its own kingdom. It seems there are new isles out on the sea, but we haven't men enough to repopulate them. You mustn't talk about that in the city. The phenomenon upsets the plants."

55

"Why?"

"Because of the anthropomorphs, of course. The Changed-men infiltrate everywhere that there are neither plants nor humans. They destroy everything. I've never really understood the matter of the growth on the brow. People say it's a punishment and that mankind is reverting to his original state: that of a dumb beast. And people say too that it's the continual use of opiates affecting the pineal gland. Still—I don't think the plants would encourage that, if that were the case. They're terribly afraid of the anthropomorphs."

"As they would be of any failed experiment," Aran said between his teeth.

"Then you think…?"

"…That they were expecting some other result? Yes. They doubtless wanted to bring on a mutation. This pineal tumor looks very much like the honeycomb facets of an insect's eye."

A silence fell. The two Sunborn understood each other.

At the burial vaults of the 12th dynasty, tombs crowned with eagles and guarded by jasper lions, Atlena stepped down from her litter. In the fore of an empty crypt she located a stone carved with double serpents. She stroked their scaly heads and activated a spring. The glow of the bearers' torches lit a stairway which plunged down into the dark.

Aran assured himself that no moss or sumptuous lichen carpeted the massive porphyry steps and the whole cortege began the descent into the passage. They passed beneath vaulted ceilings glistening with dampness. Blue and rose stalagmites glittered in the torchlight.

"We're under Mylne Lake," the prince surmised. "The water is eating down into the granite."

"This is all going to collapse someday," the queen said, with an indifference which was not, however, resignation. "I told you that the sea was everywhere retreating and that island chains were rising? But everything seems to go against my city. Recently a whole district—the Ahuahua, you know, where our last libraries stood—fell into the Lake. Ah, it happened without any storm or earthquake, just as it did with Hellemar. The ground beneath simply gave way as if it had been eroded deep below by some rottenness. I wonder…"

"What do you wonder, Atlena?"

"Oh… nothing. I floated out over the Ahuahua. I could see it all very clearly under the water. There was the entrance of the royal library, the ivory cases, the mosaics…"

"You could do nothing to save it?"

"Nothing. The plants insisted we had no diving suits. And besides, the microfilms must be soaked."

"Someone should have tried," Aran insisted. "Our forest armor might have worked. And there were pearl fishers once. We're talking about a treasure more than pearls : the remnants of human wisdom—"

"Some of my guards," the queen said, "did dive. But none of them came up. The lake bottom is covered with algae and eelgrass." Her steps faltered.

"You're not tired?" Aran asked anxiously.

"No. We've reached the end. It's here."

The corridor had forked. A vast flat expanse fell away at their feet.

"I'm afraid," Ramessa said. For some time, Ramessa had had herself carried by one of the mahogany warriors. She ordered him to set her down. The queen forgot her majesty long enough to make a face at her, then turned to Aran with a truly royal gesture.

"I give you all of this." She indicated the gulf which opened before them.

The prince gazed intently downward. In boyhood he had dreamed of secret valleys where legend said the god Hellemar had entombed the thunder—for fear blind children of men would use it.

Before his feet extended a teeming chaos. The motionless torches of the bearers drew from the shadows dreadful secrets: lizards with portholes, carbon-steel alligators, polymer cylinders, cones glowing blue and sulphurous green and filled with death. In this giant storeroom fearsome powers mouldered away—phantom rockets, flying saucers obscured in dust, atomic cannon, rust-shrouded. All that man's fevered imagination could invent on his way to the conquest of the stars, was there—and Aran, with a jolting shock to his heart, realized that some of these machines might still be in usable condition.

But it was Earth he dreamed of reconquering, not the stars.

"What do you think of my gift?" Atlena asked him.

He looked at her abruptly. "Why do you give me this?"

"You're supposed to take Mega. I'm giving you the means."

"Oh. That village. I'd have taken it anyway."

She shrugged. "We have no time to waste here. Our comrades back there seem uneasy. And I begin to understand the reason for their anxiety. This tunnel, Aran... there are strange things, screens that open on nothing, mechanisms that sense the approach of anything living. But, most of all, these silver fish, these needles meant to stitch the clouds. Wasn't it in such machines that men once conquered the stars and set their power there?"

He turned to face her, stunned. "Who told you so, Atlena?"

"The books of the Ahuahua. And I have stood before these machines and thought. Humankind was very powerful at the last, wasn't it? We swarmed across the galaxy. We founded colonies and kingdoms. I've often looked at the stars and told myself they might be other suns, dragging along with them other Earths, people with beings who look like us. But men who went their own way, who escaped before the domination of the plants, men prouder and braver... Earth after all is their home. Some reason out there must have kept them from reaching us—a reason that may no longer exist."

"Why do you think that?"

"This retreat of the waters," Atlena said fervently. "This mad, unreasoning haste on the part of the plants. And it seems to me that the nights are not as green as they were, that the stars shine brighter. It almost seems some shroud had parted between us and the Heavens. Haven't you seen it?"

"Yes. Perhaps I have."

"Just imagine that our kinsmen, our brothers, are watching Earth at this very moment. And that they're coming home…"

"It would be too beautiful," Aran said, his teeth clenched. "We can only rely on ourselves. We have to fight and hang on."

"Yes. You have to take Mega. Come."

She led him up to a machine that had the look of something simple—its club form, braced on a tripod, had scattered pitiless destruction on delicate organisms. Aran's eyes shone. He went ahead of the party and knelt down in the dust, his sensitive fingers probing shielded switches.

"Do you know what it is?" he asked. "Do you know, my queen?"

"How should I? The thing does seem to me to be in good condition."

"It is. Remember the legend of Hellemar. He advanced, armed with the crudest, simplest of weapons—the maul. But a light went out from it and set forests ablaze, reduced beasts to ashes before him…"

"Then it's a terrible machine of destruction."

"To put it simply, a field disintegrator."

And such a delight rang through his voice that Atlena grew pale. "You're not afraid," she said, "to loose the death that sleeps in this thing?"

"I promise you," he said fervently, "to use this only against the enemies of humankind. And I swear that to you. Believe me, I swear it by your own self."

VI

The dawn of the sixth day (since the court of the Agora) was reddening the sea when Aran's fleet hove into sight of Mega.

The place was a termite hill, surrounded by black sands. Its bamboo-trunk ramparts and domes of strangely smooth clay had the disquieting aspect of things not made by human hands. The doors were at frightful heights, which were more than the height of malthodes and magdalin beetles.

The ships had deployed themselves majestically across the harbor when an unspeakable stench reached them. The sea lord called his first captain, Tzental, who in turn questioned the slaves. The slaves explained that the zone of black sand defended Mega: The Ring of Death, it was called. It could not be crossed. Its blackness and its fetid stench came from certain plant juices. "Anything living," Tzental translated, "dies the instant it draws breath there. The vapors make a wall."

"It might be useful," Aran said, "to ask Peyotl A for more exact descriptions."

He passed an order for his ships to anchor and blockade the harbor. Under the bloody Sun, Mega looked dead. No movement stirred in those passages that went deeper than humans liked. Aran considered the situation. He knew the malthodes well enough—Mega's presumed masters. They were soft-shelled beetles with thin antennae and frail bodies which wild mutation had brought to a height of two or three meters. The magdalin beetles, common pests, served the malthodes as cattle. Neither of these species deserved the kind of panic reaction which had destroyed Mega's will to resist

As a precautionary measure, the sea prince ordered that no galley fires be lit, and his ships stayed out from shore. What did he know, after all, of this impregnable town of Mega? The whole planet was in ferment. Mutations seemed to come about by pure chance. Once certain sulfamides and phenols had helped create double flowers or vertebrate monsters; the plants, Aran suspected, had enlarged the field of their endeavors.

The night was hot. He climbed to the bow of the flagship, where Tzental joined him, carrying his small lute with him. Tapestries were hung there on a golden frame. The sky was green shading to black and spangled with stars. They did seem closer, and they shone like diamonds. Hour by hour the nightwatch called out to his comrades.

And attack came, as morning neared and a breeze swept away the miasmas of the black zone.

Aran woke from his sleep like a swimmer coming up from die deep. A buzz of chitined wings surrounded him and a dark mass rasped past him at deck level. Heavens, *no!* That was no malthode. A flying dragon at the least. The prince of E-enor sprang to his feet with a dismay next to nausea. Recovering his senses he realized what had seemed most sinister in that passing shadow: a clicking sound... castanets striking.

At the foot of the mast Tzental was on his feet, whey-faced.

"A scarab!" Tzental stammered. "Eighteen cubits at least! No such thing exists"

"But it does," Aran said. "One species reaches that size: megalosomes. The name signifies that they were—even before the cataclysm—*giant* insects. Mutation applied to such a mass gives us..."

"Flying elephants!"

"Or dinosaurs. Terribly armed. The male's prothorax has spined horns. But the wings don't match their weight. Their chitin segments have to be too thin. I predict for them the same fate as the dinosaurs of the Tertiary."

"It could be," the Elnyan mused, "that there were scarabs in those days..."

But they began to understand Yklantekli and his failures. Fearsome cries arose from the ships nearest the shore. Other black shadows were breaking the masts, beating at the hulls, their horns encrusted with entrails. The megalosomes passed, disemboweling their victims.

Aran ordered fires lit on the masts. Then the men saw a fearful sight: The shore was acrawl with hunchbacked masses, a torrent rolling down to the sea. It climbed the mound. *Mega was only an airhole,* Aran thought. *The whole countryside must be riddled like a honeycomb—and filled with monsters.*

On the plain, living waves surged this way and that. To their horror, the men recognized human shapes, naked and gaunt, perched above this moving chaos. Allies or prisoners? Few megalosomes reached the air. Most sank. Aran pointed out for his crews the vulnerable points, the joints of the armor, the faceted eyes. Snatching from Tzental's hands the crudest weapon—a boarding pike—he hit the first megalosome in full flight.

Shadows and chimeras flowed into retreat.

The next dawn, the beach was clear and the ocean was blue. Everything that had gone before seemed a horror born of the night. But Aran looked out on the reefs and remained convinced of danger. Amid blocks of granite torn from the cliffs, black masses swirled in the eddies. The megalosomes had begun to build a bridge—with corpses.

He had the strange maul fixed on its tripod and brought up to be set on the bridge of the flagship. The seamen hardly looked at it. Nerves taut, they kept watching the forest, waiting for some sign from Yklantekli and his men. Tzental, the charming young Elnyan—slightly mad like all the young folk of his caste—passed his lord what information he had gathered from the slaves. Many of them had fallen into the power of the insects and lived after a brutal fashion. They had learned from their masters certain rudimentary secrets of spinning and of pottery. They lived in the tunnels and left no offspring. At least they hoped so.

"I think," the navarch Tzental concluded, "that they must have massacred the slaves at certain fixed intervals—feasts and solstices. Then they would get more of them. Even a slave couldn't bear such things forever."

Aran clenched his fists and held his silence.

The Sun was settling to the horizon when cries arose from the galleys. Something was happening in the termite mound. A strange procession was ascending the ramparts of Mega... human silhouettes, bowed, bound with polished collars and smoky jewels, bearing flat stones on their backs. The sailors groaned. They saw on metal frames other figures, puppets, dolls gnarled, posed in strange postures that meant their bones had been not simply broken but shattered. The leathern color of their skins indicated that they had been warriors. And they were newly dead. Darkened blood spattered the pavements.

A mournful silence fell over the ships. The humans leaned on the rails and watched. But when they saw bunches of heads lifted on the ends of pikes and recognized their comrades of Yklantekli's army, they went wild.

The stands and lances were followed this time by two porphyry slabs borne on the backs of megalosomes. One enthroned a black stone, a cone, a meteorite most likely, smeared with blood. On the other stone a living form writhed in its bonds, red hair dragging in the dirt. Aran and Tzental looked at each other: a woman, an Elnyan woman! They were petrified with horror.

"I hesitated to destroy them all," Aran said between his teeth. "But I think it's called for."

The Sun plunged into a sea red as blood. The ramparts of Mega where the pyres were alight sent up savage cries. A horrible stench of sweat and burned flesh rolled over the flat shore. And they could do nothing. The warriors of the fleet could only swear and turn their faces away. Behind its girdle of mephitic sands, Mega foreshadowed the world to come, when insects would be kings.

When two thin crescent moons appeared over the jungle, the watch aloft reported a man adrift in the sea. They drew out of the surge a nameless rag. Pincers and antennae had flayed the wretch. But amid the red pulp two human eyes still lived, and the warriors recognized the general Yklantekli. So Aran learned the fate of the army of the land of A-atlan.

The chief of the red Giants was dying. They laid him at the foot of a mast. By an incredible effort this bloody figure, torn and seared, managed to focus his eyes on Aran.

"They betrayed us," the sea lord heard him say. "The plants—for them, men and insects are the same—things to use, master, but never—"

His head rolled back.

"No. It will never happen," Aran said. "Sleep in peace, Yklantekli."

Such was the funeral of the foremost warrior of A-atlan.

Night had come completely, and when the sea lord cast his cloak over the pitiable body, Tzental was the only one who saw his face. *(The face of Hellemar,* the Elnyan thought.)

"To me," Aran cried, "*A-atlan!*" And at his signal the warriors moved the sun maul to the prow—placed it there to face Mega, the great termite mound of Mega—and blew it away.

Tzental told the rest.

"Suddenly there was a great light like that of a deadly sun—

"And the night of Mega was cleft with a sword stroke—

"And lo, there was no more hive, no more ramparts.

"The very Earth appeared to split, and then—

"It was indescribable. The cliffs split in two. The attack the night before gave no idea of the flood that came out, hurling forth tides both shaggy and shining, vast carapaces, threshing antennae and chelae—thousands upon thousands of black geysers vomiting them up. A clicking of wings, a foul stench of burning chitin. The beaches were overwhelmed at once, waves mounted on waves and a living mountain rolling toward the sea—"

When they reached shore, Aran plied the disintegrator again and systematically scoured the plain.

Tzental the Elnyan, at his back, shut his eyes and after the custom of his people chanted the *Hymn to the Sungods.*

They are great, they are strong!
Without them we were as autumn leaves.
A swarming enemy advances,
Covering the plain.
But the Sun has arisen
And horror is no more!
We were dead, but a Sungod rises,
And wakes us again! Sing! Sing ye!

There should have been choruses. But he could not sustain it alone and the other sailors were silent, terror-stricken. Tzental opened his eyes amid a deathly hush, and saw that the port of Mega no longer existed—nor its neighboring forest. The sea reclaimed the shore. Motionless, deathly pale, and with eyes half-shut, the sea prince showered the shore with a burst of dazzling rays.

It was as if there had never been a town or an army of megalosomes.

The seafarers fretted with impatience. Aran had kept them waiting on board for a week. But a whirlwind passed, bringing fumes and radiation. The men received the order to go ashore, each taking besides his weapons a resinous torch. Everyone had masks soaked in myrrh and benzoin, cuirasses of asbestos, and bronze shields. On the sea lord's signal they lit their torches and the forces of A-atlan went ashore in a cloud of incense, like gods.

At the moment they set foot on that cursed shore, the Elnyans hesitated, but the prince of E-enor went before them. Many thought that they saw shining on his brow the starry crown of his ancestors.

Little remained of the monstrous city. The heart of the town had been razed, cauterized like a suppurating wound. A stinging reek of chitin came from all the vents. On Aran's command the warriors lit pyres of myrrh and incense in all the plazas.

With Tzental before him, spear in hand, the sea lord raced along what had been the grand avenue of the fortress town of Mega, amid its empty cells.

"We are, for all of this, the stronger," panted the Elnyan, who had seized upon his master's thought. "What was done here—what they tried to do—will never work."

"Man at the mercy of the lower orders?" Aran re-plied, grim of face. "No. But don't put overmuch faith in this machine. It could break down, and no one knows how to build another."

"No," said Tzental. "I say so because of Yklantekli. They tortured him, tore the hide off him. But they never broke him."

Followed by warriors who explored every fold of the terrain and dispatched what hideous survivors they found, they reached that gaping mouth on the very site where the termite mound had once reared itself. Leaning over that abyss, Tzental saw a smooth slope and crawling shadows. Aran pushed the young navarch aide and kept going. He knew well enough what he was going to find in this hole: a breeding ground of monsters. His torch lit enormous cocoons, a moving mass of white grubs, a gutted human form with long red hair.

He aimed the disintegrator.

For three days the men fought on shore, destroying the megalosomes, frantically searching for any trace of Yklantekli's camp. Here and there in the forest they came upon devastated clearings, trunks of trees stripped of bark, witnesses to some fierce battle where man had fallen. But nothing living.

In the tunnels of Mega the conquerors found a fabulous treasure trove of gems and crystals which served as currency, and bags of mescal, chica, opiates, clearly furnished by the plants. They brought these things aboard, along with the flat stones which had served as altars and stands, and the celebration began.

For battle now gave way to orgy. Great red fires reflected off the black waters; men drank palm wine and chica from wineskins or munched barbary figs. Seafarers gambled for jewels on bloodstained altar stones while others slept in fevered dreams, wracked with delirium.

Skirting the knots of drunk and drug-dazed sailors, Aran observed with sorrow the ease with which his graceful Elnyans, his disciplined warriors, had changed to savage beasts. They had pillaged, burned, murdered. Of course the megalosomes were filthy brutes, but they had not spared the captive slaves either, and he himself... He retired to his tent on the bow.

But Tzental appeared, bringing with him two little girls, probably mongrel Elnyan. Tzental had found them in a tunnel where the novice priestesses wallowed in their nest. Accustomed to darkness, the two little girls pressed close together, shut their great eyes, offered their amber bodies which smelled of herbs and smoke. They had likely been stolen from some village, or needy parents might even have sold them... transactions with the higher plants were a common enough thing. Tzental left them in the doorway and discreetly vanished.

The elder of the two had long black hair falling to her knees; her skin was the color of magnolia petals. Aran was lifted on a burning ride. Ah, he was not proud of himself! But this resemblance was more than he could bear—such a delight—so deep a wound—

He realized he had lived all these days with the image of Atlena at his side, under his eyelids, and that he had become mad. *And might this not be,* he thought, *the better way out? She will never love me. We will never in this world know that sweetness and that fever that mode the ancients like gods. To have an illusion, that's all there is left for me.*

With infinite gentleness he leaned forward and took the little girl's face between his two hands like some delicate fruit. Under trembling lashes two vast and empty eyes opened. Never having seen one of the Sunborn before, the little captive believed that someone had sacrificed her, and she offered herself, arms wide, aglow with ecstasy.

"Orchid god," she lisped.

He hurled aside the offered body, the face uplifted like a flower, this human child vowed to the green gods. The spell was broken. What? To dream of Atlena in the arms of this docile animal? Shuddering with disgust he called Tzental and bade him take the child-priestesses away... find their families, return them to the city.

At the prow of the flagship the sea songs, wave kisses, siren sighs... rocked the little ivory goddess under the bowsprit. She too bore Atlena's likeness. Aran had designed it so.

He bit his lips. Where to go? From now on the whole universe would remind him of that royal, inaccessible child. The black water was smooth as her hair; her face came to him amid the bubbles of the foam and among the stars. She followed him everywhere. Death itself was nothing against this slow and wondrous torment.

Suddenly on the shadowed shore rose a dire murmuring. Tzental froze halfway up the steps and the two humans shuddered. No, it was not the groaning of a megalosome, nor the moaning of slaves. There came a chanting, a few words of the Elnyan tongue quite distinct...

A phrase.

"They're—" Aran said. "*What* are they? Listen, Tzental. I thought I heard—*They're dead at our feet And they have not the wounded brow...*"

"The man-beasts," said the navarch, pale of face. "They're in Mega. They're feeding on the dead."

VII

The news of the victory at Mega reached the city, and the queen was to spend the night in prayers in whatever temple suited her. She named, as it happened, the royal pyramid. Her plant councilors at once advised her to postpone the visit till the morrow. The edifice was old and its guards would not be expecting such an honor. Atlena gave them no answer and left that same evening, accompanied by a few faithful servants. Aran had won! The rest mattered little. A voice sang in her heart; she walked on clouds.

According to custom, she left Tlavatli, Tueni, and Ramessa at the forest edge and went alone into the white vaults. A man was sitting on the threshold, a Guardian with red-rimmed eyes. He failed to recognize her, doubtless, for he did not rise. When she was quite near, she heard him muttering to himself.

"*Here is truth, all the trut...* they've taken all my keys..."

"All?" asked the queen. "And why, if you please?" She sat down beside him, using the train of her white robe to dust off the steps. The old man did not answer. She added politely, "If it doesn't bother you, I shall stay with you a few minutes. I'm supposed to go pray in the sanctuary, but I'm quite comfortable here." She lifted her face and stared companionably at the stars: Eridanus and Aquarius, the Dove and the Sextant watching over the sleeping Empire. They had not changed for millennia, and each sun had for company its own train of planets where perhaps there were humans. She could not feel alone. A gentle breeze stirred the forest.

"If you like," the Guardian proposed, recovering a better face to matters, "I can guide you to the tombs of the queens. Those keys I do have."

"But the valley is a long walk from here," Atlena said.

"No, not the princesses buried in the valley. They're too ancient, and besides, I don't know their names. The last dynasty has its dead buried right here in the pyramid. There isn't much room left. We're at the end of the age."

"Ah!" said Atlena. "How do you know?"

"By the crypts. At the beginning of each dynasty, the plants make their calculations, and they build as many crypts as there will be sovereigns."

"And you say that all the crypts here are occupied?"

"There remain just the tomb for little Atlena and the pit of Ael."

"Who is Ael?"

"Queen Maos' son. The queen's brother."

"She has no kinsmen but the prince regent and Prince Aran!"

"Oh, but she does," replied the Guardian. "You're too young to know. The queen, anyhow, doesn't know it either. Ael's the one who turned into a beast."

Atlena rose, cold to the heart. "You're mad. If Queen Maos had had a son, he'd be a Sunborn, and everyone knows they don't get the plague."

"This one has it," said the Guardian. "Anyway, he's only half a Sunborn. Queen Maos married an Elnyan she loved dearly. Now you know, he was maybe her clerk—someone gave me to understand so, I've forgotten who. I'd gladly show you Ael, if I had my keys, though he's really not a sight for a young lady. But you see, someone's taken my keys, this very night. Will you come see my queens, aye or nay?"

Atlena followed him like a sleepwalker. She had often had the impression of living and moving in a dream, especially since Aran's return. But she mistrusted everything. She had her food tasted by her servants and at night she closed the windows overlooking the garden.

They arrived at a bronze door. The Guardian touched the delicate carvings there.

"Here we are," he said. "The first tomb to the left is empty. That one waits for little Atlena. I sweep it and keep it aired,

70

especially since there's some question about her wedding flight, because you never know, do you? Accidents happen. But it's rare that a young and beautiful princess dies at a husband's hand. All the consorts sort of let things take their course, you understand—maybe hoping for some mercy, or that it will only be a charade, a game. But there never is any mercy. They make them drink a philter *before*—and when I say *they*, I know the ones I mean. So do you. No doubt about it."

"Yes," said the queen.

"Now the last queens of A-atlan are all here," the Guardian went on. His diminutive form took on in Atlena's eyes a fearsome size. "Maos, Atlena, Atlys—and how many, many more! I mention these because they're my favorites. They died young and they're so pretty in their plastic cases. Yes, they do embalm them all. The plants use a very ancient method, excellent, oh my, yes, they do know their spices. So my queens are very beautiful in their funeral gowns, and when they sit up on their beds to speak, oh my! You'd think they were alive. Of course, they always say the same thing, and the records are a little worn. Eh, shall we go in?"

She could only nod her head.

The bronze lotus-door slid aside, raising a cloud of very ancient dust. Atlena saw before her a long corridor, dark and cold, wherein flickered globes of glowing crystal. All along the walls, crypts were hollowed out. Only the first was empty, and another—walled up. Each of the others contained a sarcophagus, lined up like beds in a dormitory.

The man pressed the heart of a lotus. On the right a porphyry coffin tilted up. The lid opened like a door. Atlena recoiled with an outcry.

A shape lay facing her on the bier. The queen was actually covered with a kind of crystalline, transparent sheath, which kept her colors as in life. She had a silver-white face, cherry-blossom, deathly white, black hair woven with pearls m a thousand tiny braids, and, beneath her half-closed eyelids,

71

irises the color of lapis lazuli. Her cloak of violet byssus swept the floor and a circlet of amethysts crowned her brow.

"Atena," said the Guardian. "She was killed in her wedding flight, by a stupid Elnyan who didn't know enough to appreciate the honor he was given. For the law says: *In unions between castes, it is the high caste that kills.* And the queen is above all castes. Since then, the plants have introduced the philter. Ah… you want to know what became of the Elnyan? Not much. He died, of course. My queen will tell you."

A voice actually came to their ears. Atlena tried to tell herself that it was only a very old record installed in the sarcophagus, only the coursing of very old grooves, for it seemed to her that the hard lazulite eyes rested on her. Queen Atena drew herself up on her mermaid's tail and spoke to them:

> *On my second flight I died.*
> *I opened gates of mystery*
> *And now I know.*
> *My slayer lies in Hell.*
> *Spines tore him*
> *And vines strangled:*
> *The power of the plants.*
> *Blessed be A-atlan.*

The porphyry coffin resumed its horizontal position and the dead woman lay still on her gold-broidered cushions. The young queen cried aloud and pressed her hands to her temples.

"The law, always the law! But where is it leading us? It's the first time I've asked that, Guardian, and I'm afraid. If Sunborn kills Elnyan, Elnyan kills his red-caste wife, and red warrior kills green slave—then what is left of A-atlan in the end? Can it be that our laws are meant to exterminate the human species?"

"Ah, well," said the Guardian philosophically, "A-atlan has lasted for 2000 years at least. There are always infractions of the rule, and, in time, one marries within his own caste. Evidently that *is* rarer now, since anthropomorphs tend to be born most often in marriages between equals…"

"These aren't human rules!" Atlena pursued, seeming not to hear him. "These are the laws of the hive and the ant-hill! What would happen if a queen rebelled?"

Her answer came in a fluid music which arose from the crypt opposite. An amber and electrum bier opened. Clothed in azure, brow girt with a tiara of turquoise, Queen Atlys, called the rebel princess, seemed to smile upon an eternity of light:

I died.
Here lie I, friend of the plants
I pass them my crown: they are the law.
Blessed be A-atlan.

"She went to the Council palace," Atlena observed harshly, "and she never came out of it alive. That's the way of it, isn't it?"

The Guardian had no time to answer. The face of the third cell slid back.

Oh! The third! Atlena thought. It was an enchantment. The music was sweetness and violence at once. Her hair was honey and her eyes nightbound lakes. Under her nacreous robes, rainbow hued, Queen Maos had Aran's likeness. *Not at all strange; we're all cousins.* Maos looked less like one asleep than like a woman hiding some unspeakable joy. They called her the Queen of Sin.

"But I thought she was burned alive," the little princess said, "because she broke the law. How beautiful she is! Are there crimes that make one beautiful? What was it she did?"

"I thought," the Guardian said, "that the whole Empire knew that. Queen Maos married three times—twice with Sunborn who died as they ought—one the father of Ael and the other of Atlena. They were profligate with Sunborn in those days. The third mate was Elnyan. She was so attached to him that she hid him a whole year in a tower... But they found him anyway, and sacrificed him."

"And the queen?"

"They never burn the queens. They save them to give advice to generations to come. Everyone can find something worth thinking about in what they say. And the more I think on it, young miss, the more I think your own fate didn't bring you here tonight without reason."

"Without reason?" Atlena could not take her eyes from this beautiful young woman—who was her mother. "Ah, no."

The ensorcelling voice sang to her:

I died; and this is why.
Judge me, you passersby.
I am Queen Maos;
I despised the law.
I failed to kill my mate;
Cursed be my name forever.

Here the record broke down and a hoarse and heavy voice (the voice of an amorous woman, decided Atlena, who knew nothing of love) began to repeat tirelessly:

I died... I died... I died...

The little queen fled, stopping her ears.

VIII

The following night Atlena came alone to the throne room. But as always the emerald shadow rustled with invisible presences. The window overlooking the garden was full of moonlight. A liana vine reached out. Atlena laid upon the last step of the throne a shining object, a ring, and then withdrew. A fountain sobbed into its basin.

"I don't understand," the queen said, "what you expect of me."

"Majesty," replied a fat green peyotl, hidden behind the pillars, and his thought waves were honeyed. "We remind you of your queenly duty, that's all. The Empire of A-atlan has always been ruled by Sunborn. The divine posterity only survives in you and in the house of E-enor. We have already spoken to you of this. Your answer has been—"

"The same as now. The sea prince is too important. He serves the Empire too well for me to think of sacrificing him. I leave it to his decision. I say so again. Well?"

"Well," whispered the gourd, dimly glowing, "Prince Aran says that he consents."

Astonished, she put her hands to her face and gasped a breath. When she lifted her eyes, Aran was there, in the shadows. He had not taken the time to put off his armor and, unmoving, he stared at the black and white patterns of the pavement.

The queen asked in a voice grown hard, "You consent, do you?"

"Yes, my queen." Aran's voice was hoarse.

Atlena recovered at once. Her short reign under the iron rule of the plants had accustomed her to contain her emotions. Since Aran had betrayed her—for in her eyes it was betrayal—she could no longer rely on anyone but herself. She nodded, extended her small hand to the peyotl. "The ring?"

"It is there," the plant hastened to answer.

"Let this man put it on my finger."

This man. She said it well: Prince Aran no longer existed. He came, he bowed the knee, deathly pale, all the muscles of his face rigid. When he passed the circlet of diamonds onto her finger she felt his hands. They were like ice. *They've poisoned him with mescal—or what more?* she thought. And aloud said, "You know what awaits you?"

"Yes."

"Swear, then."

"I swear that I am warned. The queen of A-atlan delivers herself to the wedding flight to perpetuate her race. I am her slave, and any disobedience to the rites is punished with death. I know that having received the ring and the gift, I must die before the dawn. I shall not resist. Blessed be A-atlan."

"The promise is made, and it is irrevocable," the peyotl pronounced. Triumph sang in his voice.

The queen restrained herself no longer. "Withdraw," she ordered. "I don't want any plant in my palace. This man will surrender his weapons to me and I will speak with him—alone."

"Majesty—the law commands—"

"—that you obey the queen. By the gods and the totems!"

The green monstrosity retired slowly, letting his roots trail behind. Atlena and Aran were left alone, he kneeling, she still upon her throne. She looked at the sea lord so long that her courage wavered.

"Conqueror of the oceans!" she said. "Conqueror of the jungles and of the megalosomes! What other titles does the city give you lately?"

"Be quiet."

"You give the orders here now? You've renounced your rights and your honor. From now on, you're nothing but a slave, a man condemned to death. Oh Aran!" She could not prevent a catch in her voice, and shouted then in rage: "You think this pleases me? Well, I'm crying. Be happy!"

Aran lifted his head. Something like his old smile touched his lips, and Atlena cried, "You've betrayed this land and you've betrayed me!"

He murmured, "The green dragonfly..."

The living waters wept on the esplanade of the palace. The divided Moon burned as yellow as in the first days of Creation. Atlena left her throne; in the emerald night she shone like a water flower. When she was face-to-face with Aran, she drew herself up on tiptoe, put her hands on his shoulders, and spoke in the secret tongue of the Sunborn, known long ago in the company of Hellemar.

"It's like that, then? They've stuck you down, captured you? They've forced your consent. Tell me."

"Oh, no," he said with vast weariness, "you still don't understand. I love you, Atlena."

The migration of the moths began very early this year. They passed in grand, gliding flights and shadowed the Sun. Certain particularly lovely species, the velvet io's, the thin-veined luna moths, the flame moths with yellow eyes and tiger stripes flew over the council gardens like airships, and the red eyes of sphinx moths blazed in the night.

But these grand and noble flying creatures gradually weakened. The sudden mutation had drained their powers of resistance, and at any instant some cecropia crashed against a garden wall or tumbled out of the sky to drown in the sea. Atlena watched them from the terrace of her palace and observed with horror that they were too beautiful to survive, like the Elnyans they resembled. What would become of them then? She knew that there existed secret enclaves where the most luxurious orchids—and the most carnivorous—awaited their levers. Until now the mating customs of insects and flowers had never moved the pure and cold Sunborn. But now these terrors stared her in the face.

Clouds of little red and night-blue bombyx passed, encumbering the public thoroughfares. They flew in a straight line, seeming to follow some secret summons. In vain, red

Giants posted at the four corners of the city tried with trumpets and sea conchs to herd the swarms landward. The masses flew over the Megalopolis, littered the plain with little brown velvet bodies in a dark rush seaward.

"Love and death," Atlena said to herself. She clenched her hands and bit her lips. "Is that all we have left now, love and death? The two doorways, the two trials—like birth— where a creature uses both body and spirit?"

But abstract philosophy was not Atlena's strong point. She was restless everywhere. Why did the plants, who could not survive without the moths, let them grow so delicate, so vulnerable and frail? Their lives scarcely lasted any time at all. Their migration was like a mass suicide. What did the orchids *do* in their enclaves?

She was suddenly cold.

For three days and three nights the thick, unbroken wall of moths flew to meet the two moons reflected in the ocean, captives of the glows, of the reflections, and of death. Some, seized with madness, began their spirals early, over the city, and fell to their deaths.

The water of the cisterns quickly became undrinkable.

The signs in the Heavens were dire. The divided Moon rose half black, half scarlet, and the two crescents fled each other.

They brought the queen's wedding gown to the palace. Starred with opals, it glowed like a lake. The last Elnyan embroiderers had spent ten years and all their care upon it. The crown bore seventy antennae, ending alike in huge diamonds, and a cascade of pearls held the veil in its folds.

The weight of the jewels was such that, once dressed, the queen could not walk. They carried her in her sedan chair. Seated between a mottled python and Tiouy, her island pygmy, amid the iridescences and the jewels, she looked at once like a goddess and like a child.

Whirlwinds of red sand and the cyclonic spirals of butterflies turned the procession into a panic rout. The queen laughed at the sight of cacti overturned, roots in the air. The streets were deserted, for all the population of the city was gathering at the temple. A double hedge of Elnyans and distressed warriors massed along the triumphal way. They wore their parade uniforms and had ashes in their hair.

Prince regent Uxmal met the queen at the threshold. He wore mourning, as befitted a father who was sacrificing his son: saffron garments and a gold mask. Atlena set her hand on his fist and tried to smile at him. The waves of her thought hurtled vainly against a mental barrier.

"See here," she said, "you know well enough it's Aran who wanted this. He's mad, oh yes, but so far as I have any power, he is in no danger. Only, see—I speak for myself, not for others. If you can talk to him—stop him."

They entered beneath steep, pointed vaults. This temple built by men belonged to them so little now that the divinity lacked a face. In the moving light Aran, stripped of insignia and of weapons, resembled a statue. Atlena clenched her jaw, lowered her lashes, and walked toward the double gleam. On either side of the altar Uxmal, prince of men, and Peyotl A master of the plants, had taken their places. The queen addressed the prince regent in the ancient formula.

"Is it by his own will that this man is here?"

Before Prince Uxmal could give his response, Peyotl A said in a triumphant voice: "Is it indeed of your own will, Aran, prince of E-enor, who were lord of the seas and master of the legions, chief of the warriors of A-atlan, conqueror of the oceans and of Mega—that you stand in this place?"

"Yes," Aran said.

Atlena cast to the officials the symbolic ring. "Put it on this man's finger, for I am the queen of A-atlan. Because I must continue the Sunborn race and keep the throne pure of taint I accept his life. He will share my wedding flight and die. Blessed be A-atlan. I have said. May the gods hear me."

A green phosphorescence passed over the peyotl gourds. Peyotl A said in a loud voice: "The gods have heard you. Blessed be A-atlan, land of plants and of men! Henceforth,

Aran, who were prince and chief of warriors, I salute you as dead. You are vowed to the infernal gods. Rest in peace."

The conchs and tympani rumbled. The ministers presented the queen the axe and the blade, the keen edges of which she regarded as in nightmare. Then a cup was offered them each. Atlena scarcely brushed it with her lips; when it was Aran's turn to drink, she staggered and caught herself on his arm. The black and burning liquid spread on the stones.

"Fatigue," she murmured. "It's the weight of the crown." From the mob crushed into gloomy silence rose a sigh, and the flowers, the leaves, and the tendrils rustled as in a storm.

But anticipating the movement of the warriors, Aran had leaned toward the queen and lifted her in his arms like a child. Head and shoulders he towered above the mob. Her delicate face, haloed with diamond antennae, leaned against his chest.

"Make way!" He used that well-known voice, that of the battlefields.

And, opening the sea of Elnyans and plants who stood stupefied and bewildered, he carried the queen like a plaything or a prize.

IX

She was raving for long days coming out of a stormy and shoreless sea. She brought out of it a ballast of visions which drew her back toward the depths. First and always, there was Aran. They had returned from the temple in a closed litter around which the people danced and yielded themselves to excesses. He had carried her in his arms through the deserted halls of the palace. But had they truly been alone? She had had the terrarium removed, but there remained vast windows open on the night, the mysterious garden and its orange lilies. Atlena saw only Aran, stretched full-length on the petals that strewed their bridal bed. His face against her bare elbow had a frightening tranquility, that of the blessed dead.

"You didn't let me drink the philter," he said.

"No."

"Why?"

Did she even know? All in her was storm and darkness. She begged him to flee with his ships. He laughed and refused. Then he took her suddenly in his arms. She fainted at the touch of his lips, sweet to the point of dying...

After that, she did not remember clearly. There was a wall between them, a physical and mental defense which made human contact hateful to her. A cry—perhaps her own, but she did not recognize her voice—a rush of shadows and a struggle... And in the wild night wherein she felt a lancing pain, a flash of steel...

Suddenly she lifted her hand to her throat, found a bandage, and was too weary to cry out. The night and the fever closed again upon her.

The first time that, with bitter mouth and bruised body, she left the nightmare, a green mass was watching by her bedside.

"Peyotl A," she said. "Am I dead and in Hell, then?"

"No, my queen. You are alive."

"But I am going to die?"

"No."

"The wound at my throat?"

"Be brave, my queen. He meant to kill you. But you are safe."

"*Who* meant to kill me?"

A silence. A name poured forth like a droplet of lead.

"Aran."

"You're mad!" And rising with a vast effort from her sweat-soaked cushions, she said, "Where is he? What have you done with him?"

More silence.

"Have you killed him? Answer me!"

Images and sensations of the previous night scattered from her grasp. She was sure of one thing: She had not struck him. But the wound was there. She recalled the brief chaos of shadows and cried as she had cried that night: "Aran, save yourself!" But the green glow which flowed over the peyotl's tumescences grew, filled her eyes, and drowned any slightest impulse toward rebellion. She was very weak from loss of blood. She fell asleep.

She took with her into the shadows a single image, a blade-edged certainty: at one moment of the struggle, she had hurled herself in front of the weapons that threatened Aran.

The world ceased to exist for days and days. At her bedside green figures took turns, repeating: *He struck you. He meant to kill you. He resisted the laws.*

Clenching her teeth, fixed in her obduracy like a little bandaged idol, Atlena repeated to herself, "They're lying. Kill me? He? He would rather die. He was gentle as a fawn, as a rose petal. He was—honey on my lips."

"Who else could have attacked you? You were alone."

"When I opened my eyes, the room was full of shadows."

"The guards came to your rescue. They threw themselves on the blasphemer."

"What guards? No red Giant would have laid hands on his commander."

"Council guards."

"Ah. Cacti. The long-spined ones."

"There was a frightful slaughter. But they got his weapons away from him."

"*I* gave him those weapons!" the queen cried. "Aran could never hurt me. He loved me!"

"Exactly. He struck you, mad with rage and passion. His morals were abominable and you know it."

She fell back into the hell of green shadows.

Finally came the real wakening, at the golden end of autumn, the crystal days of icy breezes. Atlena lay whole days on her terrace, watching the fall of the purple and rust leaves that announced the death and birth of the plants. On the lawn, peacocks spread their blue and green fans. Ramessa caressed the hieroglyphs of the singing books. They brought the queen some Elnyan children, charming and grave, whose brows were pure, who played at her feet with mysterious laughs. She knew that they were trying to console her that her own little child would not be born. But that was all right with her. Indeed it was all right.

At twilight she began to be afraid. They lit candles and the maids danced on the margins of the pools. A little peyotl played with images to dazzle their eyes. The queen had grown so weak that affairs of state had become an intolerable burden for her. At least such was the opinion of the Council, which had made decisions during her convalescence.

It seemed that Aran had never existed—or indeed that he still voyaged on unknown seas with some ghostly fleet. So dead men do, on the barks of the night.

The day came that they could carry Atlena to the temple, to thank the gods for her healing. She seemed languid, indifferent, but her glance, sliding between thick lashes, remarked countless mourning tunics along the road. The people seemed crushed by terror.

But the queen ordered mangoes thrown to the mob, breadfruits, and pearls glued to shells. The slaves fought over them and the Elnyans danced.

On the steps of the temple a pale, very old-seeming man tried to cast himself at her knees, but the human guards of the Council (who lately watched over Atlena) seized him and hastily bore him away. They had thrown a cloak over his head.

"Who was that?" the queen asked languidly.

"A beggar," said Tueni.

"A leper," said Ramessa.

They offered sacrifices and incense to the Unnameable, whose rites drew near—a secret divinity whom men and plants alike venerated, for no one knew if it had face or calyx. When the queen was returning to the palace a peyotl B discreetly dropped a word to her concerning the abandonment of a town called Mega: The enemy was too powerful, and it was better to break off the war.

"Mega!" the queen exclaimed. "But I thought that town had been destroyed."

"My sovereign has been dreaming."

"Then who commanded my armies?"

"General Yklantekli. But he is dead."

She shut her eyes and seemed very weary. In the depths of her burst forth a great mad laughter. She had caught them in a howling lie! They believed she had forgotten the campaign of Mega. They lied, they had always lied. Under her gossamer tunic her hand stroked a scar, not the mark of a knife, but of a spine, a plant's claw. She knew now who had wounded her, and in what struggle. She returned to the palace and took pains to seem languid and goalless, played with her mottled python a while, then declared that she would sleep.

Toward midnight, deceiving her guards' wakeful surveillance, someone came into her room—the pale old man of the Temple, Uxmal.

She sat up in bed and choked back a cry of horror.

Uxmal had wakened her suddenly. He looked like a ghost, an ancient mummy. His tunic was foul with ash; his head was shaved; blue veins stood out at his temples. He crept to Atlena's knees, not daring to speak. It was the queen who leaned forward, who seized him by the shoulders and stared into the depths of his yellowed eyes.

"Where is Aran?" she asked with unspeakable anguish. "Have they killed him?"

"Ah," cried the Sunchild. "You don't know. You, the queen—"

"Speak quickly," she shot back. "I only know this: that he never lifted a hand against me. What happened that night?"

"No one knows for sure. It seems he defended himself. Ah, not against you, no! But listen to me: For centuries they've put something into the groom's cup, opium, aconite, mescal—and the queen's husband is unconscious by dawn. Then the guards carry the body away. The Queen never remembers the struggle. Three princesses have resisted the law…"

"I know," said Atlena. "Maos, Atena, Atlys—"

He stared at her a long moment. "You didn't let him touch that cup, majesty."

"No."

"And you were wounded."

"Not by Aran."

"They struck you without meaning to."

Atlena smiled oddly and looked at her hands, her frail wrists. A nail broken off cleanly—she remembered—she had thrown herself between the guards and Aran, impaling herself on the thorns. All claws bared! Well, no one could reproach such behavior in the queen.

"All of that matters little," she said. "What did they do with him, Uxmal?"

"When you fell, he stopped defending himself. They took him but they dared not kill him. The hour of sacrifice had passed. So they took him away with them."

"You think he's alive?"

"I would give my heart's blood to know that he was dead," cried Uxmal. "You *know* the plants—"

She pressed her hands to her temples and choked back her sobs. Her brain, clear till now, struggled feebly to think.

"So," she said, "if he's alive, where did they take him? Into what pit of Hell? I could have my guards seized one by one. They would talk—"

"I don't think so," Uxmal said dejectedly. "How could they tell one plant from another? Besides, they were only barbary figs and prickly pears; they've surely disposed of them."

"Yes. The cacti can be thorough when they set their minds to it. But you must have an idea. Speak, try! You're his father, Uxmal!"

"The sailors of his fleet surprised some goings and comings of the higher plants at the edge of the Valley of the Dead. But no one has seen them cross the city."

Atlena thought, a line drawn between her childlike brows. "They didn't cross the city. They fear the mob that loves Aran. There must be some underground passage from the Council palace to the Valley. This continent is honeycombed with them. So! You're surely watched very closely. Send me one of his captains, then, a man you can trust. Ah, there is one Aran often mentioned: Tzental-ten-Helion. Hurry!"

Uxmal prostrated himself again. "Heaven save you, Majesty."

"Me?" she answered with hauteur and unbearable intensity. "What do I matter? But Aran—"

One thing was clear in her mind: the horror that burned in her upright as a candle flame. Aran was alive and a prisoner of the plants. She knew that he would have preferred to die.

The moment the prince regent left her, she called Ramessa with Tlavatli, the only red Giant they had left on guard at the door of her chambers. The Giant presented to the queen the expression of a faithful dog. The two servants were of limited help to her. Ramessa brought only a single piece of information: since the wedding flight the doors of the Council palace had stayed adamantly closed, as if the plants had feared a rising of the people.

Seated on her bed, her chin on her fist, Atlena reviewed what she knew of the dread palace: Even the queens rarely had access there. It was a fortress within the city. One entered it openly by the Stairs of Uncountable Steps and by the amphitheater where Aran had once defied the enemy. Two of its wings disappeared into the enclaves of the moving orchids... one abutting on the Temple of the Unnameable, the other on the Valley of the Dead. Whispered rumors said Queen Atlys—bravest of the queens—at odds with her Council, had once stolen into the fortress never to be seen again... at least, not alive. For six days the people and the queen's loyal guard had besieged the Agora. On the seventh, conchs and kettledrums at all the street corners heralded the terrible news: The Guardian of the Keys had found Atlys in the pyramid at the bottom of a sarcophagus, embalmed like the very ancient dead.

"And that much is true, because I've seen her," Atlena said. "So," she knit her delicate brows, "Atlys never passed through the city—no more than Aran did. She simply went into the Council palace and ended up in the crypt that waited for her. I think I begin to see things clearly. But the necessary matter—"

The next day Tzental-ten-Helion turned up at the queen's palace. Tlavatli, the Giant guard, and the dwarf Tiouy the clown, said that *Hummingbird* was at the doors of the room where the queen happened to be pretending a game of dice with Ramessa. It was a true palace intrigue, pathetic and ridiculous. The navarch Tzental had no more than approached Atlena before she knew all about him. He loved Aran with a devotion and a terror that undermined all his indolent Elnyan nature. He fell to his knees, burst into tears, and laid his dark young head at Atlena's feet. She was pleased to read in his brimming eyes the exploits of the sea lord, events wrapped in legend—the ships shuddered under the purple triangles of their sails, the sun-maul hurled its fires, Mega vanished in a sunlike death.

"You still think of him?" asked the queen. "Aye, so do I. We're going to look for him, you and I."

No name was spoken. They had no time, and the park surrounded the palace. The arrangements were made for that very night.

A last matter completed! her arrangements—a weakness of Peyotl A. *(A is so sure of himself,* Atlena thought wryly.) The great plant arrived in the afternoon brimful of agitation. They had found traces of a landing in the Valley of the Dead.

"Megalosomes?" the queen asked anxiously. She was playing at a game with Tueni.

He did not yet know. A shining object had been sighted over the desert and there were striations in the sand.

"Surround the Valley," Atlena proposed. "Ah! I forgot. Dry sand disagrees with you. Well, you have to wait, then. Defending an empire isn't so easy. One day we'll be attacked in this city and you'll be sorry to have gotten rid of Aran."

The huge globe darkened. "My queen," it murmured.

"Your queen?" Atlena asked impertinently. "I just like things clean and above board. It's not just with your roots and your perfumes you ward off insects and other high Strangers. According to my information, the Empire had only one being able to protect it: Aran. And you succeeded in destroying him. The wedding flight, indeed! That was nothing but an excuse. I never touched more than the rim of my wedding cup and I remember everything. I never fought anyone. Even if I'd wanted to, I could never lift weapons, and what kind of danger could a frail little woman be, facing a warrior of the sea lord's mettle? All the same, Aran has disappeared. My conclusion is simple. You killed him. Am I right or am I wrong?"

"He committed the crime of attacking you," the plant objected.

"So *you* say. *I* don't remember it."

A silence fell. Dead leaves skirled on the terrace. The queen faced Peyotl A with an expression so empty and a spirit so distraught that the great plant made the first mistake of his long career. He said reasonably: "We didn't kill Prince Aran."

"Oh? What did you do with him, then?" The queen seemed elsewhere. She took off her crown and counted the points of it. Her self-control was so great that Peyotl A walked straight into the trap.

"No one can see him," he said slowly. "And when he does come back—he will no longer be Aran."

X

Tzental-ten-Helion brought his skiff in as arranged, into the sleepy cove behind the royal gardens. The blue cliffs shielded him from indiscreet pryings, and flying fish played there under the divided Moon. The cove was familiar to him. He had often landed there with Aran. He knew that the tendrils and tentacles of the plants were powerless here at the edge of the dry sands. But it was in this sheltered corner and on this night that he met the greatest astonishment of his life.

A creature was standing in the middle of the beach. It was tall. Its armor glittered. The navarch took it at first for Tlavatli, but it was busy with a sort of silver dolphin. At the instant Tzental hailed it, the Stranger retreated and Tzental swallowed his shout. It was like a statue made of moonlight, shining metal, iridescent A short sun-maul swung at its hip. Beneath its lifted visor its features glowed white and gold. A god. Was it a god? The navarch dropped his oars and fell on his face in his boat. A sighing filled the air and a lightning flash set the sand ablaze. When Tzental sat up in his boat, which was gently tending out to sea on the backwash, he would have believed he was dreaming. The Stranger had vanished and so had the dolphin.

The Elnyan had not yet recovered from his surprise when the sands whispered and Tlavatli appeared, on reconnaissance. Trembling, Tzental mimed the encounter, the glowing apparition, and the silver fish darting toward the stars. Had a god descended to the desert rim? But the red Giant experienced neither the dreams nor the troubles of the golden caste. For him the matter was simple and the gods were dead with Hellemar.

"But there *were* other Sunborn," the navarch dreamed to himself, having cast anchor, "once, scattered across the Pleiades. If they still exist, they might send a messenger—"

"They'd have done it long ago," said Tlavatli, "if they could have."

The unknown machine, a needleship, as the pilots of the starports called her, had plunged through Earth's ionosphere, and when she had succeeded in forcing the magnetic field, the pilot had sighed with relief. The man's name was Victor Novy. He was the second officer of a reconnaissance ship stationed about Deimos, a spaceborne laboratory which had been observing Earth for many months.

For since the day the computers of the colonial worlds had noted perturbations of Earth's magnetic field, the web of observations had slowly tightened. Satellites and automated probes were launched daily toward Earth. The galaxy blazed in reverse the trail laid down by men of the 20th century.

But it was the first time in known history—for how many records and chronicles had been erased?—that a stellar emigrant had set foot on the soft and stable earth of the motherworld.

Victor Novy had staggered a little. He had not dared remove the suit. But he took among his gear samples of Terran air and sand. Before beginning his descent to the desert he had slowly overflown the dense jungle and once, a huge mound. His cameras and spectrographic equipment had worked frantically. But the moment he crossed the last barrier to Earth, he realized his eyes had captured the essential image of that rediscovered planet: that of a man standing in a fragile boat.

The queen appeared on the beach, veiled and wearing Ramessa's clothing. Tiouy the dwarf and the spotted python followed after her. With this company, looking like something between a fairy tale and a panic flight, Atlena undertook her revolt against the greatest power of Earth.

She settled in the skiff and it slid out on the thread of the current. Forgetful already of his encounter, Tzental admired the little woman, so clear-headed, steel-solid. He wanted to speak to her and dared not. Their course skirted the sandy shore. They saw in front of them the great Council gardens, full of secret life, walls of giant bamboo which protected the orchid enclaves, and the opal dome of the Temple of the Unnameable. Something was missing between the royal palace and the Agora—a whiteness, a divine presence, Hellemar.

Even he, the queen thought, *is out of human sight and reach.* And the likeness of the linked fates struck her.

Before them now stretched the desert, the valley of dry and crumbling soil, barren of vegetation—meteoric craters and zodiac wheels scattered like broken toys. There lay the kingdom of the dead, where 20 dynasties slept, preserved in salts and spices—and to this the royal pyramid gave access.

The skiff drove up gently on the blue sand. Tzental helped the queen ashore. She looked like a little secret divinity, hunted for among the living. Her feet made tracks in the dust of centuries. Her sandals bothered her; she took them off and walked barefoot. *I always come like a beggar,* she thought, *when I meet Aran.*

The company stopped in front of the pyramid. With all its lights extinguished, the great cone was plunged into the shadow of giant ferns and none of them dared go farther. Atlena, in a dry voice, hailed the Guardian of the Keys. No one answered. Then, wrapping herself closely in her veils, she walked forward and the python rippled after her. A door gaped before them. They plunged into a corridor and stumbled upon a mummy wrapped in sackcloth. The Guardian lay before the door of the queens. That lover of divine presences had not strayed far to die.

Tzental hesitated at taking the keys which hung from the dead man's belt.

"It would be irony," Atlena said curtly, "if a sovereign of A-atlan couldn't visit her ancestors. Give me the keys."

He obeyed. They entered under the vaults carved with the likeness of lotus flowers. A fine dust filmed the stones and carpeted the vacant tomb destined for her, the little queen.

"So," said Atlena, considering the three sleeping princesses, "there they are. Only two entered by that door in full view of the weeping mob. The third was discovered—found. She had followed another road. There must be a secret exit, under Atlys' coffin. Look for it."

The dwarf and the Giant, kneeling, worked around the bier, feeling of the partitions and pressing the flower petals. Tzental dreamed, that being the Elnyan inclination. He imagined the heavy coffin of the rebel queen voyaging in the darknesses of the Earth, then coming back to daylight to demand justice. There was truth in such images, for there came a moment when—doubtless Tlavatli or Tiouy had activated some mechanism—the amber and electrum coffin raised up and opened. The men recoiled, but not Atlena. She looked closely on the young corpse, arrayed with her chaplet of turquoises and pearls, her face calm and her eyes so very blue. The plants had gained the secret which had once eluded the Egyptians: They succeeded in preserving human eyes. But the pupils of this corpse were strangely dilated.

Yes, murmured Queen Atlys' distant descendant. *No wounds. But a good dose of belladonna or aconite wasn't it, majesty?*

The melodious voice replied:

I died.

Here lie I, friend of the plants.

I pass them my crown: They are the law—

Then like a hollow cry, like a plea—the Guardian before his death must have listened so often to his ghosts—the record was worn:

A-atlan!

Tzental and Tlavatli had fallen to their knees. Atlena shrugged.

"Ah, well," she said, "it's only a record. My ancestor has been dead for 200 years, so they can make her say what they like."

As she expected, the sarcophagus hid a gaping opening. The coffin had come from that track and—mockery!—the queen herself was guarding the access.

"You stay here," Atlena told Tzental and Tlavatli. "One of you watch the boat and the other the door. Tiouy comes with me."

"But dangers threaten you—" murmured the seafarer.

"I have my python and Tiouy has his lance. I have spoken!"

The navarch Tzental watched them descend. For him, the night's dream continued. First the messenger from the stars and his flying dragon which plunged up into the infinite, and now this descent into hell. The python passed, hissing, his delicate head uplifted. The queen's bright robe disappeared into the underground darkness. The young Elnyan shuddered, thinking that everything was repeating itself. In the myths Aran had deciphered in his presence, Ishtar, Astarte, Aphrodite had gone searching for Adonis-Tammuz in the abyss. Isis received back the fragments of a martyred body. Tzental's imagination wandered. Would Queen Atlena also lose her crown and her seven veils? Would she let herself be stricken with sores?

Everything was possible in the clear night, scattered with stars which were worlds. A cyclic destiny, the same atoms recombining in an infinity of diverse combinations, then rediscovering one day a certain chosen form, a privileged configuration. But that meant then that Earth and humankind would begin to live anew, that they would witness a new dawning— or quite the contrary, like a weakening echo, having reached the end of its refrain, did this rebirth of myths herald the end of everything?

The end. Tzental felt a sudden chill. He wished Tlavatli had not gone back to the boat. Everything around him spoke of endings. The queen would never come out of the dark; or, rather, she had never gone at all. The crypt resumed its unquiet silence, peopled with dead souls. He tried to imagine the Valley, the dust devils which might be wandering ghosts, the distinct shadows of the gods of the zodiac. All of it seemed incredibly old; the eroded monuments, the rounded teeth of the eastern mountains forming a landscape like a dead planet. At-lys in her tomb seemed to sigh: *This child of my blood is even more reckless than I. I wanted only justice. She seeks love in the realm of the dead.*

Tzental was brave. But it was one thing to sail the oceans, meeting storms and monsters, and quite another to defy laws and mystery and death. Navarch Tzental-ten-Helion felt chilled to the marrow, yet he had seen neither the bronze doorway of the laboratories nor, under the left wing of the Council palace—the octagonal room and its white tumuli—caverns, torture chambers, operating rooms, and laboratories where the plants exercised their power over humans—nor under the stark clarity of the crystal lamps, the form chained beneath its shroud.

When they returned, a livid dawn was streaming over the desert. The wounded python dragged his coils heavily along. He had fought a thousand unclean beasts in the shadows. Tiouy, exhausted, fell on his face. The others walked past Tzental without seeing him. Tzental wanted to shout aloud to them the incredible news which had finally penetrated his brain: that they were not alone in their fight! Their friends, their brothers were going to come, and one of them had already landed from the stars. But what proof could he give, even to Aran—what sign? They walked away into the distance of the corridor like shadows, and the navarch could believe that they had drunk the water of forgetfulness, in hell.

Outside, the moons slid to the plane of the horizon and a nacreous radiance came from the sands.

Aran was first to leave the pyramid. When the queen reached the threshold, she called his name after him, and Tzental saw his master turn. He choked back a cry. An inhuman suffering had made him thin, hollowed his beautiful face. He was foul with fluids and blood and, between the widespread edges of a wound, Aran bore on his brow the marks of a spongy tumor taken from a cadaver.

They've tried that on him, the navarch thought, cold with dread.

The Sun rose amid violet and green mists, a great honey-colored lamp. Beyond the sphinx and the wheels, the triumphant jungle recoiled before the desert. There was only a band of green shadows to cross.

There, Tzental told himself, *waits the last refuge, the farthest reaches of Earth, teeming with anthropomorph monsters and nightmares.*

"My place is henceforth among them," Aran said.

XI

To reach the desert, one had to cross the living wall which surrounded the city on all sides.

And one had to do it quickly.

The two lunar crescents had touched. Aran walked straight ahead, and the emerald night drank him in.

Then he understood *their* strength... that of the plants.

It began with the unevolved ones, the ferns, the olives, the terebinths. Never was an invasion more triumphant. Aran crossed the outskirts of the city whose very name was forgotten, places devoured by orchards gone wild and parks gone to thickets and copses. Here and there the ruin of some palace rose under a curtain of ivy, or a tower pierced the vines. By such signs the prince of E.-enor could measure the city's decline.

Ancient fortifications yielded to a zone of quagmires. Walls had fallen; slivers of malachite and mother-of-pearl marked the moats; the reek of stagnant water and of lilies constricted his throat. Huge water lilies floated on the ponds. For hours Aran crossed the pools flower to flower.

The plants had not all undergone the same changes. Certain ones, the iris, the cardamine, the marsh euphorbia, took no part in the nightmarish battle that set plants against humanity. Others, while remaining mute, sluggish creatures, reached colossal proportions. Horsetail ferns formed the pillars of a green temple. Emerald shadow reigned over thousands of leagues.

When the Sun climbed the sky, it shone only as a yellow-green glow through the vaults of leaves, in a living, suffocating steam bath.

Aran walked the whole day without stopping. He shied from any precise thought; for the evolved plants, it was in fact their only means of locating him again. His head was heavy and fevered, a sharp pain tormented his wound, and he paused only to wash and drink in the cup of his hands.

But the water contained for him a faint taste of rot.

He had no opposition. He must only defend himself from several encounters with clouds of moths and roving larvae; their soft touch, the rustle of heavy wings, nauseated him. He armed himself with a euphorbia branch and slashed himself a path through these whirling masses. The few surviving vertebrates, small beasts, beavers, weasels, left his path, perhaps sensing the despair which surrounded him and fleeing such a walking misery.

He reached unhindered the second ring of the forest, that of alders and maples and gray and purple poplars, so densely laced with vines that he must stop, find a shard of granite, and, imbedding that in his staff, make of it a crude hatchet.

All about him the forest prepared its third assault, and the end of the daylight was surely not far away. The green masses became black, impenetrable, the musk of leaves mixed with the odor of rotten wood. A cloying flower scent joined it suddenly and he looked over his shoulder, prepared to run. He lifted his face, drowned in those merciless perfumes, and saw there among the treetops a traveling colony of dark orchids, green and violet. Was it a patrol, or some greenhouse wherein a new species finished its mutations? Huge flowers opened waxen cups large as waterpots, thrust out stamens and quivering pistils, and while they were visibly occupied with their gestation, Aran felt himself suddenly weak, spent to the marrow, as if these giant mouths were drinking his life.

He began to run and saw the end of the forest. The countryside changed abruptly. The Sun set in its imperial purple over a stretch of white sand. The hunted man had still strength enough to tear through the vines, the tendrils which at the last moment wound themselves into his flesh; and to aim his bleeding body at the dunes. Now his wounds burned as if poisoned, but he knew that the jungle had recognized him, that it was too near, and he could not stop.

He walked, stubbornly turning his back on the forest, the city, Atlena, and his own past. But a long, pearly cloud over the desert reminded him of her thin body weeping in his arms, and he bit his lips furiously. He must not think of that night or its sweetness mingled with dread.

Later Aran could never recall the details of that walk; it confused itself with his personal concept of Hell.

The plants had disappeared. Here and there a few jeweled spines of crystallized salt evoked recollections of the terrible power of the flowers. Aran thought this region might be some sea bottom risen since the catastrophe. Indeed ancient lands were slowly emerging; he believed it. And when the capricious outlines of the hemispheres had been reestablished, the plants would take possession of them. There would be, in all likelihood, no more men on Earth.

He walked all night and part of the day. Other dangers lurked in this desert which must become his refuge. Here the dry, burning air tore at his lungs. He breathed and ate sand, and the heat reflections made his eyes seem to bleed. He was so thirsty that, his eyes closed, he saw at once the murmuring fountains of the city, the forest pools, pure water, mysteriously smooth. He realized this for a second, natural barrier which prevented all escape from the Megalopolis, and he forbade himself such weakness. But fever burned in him. When the Sun finally set, drenching the flats in its red glory, Aran flung himself down on the sand in the shelter of a dune and slept.

When he awoke, under the blazing of a Sun clean and clear as in the first days of Creation, he met a new suffering. His lips were cracked, powdered with salt, and his throat constricted like old leather. He hollowly mourned leaving the green Hell, drenched with humidity and sap; and painfully he gained his feet.

It was the third day of walking he remembered least. The creature who moved toward the blazing west was no longer Aran of E-enor, but a sunburned animal, an automaton. If he could have gone back to the jungle, he would have done so, running. But he was moved by a phenomenal and mindless will.

Finally the color of the Sun changed, the sky became darker and the air poorer. Under sandy cliffs appeared the likeness of a sheet of water. Drawn by the smell and a slight sense of moisture, the fugitive came down the slope. The sky was already darkening, and a bright star hung over that thin thread of crystal. A river, it was a river! He knew he was dying of thirst. *But I hardly realized it,* he told himself with fearful clarity. *Is that a sign of the vile thing they slipped into my veins? If only I knew...*

He knelt before that trickle of water. It reflected a terrible face, black and bloody, hardly human. He drank from his hands, then bathed his wound and saw his own familiar features reappear. It even seemed to him that the injury on his brow was paler and cleaner. *It's impossible,* he said to himself. *They tainted Ael, and I am damned too. Anything, anything but the torment of hope.*

But a brief glow was alight in his soul and he could no longer put it out.

And came the third night. The sky became violet, then black. In the cliffs overhanging the river Aran found a cleft in the rocks and slid down into it as into a tomb made to his measure. He found it a sensible precaution, for a few moments later the inhabitants of the sands began calling one to the other. A troop of them came down toward the watering place and in the trampling of feet and the smell of chitin, Aran realized there were beetles out there. An ant-lion passed on great outspread wings, with a frightful noise. Aran's fever populated his mind with hypotheses and deductions; he wondered, suddenly, why during the years just after the cataclysm, the more complex species, the warm-blooded vertebrates, had suffered everywhere and often become extinct, leaving their niches to arthropods and frogs, finally to plants, as if there were a reverse selection going on.

He was near a conclusion when he slid down into the depths of a nightmare. Atlena was there, but she pushed him away because of the wound on his brow, whose edges burned. It was unbearable. He tried to prove to her that the danger threatening the Sunborn was something else. Then the plants came: the gray cephalocereus, orchids trailing light, brittle filaments, like plants dried between the leaves of old herbaries. The nearer they came the greener they became. They puffed up and became enormous, as if they drank up life—his life. A green, spongy mass, an echinocactus surpassing all previous horror, crawled upon him in his dreams, insinuated itself into his veins, sucked his life like a sponge, disengaged and departed, into a mist.

Aran woke with a jerk. *But it was not just a dream, that—that horrible touch.* Conclusions imposed themselves. Dreams used symbols. So the monstrous advance of the cacti was due to the fact that they had learned to tap the life force of warm-blooded species.

First they must have killed indiscriminately, and that was when we must have lost almost all the four-footed vertebrates and that major portion of humankind Peyotl A was talking about. Then they changed their ways; they had to manage their granaries. I believe they killed Maos, Atlys, and the others. They had no further need of them and they drank them dry, that's all. But now I understand. This poor Sunborn breed of ours has somehow acquired a kind of immunity, or maybe we even manufacture some sort of toxin. That's why they're trying to destroy us.

And also because the times are turning around again. A new era is beginning.

Oh gods! It comes now that everything is lost!

He recalled the unmistakable portents: the return of lands from the sea, the stars that seemed closer, the green shadow's dimming. The planet was returning to its normal cycle. Other forces might, *must* intervene. Mankind must survive this waiting period! Aran suddenly felt a chill; his fever had broken. He crawled to the mouth of his cave. Above the river which shone like a naked blade, a blue line appeared on the horizon. The sky grew brighter and proclaimed the day. Suddenly a whirlwind rose over the dunes, tore off a bit of the cliffs, raised a curtain of sand, sank toward the sheet of water. And there was no more silence.

At first glance, Aran saw simply a whirling shape which grew tendrils, green horns, velvet feet, ending in strong claws and a long flame of red hair. Then he realized it was some great ape in the clutches of a horsetail fern—one of the mad ferns, of which even the plants spoke with a hint of disgust. A green giant, carnivorous, restored by the caprices of mutation to its size in the carboniferous era, half maniac, half vampire. The chances of its prey, even a gorilla, were scant in such a contest.

And yet the ape took the offensive. It went at it, hanging from the plant; it dug in its nails, wounded, tore bits off. The plant squeezed its adversary in its green fronds. They passed, one dragging the other along the shore, and Aran jerked—he had just seen, tightly bound to the trunk, a thing like a puppet that the plant carried along in its rush. A human child! The little body was smooth and golden—red hair swept the sand. Aran raced after it, forgetting his weakness and his wounds.

He fell with all his weight on the mad fern, which brought its fronds about and wrapped a tendril right where the torturer's collar had galled his neck. Aran felt an incredible pain, as if his body were suddenly being drained of blood. But he did not relax his grip. His hands closed on a green node as once they had on the sea monster's scales.

With a terrible effort, the plant fled farther, bearing along three intertwined bodies, but doubtless it overestimated its strength, for an instant later, it fell with a thud to the sand. Aran had time to free his right hand and, finding in his belt the polished stone fragment which had served him as an axe, he took several blind blows at it.

Thick sap oozed out. Green limbs unfurled and flung to Earth the ape and the human doll. Then, breaking in twain, the plant utterly collapsed.

The great ape scrambled up and ran to the child—no ape it was: Its eyes and brow were invaded by a wine-red tumor.

So then, he had arrived. He stood in the presence of the anthropomorphs. And he found nothing to say to them. For the moment he was paralyzed, frozen in horror.

A hoarse, hot voice. "I am she-born-without-blemish."

The little golden figure had risen. She was no child, but a very young girl, probably Elnyan, with a flower-petal skin, blood-red lips, and dark, sober eyes. Her brow was pure. The man-ape had fallen at his feet and sobbed something desperately. The girl repeated it, searching for words.

"Friend. I am a friend." Then: "You also have no tumor."

"But I do," Aran said; and, parting his hair, matted with sap and blood, he uncovered the wound. But the girl felt the injury, traced the scarred edges with her finger.

"It's only a cut," she said. "Somebody put something nasty there, but it's fallen out. You were hurt and you lost a lot of blood. Come with us. I'll care for you. You please me."

"You're sure?" Aran murmured. "It's not a real cancer?"

"Already dry. Your skin is nice. The real thing—it's like a wrinkly sponge. You stay with us, all right? I'm Naja. Him"—she indicated the blind man—"he's Naj. He says he's my father, but I doubt it."

Naj and Naja were part of a band, he learned, that was passing upriver. They had fallen behind, for Naj, being blind, hunted night as well as day, and the girl served as beater. Was he really her father? At any rate, Naja was clean, and that proved the blight was not necessarily hereditary.

She washed Aran's wound and cauterized it with desert salts. His fever rose dizzily and Naj carried him into the cave. Naja skinned the mad fern and the two anthropomorphs feasted on that suspect flesh, but Aran asked only water.

When night came again, one savage night succeeding the other, with beetles coming to the watering place and moths rustling, sighing, fluttering, Naja slept curled at the feet of her rescuer. A hundred times that night, calling Atlena's name, Aran pushed away that hot, thin body and clinging mouth.

But he told himself that Naja was used to monsters and that he failed to frighten her.

At dawn, sliding down to the river, Aran saw in the rainbowed water a face purged by suffering, pale, with—about the level of his brows—a pink scab which no longer oozed. He was seized with a powerful joy: Was it possible? The plants had been deceived—definitely—the graft had not taken. He was healing.

When he climbed back toward the cave the hot wind brought him a fearful animal stench. The dunes were crawling on all sides of him.

He saw them.

He had first the impression of a single face, inside out, pathetic, horrible, features invaded by a suppurating tumor. It had the look of a boil ready to burst, a green sponge, a third, faceted, pineal eye. The true eyes were nothing but bloody pits, the mouth a slavering cavern whence came a sometime rattling.

This terrible face, this symbol of human suffering, was repeated across the horizon. Truly they were beasts... and no, they were not. Standing on the hill, clenching his nails into his palms, Aran felt a piercing anguish in his heart, rage mixed with ancestral emotion: pity.

He wept over these monsters who rose out of the desert, spines bent to the Earth, black and burned, horrible. They walked, tearing themselves on rocks, descending the dunes, bloody rags and fur. Sometimes in the grip of demented rage they flung themselves to the sand and rolled and howled. Other tides flowed in—a living wave. The weakest were trampled. So operated a frightful selection. The rage of destruction drove them to annihilate everything in their path.

They never wept and never laughed.

The prince of E-enor was indifferently accepted by the clans. If he had thought he could rewaken these devoured intelligences, he forgot that hope. It truly seemed that the tumor had destroyed the cerebrum of the Changed-men. There were rare ones who, like Naj, had a name. They forgot concepts just learned and recognized no connection between cause and effect. The only things that fascinated them were forces of destruction—a landslide, an earthquake, a river in flood. Aran won their hearts from the moment of his first combat.

XII

Two moons had passed since Aran's meeting with Naja. The anthropomorphs flowed across the desert like a sluggish river. They traveled west, but they habitually delayed and strayed off their path. One day, Naja, who traveled on her blind friend's shoulders, lifted her hand and, through the golden dust, pointed something out to Aran.

"Andrada!"

It was a city of the Sunborn, buried in the sands. Aran, who had seen so many cities, regarded this one with admiration—its lacy walls and alabaster towers. What king, what queen had built and then abandoned those white marble terraces, those mosaic courts, those star-patterned squares? At a distance the mirage dazzled the senses.

Seen close at hand the city showed destruction worse than the cities under the domes. Parts of the walls threatened collapse. Dunes crushed the fallen vaults and along the public thoroughfares ran the careful glidings of serpents.

But there was something else. Passing through the city gates, Aran felt suddenly surrounded by shadows. A fearsome and hostile strength existed there. It was with them instantly and then the impression lightened just as suddenly as it had come. White walls blazed under an implacable sun. The grand avenues were empty and the plazas stood deserted.

Andrada looked apt for a meeting place, and yet the clans did not enter here. They stopped in the shadow of the ramparts. Was it because the anthropomorphs felt an instinctive dread of enclosures?

That evening Aran was compelled to attend a strange ceremony, the sole, dreadful ritual of the Man-beasts, the name they called themselves.

Whole tribes marched, shoulders bowed, dragging with them human corpses or great frogs. (What slave villages had they destroyed? What Elnyan outposts had fallen?) It was neither burial nor celebration. They dragged the naked bodies by the ankles or by the long, braided hair, panting with the effort. Corning up onto the ramparts, they hurled them off. It was impressive and rather frightening. Naj broke away from the horde and, with Naja's leading, passed his hands over the faces of this army of dead, feeling in turn their snouts and faces. Doubtless this horrible inspection satisfied him, for he turned and gave a guttural cry.

Then from the moats of Andrada, from the dunes and dead sands where the dark hordes had encamped, rose the dirge the prince of E-enor had heard once before at the walls of Mega, a wild, hoarse chant into which occasional human words were woven:

They have not the wounded brow.
But they die like we do!

The red and lowering Sun drowned the town in blood. At the ramparts the slave-caste corpses fixed glassy eyes on the vast sea which advanced, receded, marching in place before them. The living waves swelled, then broke to the rhythm of a terrible triumph:

They have not the wounded brow.
But they fall before us!

There was in that song an anguish without resignation, a bestial fury. They meant to prove something, to find in blood and death some primitive dignity. *Well,* Aran thought, *they do their best.*

At that moment of dull exaltation, amid the purples and flames of the setting Sun, a huge anthropomorph came forward. His brow was one massive wound, his hands hung to his knees, and he cast lustful looks on Naja. He pointed his hairy paw at Aran. In the tangle of his face shone a red glimmering. The fugitive prince understood in a flash the profound meaning of this ceremony: The inspection of the corpses tended to identify the enemy and to reassure them of their vulnerability. The black giant demanded that the stranger submit to it. The mob affirmed this demand in its vast dirge:

See if he has the wounded brow,
Or his place is not among us.
See if he has the wounded brow,
Or else he dies before us!

I have to silence them, Aran thought.

Things went very fast then. Naja cried out. And the prince of E-enor faced the colossus.

They were of roughly equal height, but the man-ape had longer arms, muscles like blocks of granite, and soft fleece protected his torso. They measured each other with their eyes and Aran coldly made his decision.

Either I take him in the first rush or he'll deck me and the mob will finish me.

The Man-beast sprang to the attack—his weight alone was enough to crush an enemy. But the Sunborn, lighter, countered with a feint and his arm shot out like a steel spring. The lightning blow struck both left eye and frontal tumor. Blinded by blood, drunk with pain, the monster tottered, crumpled. Aran was on him at once; his sharp stone axe cut the thick carotid. The conqueror arose, covered from head to foot with gore.

He expected an explosion of rage, a mass rush—but no one stirred. Only Naj, led by his daughter, came and in slow cadences sang bewildering things. Naj leapt up and down, hurled himself to the ground, mimed battles he had never seen: that just fought under the ramparts and the one wherein a mad fern might have devoured his child, but for the stranger's victorious intervention.

Around them the vast horde wavered, stamped, as at the edge of some chasm. Naja cried out suddenly in a shrill voice:

He has not the wounded brow—
But he kills better than we do!

And suddenly from the very depths of the desert arose a hoarse cry, a chant of victory. The whole flatlands howled... the death rattle of the dying was lost in it.

He has not the wounded brow,
sang Naj.
But he travels with us.

And the horde:
He has a hurting in his brow
But not a wound like ours.
An evil someone did him
That he does not forget.
And he kills better than we do.
He'll lead us to the town,
Kill those who hurt him,
Who took away our light.
And he kills better than we do!

Lifting his hand toward a Sun of bloody flame, Aran gave them his answer.

"Yes, I'll lead you to the town!"

One night he wandered with Naja through the ruins of Andrada. The city had been abandoned in a panic. All the doors gaped wide. The sands buried debris of statues and broken pottery. Serpents hissed under the doorsteps. From an altar hollowed like a cup, Aran gathered a fistful of incense.

Why had the inhabitants fled this town which bore no trace of burning and whose gates still hung on rusty hinges? The heavy impression of a hostile, veiled force persisted. In tunnels which must once have served as warehouses the explorers found dried fibers, a light dust, likely what remained of provisions. Andrada had not died of famine. Nor of poverty. In the same dust were hoarded piles of dulled jewels, dead turquoises, and chains of aquamarines, which Naja hung about her neck and arms.

They went farther and Aran discovered under the lower vaults, which led to unguessable depths, several heaps of whitened bones, of human skulls, vacant-eyed—and beside them, abandoned weapons beginning with the most recent (the most barbaric), arrows with poisoned barbs, clubs of the red Giants, studded with nails; and finally the dreadful little flamers and scopes of another panicked age. It looked like the leavings of several lost patrols, of various armies which over the centuries had come to rest in the same pitfall.

Aran stooped and picked up a small flamer. The weapon was in good condition.

He looked on these relics and his irrepressible instinct for leadership began to function.

We can sharpen the steel, he thought. *Bowstrings can be replaced. I can choose among those less afflicted with the sores, and teach them to use the clubs and maybe the spears. The hunts will be more abundant and in an attack, they'll defend themselves.*

For he used subterfuges even on himself. Since the triumphant and bloody day of his first fight, when all the bestial population had recognized him as master, he had forbidden himself certain thoughts. He tried to live as if his promise to them did not exist.

He never said, *I'll lead them against A-atlan,* but, *I'll turn them against the plants.* Yet he knew it came to the same thing: There was never a torrent harder to dam.

Perhaps it was not entirely conscious. He still had a fever. True, the cancer had not taken, the flawless body had rejected the poisonous graft, but something in Aran was broken. He knew henceforth a human weakness in his flesh; he knew he could be a prey. Not only his pride but his humanity was slain forever. Sometimes a brief nightmare rewakened in him his sojourn under the Council palace. He regarded it with a shame mixed with horror.

But there was worse. Throughout his nights in the white desert under the conjunction of the moons, he realized he could not live without Atlena. She burned in him like an upright flame.

He saw her everywhere, in the clouds racing over the double disc of the moons, in the clear dawn—all the marble of Andrada had her whiteness. He looked with rancor at Naja because her shadow, at evening, elongate on the stones, briefly evoked the little queen. Hardest of all, there remained their shared memories, things they had loved together—the pearly tints of the evening sky, a certain song, the fluid movements of waves. He could not forget the way she had of clasping his arm when, in the night, she had wanted to know he was there and that it was truly he. But he had been the one most comforted by such a trust.

Then accesses of cold rage would seize him. He would see Atlena standing on the threshold of the pyramid, while in the dim glow of dawn her eyes fixed on his wounded brow. There was in her violet gaze neither revulsion nor horror, only a terrible anguish and pity—but he wanted no more of pity. He had bitter regrets. He should have seized her and carried her away with him. She still loved him, for she had come to save him...

Stupidity, he told himself shortly. She could never have endured a trek through this desert—or living near these beasts.

But he knew other dangers pressed close upon Atlena—and he was not there to protect her. That was killing him.

The anthropomorphs lent themselves readily to war games: It was a new way of destruction. Lacking artillery, the younger ones wandered to the edge of the desert and uprooted some small palm trees. Naj and the other blind ones—they were numerous, for the tumor attacked the optic nerve—polished the knives. They made hatchets out of flint.

To teach the horde how to pursue and trap the rare game of the desert, Aran had to turn hard. He remarked that the red and green anthropomorphs (warriors and slaves) made more rapid progress than the Elnyans. The latter even as shadows of their former selves still kept their versatility and their insolence. They went often into the forest and whispered together interminably. One day the main cistern of Andrada turned up full of vipers. Several blind ones drank the poisoned water and died. Slaves talked, indicated the culprits.

Then knowing henceforth what would make an impression on the horde, Aran set up on the ramparts stakes with a horizontal bar. He hung the rebels there and let them die.

His renown grew, and filled the desert.

XIII

The first expedition Aran risked, he directed at the deep, secret harbor facing the Valley of the Dead, where his fleet was anchored. At the time of his parting with them, the eve of the wedding flight, his father, Uxmal, had murmured, "Every night your ships and I will be waiting for you." Maybe they had gotten tired of waiting. But there was still a chance.

So Aran formed a warrior band of those least touched by the ulcer, those who could still take orders by telepathy. He hunted the skies, killed bombyx and giant beetles which he left to the horde. And the feast began. *They'll stuff themselves,* Aran thought. *Doubtless they'll be sick, but they'll not leave Andrada.* Then he set his curved sword in the middle of a public square, thereby creating a totem, and trusted it to Naj and Naja.

He drove his little platoon across the desert. When evening came, the wind brought them something different from the forest resins and the heavy staleness of Andrada: the smell of the Megalopolis; and the anthropomorphs shuddered. Some crouched to the ground and refused to walk. He killed two of them as an example. The rest arose, submissive.

At the edge of the Valley of the Dead, Aran climbed a hill. Alone. He wished to show no weakness to his followers. It was a fortunate decision. In the black harbor, wherein the double Moon reflected, lay his galleys, rotting. The crews had gone. The ships drifted among the weeds and the sea rolled in the between decks with an oily sliding. So this was what A-atlan made of his exploits and his glory. He had foreseen his death, but not this oblivion.

Guided, moved by an unknown impulse, Aran leapt to the bridge of the first moored vessel. The hull was bare. There was left on deck not a solitary coil of cable, not so much as a boarding pike. Nothing. It was all stripped. Ten years of his life had gone into this void, and it seemed to him that his very life's blood flowed away through the gaping holes the reefs had made in the ebony hulls.

The great corpses lay shoulder to shoulder. Aran crossed the deck of the *Hope* and the *Anger* and came to the *Queen of A-atlan,* his flagship. Here the destruction had been plainly deliberate: masts unstepped, the majestic trireme listed to the port side; he could see her figurehead underwater, mutilated. Mussels and barnacles ate away the crescent moon she clasped.

"Meryem," he said softly. How many voyages they had made together. And here she was dead, like all that touched him. In passing, he looked down into the main cabin where he had spent feverish nights dreaming of Atlena. A cloud of silver fish danced around the rudder.

And he saw it.

A pale figure floated gently, pushed by the ebb tide. Eddies spread a saffron mourning cloak. Neither water nor sharks had yet unfleshed it; Ùxmal's face was recognizable.

The cabin doors were sealed. Aran struggled desperately to get the corpse in through a porthole. Although it was recently dead, the limbs had gone brittle. The body was drained of blood and shriveled. Fearful of mutilating it, the prince of E-enor broke the bulkhead with his axe, dived in, and finally brought his father ashore, carrying him like an infant.

He acted like an automaton; a living man would have shrunk from this dire specter, this face white and hard as onyx. So the plants had won. In the eyes of A-atlan, Uxmal had been the last male Sunborn. Laying his father on the sand, Aran looked long into his face. He knew this manner of death. Once most of his line had died so—had grown pale and weak, complaining of nightmares and dimming eyesight. It was not that they were sick, it was that something drank up their life. At a distance. And there was no defense.

Aran knew he could not carry this brittle body with him into the desert. He wrapped it in his cloak and carried it toward the royal pyramid. His anthropomorphs followed him in silence.

The edifice reared its cone amid clumps of black and green. Nothing recalled the night of his escape. The plants could not be taken twice by the same snare. The entrance to the tomb of the queens was sealed. But he struck imperiously at the iron door and after an eternity of waiting, another Guardian of the Keys came with his key ring and his torch, and prostrated himself.

"*Here is truth,*" he recited, "*all the truth—*"

A dim rasping came from the shadow. The man lifted his eyes and beheld the monstrous shapes at his door, and fainted with an owlish little gasp. Aran entered the pyramid and walked to the queens' crypts. Atlys' bier was vacant and the tunnel was walled up. He laid Uxmal on the shrouds, which still smelled of nard, of benzoin, and spices, and, as children do with their dolls, he arranged on the neck of the dead prince some faded garlands.

There was no speech to make; all that was settled and foredoomed. And Uxmal would have rejected any vengeance he could have promised.

The rest was nothing but reflex.

A cold rage gripped Aran. But he delayed to order the opening of the deep pit where raved and howled a white beast. It took three anthropomorphs to drag out that convulsing body.

In the glow of the torches in the outer court Aran could compare their two wounds. Ael had simply undergone a lobotomy. They had worked on the cortex, but he had no trace of cancer. *They wanted to make us think the blight had reached the Sunborn, that's all,* Aran concluded. *They reckoned it was possible with me, but it didn't work.*

His eyes suffused with blood, the last-born son of the queens of A-atlan snarled like a cornered panther. The anthropomorphs carried him on their shoulders. They put the place to the torch.

And the desert received them back.

The war had begun.

At Deimos, the galactic war council closed without reaching a decision. It was officially acknowledged that a landing on Earth was now possible. The pilot Novy had returned. But the documents he had brought back still lacked the necessary information. The enormous machinery of interstellar politics set itself ponderously into motion. The hearing was over. The humans who had gone out from Earth (and who indeed bore scant resemblance to their ancestors, who had through mimicry and the instinct for self-preservation taken on appearances and manners so diverse that it was hard to tell them from spider lilies, Hyads, or the blue-violet pyramids of Foramen)—these sons of old Earth then adjourned, murmuring diverse opinions.

Victor Novy, who had sat in on the disappointing hearing in the galleries reserved for humanoid listeners, felt the hand of his co-pilot, Roger Kairn, touch his elbow.

"Let's go," he said. "These intrigues make me vomit."

A needleship, which was to bring them to Marsport, was waiting for the two men, and they headed directly for it.

"Blast!" Kairn said. "Your documents weren't sufficient! That's what they wanted, wasn't it? They have to run tests and surveys. They're quite willing to liberate Earth, but in total safety. And meanwhile men down there—real men—are dying!"

"There was once," Novy said, handling the ship with reckless abandon, "once in ancient history, a little king who swore that a whole nation wasn't worth a bone of one of his grenadiers. The face of the world may have changed, Kairn, but human nature hasn't."

"But," Kairn retorted, "what are they waiting for? Till the last Terran worthy of the name is devoured by sundews and beetles? Why have they waited so long? Two thousand years, Victor! Think of it."

"Roger," said Novy, who was the elder of the two, "don't talk nonsense. The fact of the magnetic field increasing a hundredfold, the existence of the particle barrier—that's no invention. There's a story in my family that one of my own ancestors is still drifting in Earth's wake."

"Same in mine. They're the stories we enjoy telling—but we sit still; we have our courage and our nerve rationed out by political imperatives. But now there's no excuse left. The computers say that landing is possible. We've touched Earth. And I still say—what are they waiting for?"

"Federal interests," Lt. Novy said, "and things simple lads like you and me aren't capable of understanding, but those things weigh heavy—treaties, borders, business manipulations. Retaking Earth is an expensive operation." He stopped and clapped his young friend on the shoulder. "I know what you're thinking. We're just spacers. But in the crunch, things depend on us. And if each of us does what he thinks he can…"

They looked each other in the eye. Novy held out his hand, and Kairn gripped it.

It was an oath. It was kept in days to come—tragically.

The next day Roger Kairn drew a routine mission—simply to make a camera pass above the upper layers of Earth's atmosphere, leveling out at about 80,000 or 90,000 feet. At that range he had gotten some good shots, but inconclusive: great fires red-spotting a black landscape, whole spruce trees, laden with resin, flaming up on mountaintops, clouds moving across the desert.

Likely that was not enough to make the Federal delegates understand that there was something drastic happening on the dreambound planet. Not enough to launch Operation Earth-save.

Well, he would get them better pictures.

He bore like a drill toward the motherworld, toward what looked like a continent lost in the expanse of seas, and discovered a vast migration, the variety of which astonished him.

He hurtled first upon a thick aerial obstacle—a flight of hundreds of kilometers of moths and bombyx, which darkened the sky with their heavy clouds. Going lower still, he saw strange green shapes which passed at low altitudes, trailing a

floating web in their wakes. (*Roots? I must be dreaming.*)
Monstrous things bulging with growths tore themselves out of
the ground and moved; the camera shot green faces, phosphorescent gourd shapes.

Kairn dived lower. He was now 20,000 feet from the surface. He could photograph herds of beetles, great plant lice.
Carts followed, carrying creatures of froggish aspect. *Mutants?* He shivered. The scientists of the Balance and the
Herdsman would have themselves a field day unraveling these
puzzles. He began to understand the hesitancy of the council at
Deimos. But Novy and he would prove right in the end. His
cameras went on shooting at 32 frames a second.

Now low enough to be seen clearly from the ground,
Kairn's ship crossed the track of a flood of Elnyans, whose
cuirasses imitated the wing cases, the blue and red crests, the
floral patterns of hordes of warrior scarabs and green slaves.
The living sea flowed toward the Megalopolis.

"A city of bizarre beauties," Kairn told his recorder.
"Statues. *Human* buildings." Then a phrase occurred—an af-
terthought. "A place no longer in human control."

Night lay ahead. Kairn had been ten hours at the controls. He felt both nervous and exhausted. He began a steeper
descent. The jungle opened like a well before him, drew him
in. He dared not—would not—change course.

What he filmed then was indescribable—worse than a
civilized man could imagine.

Kairn gripped the controls, drenched in cold sweat; curiosity drove him. This then was Earth—but what about humanity? This mass, this moving sea, these bowed backs, these
white flittings in the shadows? A flash of his lights ripped out
of the night distressed faces, bestial, white-eyed, brows invaded by a spongy tumor: the army of anthropomorphs on the
march.

He choked with nausea and felt in his pocket after his
euphoric pills. But he resolved to go on filming to the end.

It was the greatest footage in the universe.

The sky veiled itself in heavy cloud and the darkness became complete. Kairn's ship plunged into impenetrable shadow, toward the Megalopolis. A great four-sided structure was the heart of it: the Council gardens. Kairn veered that way. Now he skimmed the buildings and saw on the ground a vast and mysterious garden, every finger's width of ground covered with strange and terrible plants.

Frightfully alive, they reached the size of towers, raised metallic spears dusted with bizarre flowers. Some looked like strips of raw meat, with violet veins laid bare; others spread themselves in sumptuous molds, and still others draped earthward fringes of transparent membranes in which beat lacquered hearts, horsetails and tubes filled with phosphorescence. None of them really looked like a flower at all—rather open wounds, lips, instruments of torture. They truly beggared all description. He could not look on them without a disturbed, nightmarish dread. They were—it seemed—like huge televisors—but aimed where? And at whom?

Kairn did not know their names, but they seemed to know him. His ship whipped at treetop level over that surface of vast corollas: stalks sunk in plastic vats, flowers like lips and jewels quivered.

Slowly, as if conscious or directed, they turned toward him. The cups angled up, became frighteningly human. Frighteningly? No. The flowers seemed now as alluring as women; had the whiteness of ivory, glimpsed amid the shivering of great tiger-striped leaves. Mouths opened to kiss or bite, scarlet or orange in the case of the tiger lily, purple in that of disa grandiflora. An incredibly delicate plant bestowed its pale clusters along a phosphorescent stalk. Kairn knew suddenly that her name was densiflorum. Her shape was that of a young woman. She called his name, she wanted—

Now the man from Gamma Bootis knew them all. They were his sisters, his dear friends. In a measureless past which could be the future he had lived a thousand lives among them, wrapped in a dense and charnal scent of orchids, cradled, carried away under the rosy heart of a great cattleya which was drinking his life...

The ship, a Probe K-10, could finish her mission even pilotless. She could be destroyed, but not deprogrammed. Centered on the immediate objective—the city, the Agora, the gardens—she kept shooting to the beat of 32 frames a second until her spools ran out.

She could not record her pilot's agonies, but she did note a sudden, fearsome outburst of life in the enclaves, an indescribable thrust, a flowering—

—as if the flowers had drunk a rain shower.

When the last loop was recorded, the levers resumed their launch position and in a strangely bright dawn, a silver arrow climbed straight up, plunged into the clouds, and vanished.

It was certainly the greatest footage ever filmed.

XIV

Meanwhile, Peyotl A, President of the Holy Council and Grand Master of the Cacti—his official title—demanded an audience with the queen. Atlena received him graciously—she was giving a party in her apartments in honor of the funeral of her spotted python. Her valiant companion had not recovered from the bites of the shadows.

The whole court was clothed in white and saffron tunics and the sistrum-players drew out strident flourishes.

"Take your place, Master Green Death," the queen bade her visitor amiably. "What, don't you know they call you that among my people? Join your songs to ours, to toast the most devoted of serpents, in whom I have lost a true friend."

The great globe settled between a lutist and a professional mourner, but of course he did not sing. The royal servants served their visitor some cyclamen preserves and the dancers expressed in complicated steps their grief at having lost so sublime a python. Tiouy declaimed an idiotic fable, framed in imperial rhymes, which dealt with an orchid enamored of a comet.

"My queen," began Peyotl A, "I must speak with you."

"Listen to what Ramessa is singing," she interrupted him. "It's very delicate."

Near the fountains a sweet voice arose:

—*Night,*
Oh Night,
And thou yet a night,
Shapeless shadow
Wherein I drown—

"My queen," said Peyotl A, "it concerns the city's safety."

Stretching on her cushions, Atlena gave her prettiest pout. "What did I tell you?" she piped. "I shall yet be bored. Can't you rule without me? I gave you my power and several

121

galleys. I have a Council, plants in every rank of it, and never a moment's rest. I used to have quiet. I had a regent. Call back Prince Uxmal."

"Majesty," the plant pronounced heavily, "no one knows how to do that now."

Atlena stopped playing with her necklace. "You've killed him too?"

"He expired naturally, as one must expect. The shame and despair of having produced such a son—"

The queen laughed shortly. "Shame at having given Aran life? But Uxmal only lived for him. He worshipped the ground Aran walked on."

"Let me finish, my queen. Presently the slave Aran—"

"*Prince* Aran," Atlena corrected.

"He refused that dignity himself. The law says—"

"I say *Prince* Aran," the queen insisted abstractedly. "And so far as I know, my word makes the law."

"A little matter," said Peyotl A after a silence of lordly boredom. "This man, who should have died, is free at this moment. Perhaps you didn't know, but he did reach the desert. I don't know how he did it, but there he is, at the head of the Man-beasts."

Atlena sat up. Her eyes were amethyst stars. Her joy cried out of her silence. *Ah! he's done it!*

"Your people are in flight before the menace. The forest is ablaze. He is on the advance, feeding himself off our stores and our enclaves. The anthropomorphs leave nothing but scorched earth where they pass."

"That's what they have left, isn't it?"

"My queen, you don't understand at all. There's no discrimination. They sweep over human villages as they do the gardens of cacti. They come down out of the hills and trample the insect folk. They march in a straight line. Now the city is in danger."

"Oh," she said, "Aran wouldn't threaten *my* city."

Peyotl A signaled a green slave who came and presented the queen a strip of bark rolled up like a parchment.

"A message from Aran," the plant said. Atlena read it:

I, Aran of E-enor, master of the Man-beasts, to you, masters and oppressors of A-atlan:

Inasmuch as for centuries, having overthrown the gods and ruled the sovereigns, you have been hypocrites, brigands, and murderers;

Inasmuch as you have violated both laws and souls;

Destroyed the third Empire and brought humankind to this present state of despair, to our disgrace, our grief, and the shadows wherein we are fallen;

I bring the desert against you.

I hurl against you those you have degraded and killed, beasts and slaves. You have taken these creatures' spirit; I deliver you their flesh.

And I tell you, I, Aran, who have always kept my word:
You will die by fire and sword.

It was signed: *Aran, the queen's slave.*

"He has done that," Atlena murmured, fascinated.

"He's attacking your empire," Peyotl A observed.

"Oh," she replied, "is it really *my* empire? Aran tried his best to serve it, and see what you did to him."

"No one in A-atlan shall exceed the head of the city," the plant answered. "Such is the law."

"Indeed—a law that's brought us to our present predicament. But we hardly need a profound discussion on it." Atlena rose. "This last of our race, this man of the purest Sunborn blood—you condemned to become a beast, didn't you? Don't protest, Green Death; I know. And the only regret you have to this day is not having succeeded in your experiment. What penalty can atone for the crime of lèse-humanity? A pain of equal measure, maybe to be covered with pustules and thousands of cancer grafts? But no, you're only plants and we are men. Aran has found a better way, fire and sword."

Peyotl A had not moved, had even extinguished all his phosphorescences. His voice arose, weak, but distinct: "You are the queen. You are free to pronounce your sentences the

123

day after the war—if there is anyone left to condemn—if you even have an Empire of A-atlan."

But he had made an effort at conciliation—after his fashion.

A certain morning at dawn, Peyotl A invited the queen to walk along the defenses. Ramessa and Tueni urged her to accept the invitation. For some time the fields had been a no man's land, but they were tired of being walled up in the palace.

The women put on their handsomest finery, and everyone went carried in sedan chairs. A cloud of velvety moths followed the procession. The sky was blue and calm. On the outskirts of the city, vast twining flowers—rose, indigo, azure—fluttered in the breeze. Golden daisies blazed like stars. These were field flowers that threatened no one. Atlena smiled at them.

But gradually the procession left the area of the walls and entered the devastated place of burned and blackened earth. The young Elnyans stopped singing to each other. Motionless, leaning on the cushions of her chair, the queen let her eyes wander over the trampled plain, the ruins, the skeletons of blackened trees.

"Really," Ramessa murmured, "Peyotl A made a bad choice of sites to show us."

"My heart hurts," said Tueni.

Atlena gestured them to be silent. She knew that anthropomorph scouts had come near the city. War—she had not known it was like this. Fire and sword did indeed march before them.

The land agreed with it. They stumbled upon swollen carcasses of moths and slipped in the chitinous debris of the plate-shelled beetles. A faint rotten smell overwhelmed the scent of the flowers. Then, at a turning, the escort came to a dead halt. Tueni began to scream and all the Elnyans shut their eyes.

On a gently sloping hill a few rose and mauve houses were still burning, like candles. Great columns of black smoke boiled up into a fouled sky. Doubtless the inhabitants had delayed in leaving their ponds, their lily gardens, their terraces. The Sun was high. Parallel shadows barred the plain and with a piercing horror, Atlena recognized the sign which figured on a number of relics of the ancient world, a sign of humanity and hope. Aran had called it *The Cross*.

There were about 100 bamboo crosses on the ramparts and on each of them hung a flayed body.

The court fled back into the city on the wings of panic.

Then things went very quickly. The Megalopolis became an entrenched camp. The plants must have uncovered the graveyard of machines, for they brought to light wheeled mechanisms. Everyone chattered about their use and several, the best preserved, burst in mishandling fingers and sepals. Then someone had a flash of genius and they hunted everywhere for the sailors of the old fleet, but they found no one, for, by curious mischance, those brave young Elnyans were dead. Only one was still at large: Tzental.

The savage slave-caste priests ran through the city quoting ancient prophecies.

"This world will have several ends: *...it (the Beast) causes all, both small and great, both rich and poor, both free and slave, to be marked on the right hand or the forehead...*"

Behind the shutters of the palace, Atlena remembered the Book wherein such things were written. It was in the temple, chained to the altar. Like the history of Hellemar and that of Queen Maos, in crimes or in heroism, humanity must be chained. She would have wished to leaf through the heavy Bible, to know the end of the startling revelations. But the only time she had ventured out of her palace, the mob had thrown stones at her as she passed. Everyone knew by now that she had rescued Aran.

A piece of flint hit Tiouy the pygmy between the eyes, and he died with a little gasp at her feet.

The night when she was most desperate, miserable, no longer trusting in anything, she received a message. Someone had hurled it through the window into the throne room. *Midnight,* said the letters written on the bark. *On the shore of the Valley of the Dead.*

There was no signature, only a green dragonfly, crushed.

Luckily, Peyotl A had other fish to fry, for the refugees were overflowing the city and camping right up to the Council esplanade. Atlena went alone, without Tueni or Ramessa (of whom she was no longer certain) and reached the shore afoot, disguised in the sackcloth of a beggar. She had risen suddenly, walked very fast, and now she was panting. The two moons drifted together and the ocean and the mica-scattered sand shone.

A raft rocked on the water with five or six figures crouched upon it and one standing. The queen clasped her hands to her breast and stilled her thought, an impulse strong enough to wake the whole Council. A moment later Aran leapt ashore. The others made to follow him, but his voice rang out like the crack of a whip.

"*Back!*"

It was he. He had not changed... still the image of Hellemar, made of imperishable material, white marble, onyx. Atlena looked at him, drank him in, the godlike face, the violent snap of eyes, the bittersweet mouth whose kisses she knew. He took an unfinished step toward the queen, but she recoiled and set her back against a column.

Their eyes met. It was worse than an embrace.

"Not a step farther, Aran. I'll strike—or scream. I've kept my bridal blade, you know."

"Even you," he murmured in a hoarse, brittle voice, "Atlena."

"Yes. Even I."

"But you came at my message."

I came," she said, gathering her strength, "to know what the rebel Aran has to say to the queen of A-atlan. For don't forget! I am still the queen. I don't think our aims and our de-

126

sires are in accord from now on—since you've chosen this road and these companions." She tossed her head at the bestial shapes crouched on the raft. "Until now I refused to believe it. They warned me not to trust you. They were right."

"Ah," he said. "That's the way of it."

It was as if he had received a heart-shot in the moment of stepping forward, defenseless. He found no more words. Yet he had come here, risking everything, simply because he could no longer live with this narrow fire in his breast, the few memories which hence-forth would seem like dreams. This child he had held in his arms—a single night—seemed now so far away. There stood between them A-atlan, death, and all the laws.

"Listen," he said, "since I must speak to the queen of this empire, listen. I've come to warn you. One of these days your subjects—for they *are* your subjects too, these Man-beasts—are going to rise up like a tidal wave. I don't know whether your Councilors have told you—nothing stops these hordes and nothing stands in their way. These creatures aren't simply brutes. They're mad with pain, rotting, eaten alive by a slow decay. And don't you want to know how the blight begins in these men, for whom you bear the responsibility? Ah, but it's quite simple, and there's no contagion. For centuries our human species—brutalized, degraded as we are—has had one consolation: the sap and blood of peyotls and all the plantish poisons. The brow tumor is precisely the consequence of this state of affairs. And my people know it. Someday, when they've destroyed all the hidden stores and the floating colonies in the jungle, they'll come to these walls. On that day it will be impossible for me to stop them. The Megalopolis will fall and we'll sweep everything before us as we did at Mega and Oyaxun." His voice shook. "I know the plants hold you as their most precious hostage, but the war has its hazards. Come with me, Atlena."

A silence. Then: "You're quite mad, Aran." She answered him in the same tone she had once used to dispute him over a shell necklace or a rhyme.

"Of course I am," he replied with a joyless laugh. "Your plants have seen to that. Look."

He brushed aside the pale-gold strands which had fallen onto his brow and the queen saw at the joining of his brows a thin scar. His lashes and the bow of his lips trembled.

"I see no such thing," she said. And after a pause: "You are still beautiful, Aran."

She had not been able to stop that cry; and at once he stepped forward. But the ritual dagger gleamed.

"Stay where you are!" she said with difficulty. "Don't make me do something even more painful. No one touches the queen of A-atlan."

"Aren't we man and wife, Atlena?" he asked desperately. "Don't you love me as I love you? You spared me in your wedding flight and you came to free me from my chains. My love, don't be afraid. I want nothing but to kiss you, like that other night. I can't live any longer without you."

Atlena bit her small fist. "Silence!" She was near to screaming. "Silence! Why have you done these things? You've betrayed A-atlan! *You*—who promised to restore this land and Europe—is it with these beasts you'll raise the divine continent from the floods? Here we stand, the last handful of humans left, and you're destroying us. You, the last of the Sunborn. You—who were our hope and our light! Are you deaf or blind, to lead this death against our gates? You'll die with us."

"I know," he said, his jaw clenched. "Do you think I'm only deceiving myself? Listen. For weeks and months, I've foundered in this abyss, bloody-handed with trying. I'm killing myself trying to stop an avalanche. Do you think I really wanted this horror? You know very well I didn't, Atlena. This weight is crushing me. I meant to give you hope and inspiration, I dreamed of a saner, stronger humankind. Your plants— what have they made of me?"

"So you take your revenge on A-atlan."

"Yes—because this empire is *their* creation. But not on you, Atlena. You're my wife."

"I am the queen of this country."

"You hate me."

"No," she said. "And that frightens me. Listen. I've thought a great deal on that. There are a great many things I've learned—since that night. I sent you Tzental-ten-Helion, with a message. Did you get it?"

"No."

"Of course not," she said. "Elnyans are lighter than moths. But he loved you too. He's disappeared. Now it's too late and I've no time to repeat some things to you; I can only say the essential. You see, Aran, I have learned. I think the greatest, the most mortal mistake our laws have led us to, is this shame, this mistrust of love... for these laws were made for plants and insects, and they only understand pleasure, fertilization, and death. But human love, Aran, is something else, isn't it? It can be self-denial, passion, and purity. In this, I've sinned more than you. I didn't understand. You see, I do love you, Aran. I love you to death." She held her hands before her not to thrust him away but to make him hear this remorseless and hopeless confession. "This changes nothing, for I also love A-atlan, and you've sided against it. I can't desert my people at the most grievous moment of their existence. Doubtless it's the end of us, and I have to die with them. I'll be paying—at least I hope I shall—for the wrong of countless generations of Sunborn, prisoners who let themselves be deceived by the plants. And for my own crime too—for I committed a crime for which my people hate me. I set you free, Aran."

"You regret it?"

"*No,*" she exclaimed with strange violence. "I would do it again, if there were the chance. But I've sinned against A-atlan. And now I'm guilty of another weakness: I'm sorry for you."

"No," he broke in. "Not that. I don't want any pity." He had taken a step forward and this time Atlena had not cried out. He knelt and kissed the hem of her tunic. The Man-beasts had followed him, profoundly excited. The queen looked on their pustulant muzzles, their muscles, their bloody eyes. She reckoned that Aran was their prisoner, far more than he had ever been of the plants, and with infinite gentleness she stroked his hair. She caught then an impulse of his most secret thoughts.

"*My love, if you don't come with me, I'll stay here.*"

"They'll kill you."

"No matter. I'm dying anyway without you."

There was a howl in the night. Two anthropomorphs leaped forward, old ones, doubtless, who could still catch some of the thoughts of the Sunborn. They watched their leader's movements, ready to spring if he gave any sign of betraying them.

"There's nothing more you can do, Aran," she said. "You're their hostage as I am that of A-atlan."

He rose. His eyes went hard.

"You're right," he said. "Each of us is nailed to his own cross. I have to leave you. Let me embrace you, will you?"

She let him pull her toward him, fold her in his arms. Lips touched. The lovers were alone in the world—little matter to them the presence of beasts and cacti. They knew they had lived and suffered only for this instant, and surely they would not have another.

As the two moons drew apart, drowning the sea with their silver, Aran tore himself from Atlena's arms and fled.

XV

Peyotl A mounted the terrace of the Council palace.

He was a singular creature. If the spirit is human, this cactus more than half belonged to the species he was trying to destroy. Infinitely old, surely witness to the great cataclysm, Peyotl A had devoured so many human lives that his molecular composition had changed. But he had acquired some attributes of humanity on his own: his selectivity and his logic. He had nothing but mistrust for individuals. He reckoned queens and warriors, spirits and bodies, as minor quantities and interchangeable, almost like a human gardener might his cucumbers and his melons.

He made an exception of Aran. Aran had no illusions of the feelings he inspired in plants: an attraction and a hatred, prince toward prince. It was a fascination of polar opposites (theologians had once discoursed on non-love). In this battle of giants there was mixed a negligible quantity, Atlena, queen of A-atlan, and this airy sprite might tilt the balance the wrong way.

From the height of his terrace Peyotl A could see vast space extending at his feet. The forest retreated before the desert. Fire brooded under the vines. Sandy bays penetrated to the very heart of the jungle.

A phrase thundered through Peyotl A's fibrous system.

I shall bring the desert against your walls.

Below, on the crenels of the ramparts, some old cacti were scurrying about. They had just installed here and there some engines vaguely resembling the sun-maul. The maul itself had been lost with the flagship, but the plants knew the secrets of other underground arsenals, and they brought weapons from them. Raised on their tripods, there they stood, aimed at nothing, and no one knew how to use them.

"Yet," Peyotl A muttered on a plantish wave, addressing one of the eldest Old Plants, "there were men—Aran's seamen. What did you do with them?"

"Some escaped," replied the cephalocereus indirectly.

It was better not to ask of the others.

"Who?"

"The navarch ten-Helion."

"How?"

The gray candlestick swept the stones with his woolly fibers, avowed that they had tracked Tzental to the edge of the desert, and that he had vanished—behind a shining hard barrier, a force field which emanated from a silver fish.

"Absurd," Peyotl A interrupted him. He searched feverishly through his memories. "That—that sounds like the defenses of the world that was destroyed."

"Truly destroyed?" The gray cactus hesitated. "Several nights later the same projection came from a glowing object that traveled over the gardens of the Agora. Oh—very high! There was a life form in it. It went straight up."

"You let it escape."

"Not the life form. It was—Sunborn energy. It was very good."

Peyotl A noted the changes which had come upon this Councilor. His shell was smoother and his fibers greener.

His irritation mounted.

"If you don't succeed in managing those machines," he said brusquely, "take a few Elnyan notables, shut them in the central library, and let them read the books. Then you read their minds."

He banished the images and the ideas, henceforth useless, and ordered the high priest of Mega summoned to the terrace.

This was a green slave, escaped from the siege. He prostrated himself on the steps of the black onyx throne and, for a moment, the lord of the plants considered him as his shrunken reflection. The substance of the two beings was a merciless hatred.

The master leaned over the slave. "You hate!" he said. "And you want to kill Aran of E-enor. We all hate him, but you were the first sufferer. He destroyed your temple, freed or killed your victims. You want revenge. I offer you the means. You'll pay for it with your life, I think. Do you still want it?"

"I would die," the batrachian wheezed, "blessing my gods."

"Perfect," said the Peyotl "Tonight you go into the desert. In the heart of it sits an ancient city—Andrada. Why and how this dead city was abandoned in an impulse of panic is a matter without present interest. But the inhabitants fled, abandoning our installations."

He seemed to dream.

"They are," he continued, "a hypnotic apparatus. The controls are workable. Here is my seal. If you fall into the hands of the anthropomorphs, say that you're my messenger and demand to be brought before the prince. You'll ask him to speak face-to-face, without witnesses."

"And I'll strike!" sang the slave. "I have my stone axe and my totems—"

All Peyotl A's green luminances flashed. "That you will *not*. The guards will have taken your axe, and Aran killed a mad fern with a blow of his fist. But you will recite him this message. Learn it by heart:

"*Peyotl A, master of A-atlan, to Aran, master of Man-beasts: salutations!*

"*Peyotl A speaks, and says: When you lead your hordes against our walls, a white totem will go before our warriors and at the instant our ranks waver, she will be thrown to the beasts. I, Peyotl A, the Green Death, I swear it!*

"I think that will be enough," he added in a dreaming voice. "He will submit to his fate."

The cactus was vastly astonished then to see the slave sit up. "And if he *doesn't* hear me?" demanded the priest of Mega. "Then what do I do?"

And the master knew the slave had understood.

"Listen," he said, sliding as low from his throne as he could toward the kneeling slave, "Andrada has at its heart a round temple, where Aran lodges. We know it. It's a question of pressing the seventh stone to the left of the altar."

The slave kissed his roots—and their wake on the terrace.

Wearing the jewels unearthed in the dead city of Andrada and daubing herself with antimony, Naja had ideas of grandeur. The day the prince of E-enor sent word that he was returning to her tribe she declared, "See! He wants me. And he's a *sun god*, too."

On the marble of an abandoned lararium sprawled a great silver beast. Ael followed Naja with his eyes, and it was unbearable, this likeness in features to Aran, this human desire.

"You can take her," Aran of E-enor had said.

In Aran's absence, they all lodged in the circular temple of Andrada: Ael, Naja, and Naj. From that first evening in the town, the savage orgy had begun. The anthropomorphs occupied the city in an incredible disorder, in a heavy rank smell of sweat and wet fur. They blocked the streets, dragged the carcasses of butterflies and moths into the squares, drank the forbidden juice of the peyotl and gorged themselves prodigiously. They trod on the crushed blooms of prickly pear and fruit of barbary figs, the only flowers that survived the desert, and their sickly sugar aggravated the most afflicted ones, who rolled on the ground and groaned. Others broke the ivory screens of the palace, sacked the altars and howled at the stars. Unmoved, indifferent to this scramble, the blue moon caressed the marble lacery of the balconies and the crumbling wind harps.

A certain night the watchmen pushed and dragged a slave into the temple. He had been caught on the ramparts, he panted, and he groveled helplessly at Naja's feet. Under his torn tunic his body was a mass of wounds. But the narrow eyes of the high priest of Mega recognized the round temple and sought the seventh stone.

Naja stood, her back to the altar. He crawled to the feet of the young savage.

"You are beautiful! Your hair is the sun and your arms—lakes of delights. You're so beautiful. Be merciful."

"More beautiful than the women of your cities?" Naja asked, interested.

"No one equals you. Not even the queen."

"And yet," she said, taking a studied pose, chin on fist, "yet he doesn't love me—he—Aran."

Imperceptibly, by a slow creeping, the captive was approaching the stone. Suddenly Naja shouted. Naj leaped with his frightening blind precision and brought the panting body back to her feet. Then, squatting in front of him, Naj watched him.

Feeling his strength ebbing from him, the Megan changed tactics.

"Yes, you're the most beautiful, but he doesn't love you. I—I know charms—"

"Truly?"

"There's a very powerful one—here. In a coffer buried under—under the seventh stone." He improvised with a madman's swiftness. "Let me go find it—it's a necklace. You put it on your neck and the prince will see that your beauty is unique. He'll set a crown on your brow—"

"I already have crowns," Naja broke in suspiciously. "What I want is to lie in his arms."

"By the gods and the totems, I swear it! You'll lie there tonight."

This time it was Ael's turn to growl. He had followed this game—his green eyes flickered in the night, and he recognized the unpleasing words. The Elnyan woman turned, stroked the cat's nose with her hand.

"He lies," she said. "If there's nothing there, I'll let you play with him. Naj, here!"

And Naj bore the prisoner to the seventh stone.

The prince of E-enor returned to Andrada past midnight. He was tired. The faint smell of dead flowers, of flesh and incense adhered to his steps. It was the very perfume of the Megalopolis. Wherever he went henceforth, whatever his weariness and his anger, this night in A-atlan shrouded him, sensually. So smelled the orchids of the secret enclave, so smelled the cup the plants offered and the blood spreading by Atlena's bedside. He clenched his teeth against an outcry. The torture began again, worse.

He had thought that seeing her again would help him, that he might worship her henceforth distantly, as a goddess. But everything conspired against him. He walked a long avenue sown with long, moon-silvered bodies. Andrada breathed a perfume of bestiality and orgies. On its sands dark spots spread—forbidden liquor? Blood? In the black sky stars were dead worlds whence no help could come.

Aran entered the circular temple. In the atrium Naja slept in Ael's arms and in her flowing hair, as in the middle of a pool of blood—or perhaps it was blood. The two young people had taken refuge on the very altar, as if terrified, and the blind man lay at their feet. In the doorway Aran stumbled against a horrible burned puppet.

"Yklantekli," he murmured.

The resemblance was great

But a black claw scrabbled at the stones and, leaning forward, Aran recognized the jewel it clutched: Peyotl A's seal. By a just reversal of fortunes, the high priest of Mega was dying gut-wounded, burned—like his victims. But his hate was so strong he could still pronounce: *"Peyotl A says: The white totem will be given to the beasts—"*

Then he fell back, dead. On the seventh—shattered—stone.

The sea lord walked into the open hall adjoining. From the crest of the hill the temple overlooked the desert, and a graceful colonnade opened upon a Moon-dusted sky.

A mortal silence lay on the place.

Filled that morning, set in their marble niches, the water clocks were empty. Aran trembled. How time flew! He knew what a monstrous pillage the next hours would bring the horde. He felt crushed by so much of violence and horror, worse than a drowning man carried by the floods. He remembered bitterly the mornings of other leave-takings, other battles, and the joy that roused the blood and swelled the muscles: the anticipation of victory.

Today the absence of all exultation left a frightening void. A longing to sleep. An anguish.

When he lifted his eyes, he saw her.

His first impulse was of revulsion: another plant!

It seemed to rise between the tiles on a living and powerful stem, silvered just enough to evoke human likeness. Pale leaves, scarcely streaked with green, gave it a strangely mutable look. The phosphorescent ghost rose from a sort of pearly disc. Black, shining filaments like those of orchids fell to the ground, and at once the temple was saturated with a scent of primeval forest, of water sun-warmed, and orchids.

Three spots of shadow marked the approximate places of mouth and eyes. They pulsed and grew. It seemed the entity hesitated to make a choice of a form and a mask. But under Aran's eyes, the transformation progressed. It was as if the plant, plunging its tentacles into his brain, had drawn up Atlena's image.

It was she. *She* had come.

And that dreadful night was gone. There was no battle, no Empire of A-atlan. Aran weakened in a terrible delight which reached the very roots of his being and touched all his desires. The sheet of blue-black hair blew aside and he recognized through a yellow-green mist the supple, sweet body of the child he had held in his arms, the willow-waist, the pointed, lovely breasts. She spoke no word. Orchids are silent things; but tears flowed over her upturned face, blind, magnificent, that of a woman gripped by deepest passion.

He stayed there, statue-still. The ancient mental barriers, forged by a strong and knowing race, stirred an abrupt reaction. *Be careful,* said a voice which was like Uxmal's. *This is not the queen. When you see her eyes—*

Slowly, slowly, with the imprecision of a phantom (or something remote controlled) the lovely figure moved toward him. Her presence roused in him a dizziness, the hot tides that precede a mortal joy—she left him bound and drained of will. Her rosy lips were very near (or was that an opening calyx?). They rose to join his and to drink his life. He longed passionately for this kiss, this death. All his struggles and his flight seemed vain. He had always chosen this end—yes, the wedding flight was just, the law was just.

He spoke her name. "Atlena."

By what drowning reflex did he call for help on her who was offering herself before him? He had the impression that shadowy abysses and ages separated them. And he knew that this was true. It was then that the shadow-fringed eyes lifted, with a dreadful slowness, then that the strange eyes opened, pale stellar seas. There was nothing there of the regal little woman, but promise of inhuman pleasure, floral gulfs, lightning-riven abysses where one might fall, soft whisperings of stubborn species and flesh eatings—*in which one can share, in which one can sink—and reign—if one wishes—*

The pearl-skinned hands, the petals, the tendrils enfolded him as he set off his flamer.

The "hypnotic apparatus" was destroyed in a single blast.

Atlena wakened in the middle of the night, shaken, ice cold. Someone had called her and she had come to his aid. Aran, surely, but the rest was nightmare. She did not know if her aid had been enough. Nor if he was still alive. The danger must have been terrible, if Aran... She sat up in her bed. The night was strangely calm. The very park seemed asleep. The moonlight wandered over the lawn and in the center of it rested a strange object, a flat disc, rimmed with slightly convex light which recalled the ancient prophecies which the people sang in the streets:

"And I looked, and behold there were four wheels beside the cherubim, one beside each cherub; and the appearance of the wheels was like sparkling chrysolite. And as for their appearance, the four had the same likeness, as if a wheel were within a wheel... And their rims, and their spokes, and the wheels were full of eyes round about—"

The man or the cherub who stood armed before the strange machine felt a Sending fixed on him, a human thought of a rare quality, and fascinated as he was by the opal façade of the palace, he turned.

It was Victor Novy. The terrible and mysterious end of Roger Kairn, whose records and bloodless body had arrived at Deimos, had drawn him to this venture. He had made a pact with the lad, mutual defense. Kairn was dead. He felt obliged to go on.

Kairn's films had caused a riot in the council. If such mutations were possible, the whole human race was threatened. Novy spoke and gained an amended decision. One more attempt at verification, then the mass movement would begin against an Earth fallen victim to monsters and degenerate humans.

He had volunteered for the attempt. He had left his ship in a force field, loaded with weaponry and sensors, and rather nervous. After Kairn's photos, he expected to meet he-knew-not-what: a giant beetle, a man-eating cactus, a human being transformed into a locust. And suddenly he found himself face-to-face with a young woman of the likeness of a lily.

Worse, she came down the terrace steps and ran straight toward him. Disconcerting enough that this was a terrace, a vast garden, a lovely and noble Terran house—such as the colonists of distant worlds tried vainly to imitate—

—and the night was a gentle earthly night, blue, with normal shadows on white gravel, a solar clock which indicated plainly fourteen minutes till midnight, and a crazy owl which was drinking in the moonlight from the canal at Atlena's feet.

When she stood before the stranger—and he saw her from blue-black hair to gleaming toenails, the likeness of a perfect Terran, which the brilliant, hard, and cultured beings of other worlds had ceased to be, she addressed him politely in a short-range Sending, in perfect Galactic.

"I thought," she said, "that you'd come from Aran's side. I'm sorry."

She damped that thought neatly.

Fascinated, Novy explained with eloquence. "I come from another world, beyond the stars. We're the sons of Earth, sown before the great cataclysm, but we've kept faith with the mother world. We've watched you for a long time, and we're coming to help you."

"Only now!" Atlena said, recovering her hauteur. "One would say we were playing at one of those old dramas where everything has to happen in 24 hours, on a reduced set—and end very sadly. I'm afraid you've arrived a little late."

"No," he said, "since humanity does still survive. And you're the living proof of it. Beautiful and fragile, magnificent and threatened—"

"How finely you speak! Humanity exists, yes, decimated and hopeless. Once we fought the seas and watched the Heavens, waiting for an ally, a messenger to come to us—oh, not necessarily to help us, but to strengthen our faith in an immortal humanity. No one came. The yoke of the plants and the insects' laws overburdened us like a leaden crown. We felt we were lost, changed to beasts—and Aran rebelled and they tried to kill him. But all that is too complicated. You'll understand nothing of it. And in a few days or in the next hour, the battle is coming."

She sat down on the steps of the stairway and simply, humanly, began to cry. A cactus might have seen an incredible sight: a princess of A-atlan, that cold land void of all sentiment, pouring out all the tears in her body, unrestrained, while a monster, an angel, an interstellar messenger, tried to stop a deluge with a large handkerchief.

"Who is Aran?" he asked at last.

"The last of the sun gods. The last man of Europe, if you like. The one who might have been able to save us, if you had come sooner."

"And he's fighting—whom?"

"*Me!*" she cried. "That is—the laws, the plants, and the Empire of A-atlan. Oh, you understand nothing. I want to die—"

But she underestimated the powers of mind developed on distant worlds. Novy had understood. He got to his feet. He had the overwhelming impression of having come in at the end of the *Nibelungen*, of a tale told of heroes and of gods.

"Our fleets are near Deimos," he said. "I'm going to rejoin them. I hope to bring them here. We'll do all we can to save what's left of the human species. Thank you, dear lady—or should I say—majesty?"

XVI

In the course of his going, Novy recalled he had taken no picture of Atlena. Could one photograph the impossible?

And his previous records were still locked in the grip of the intelligence service. He had no new fact to hasten the decision of the interstellar admiralty.

But events were set in motion and no one could stop them.

On Rega, an artificial relay satellite of the Moon, where he must stop to reenergize his magnetically disrupted engines, the commandant of the auxiliary port shared his misgivings. His men had tried a prospecting operation. Non-regulation. They would be reprimanded, of course. But worse, the matter had to go to higher authority. And the reserve commandant stood by his men.

Rega had no atmosphere, being only a pebble that spun and silvered in the void. The stars from here were enormous and the Moon occupied a third of its horizon, sometimes red, sometimes black when its two halves rejoined. The station was composed of a little astrodrome and a barracks under a transparent dome. The commandant made a vague gesture at that building.

"You see—we took a prisoner. No, not the right word— the fellow surrendered on his own. He came running up like a madman out of the desert, followed by something inhuman, ghastly—so my men said. This—is a man. He's the reason they went down so low, indeed."

"And?"

"They got him. Or rather he leaped right into their protective barrier. Since then he's been half-conscious or sleeping."

"Take me to him," said Novy.

Tzental-ten-Helion, charged with the queen's message, had left the city a month ago. The first braziers were lit in the jungle, the terrible renown of the man who was master of the Man-beasts was just reaching the city. The Elnyan's excitable and volatile spirit, his slender body were afire. He believed he was living a legend.

He had to reach the dry sands, to cross a thin strip of land over which drifted a kind of green mist. He had plunged into it. As he walked he had repeated, to learn them by heart, the terms of the message, but increasing foreboding drove that concern from his mind. When he came to the heart of the narrow valley where wound a thin thread of crystal, the hunt was on.

What he had taken for a fog unfolded itself rapidly in thick layers. It was frightfully alive and damp, and as quickly as the vapor gathered on his skin it entered into his pores; another energy mounted an assault on his brain. It recalled—almost—his deep dives in the green sea—but there he had worn a suit and he had been free. Here, the green darkness drowned him.

Less strong, less stubborn than Aran, he perceived symbols according to his Elnyan sensitivity. He saw green dancing flames, wandered a terrible carboniferous forest where each fern trunk was hostile and moving; he stumbled along the brink of a primeval marsh out of which arose a foul odor. And he lived, he sensed, in symbiosis with the green entity which forbade him access to the desert, with vast and frightening things, with symphonies which set his nerves aquiver and undermined his sanity. He would likely have lost himself to this green madness, if another force had not intervened.

It was like a glowing, cold projection. The shadows opened, retreated from the passage of the beam, abandoning their fainting victim on the sand. Tzental still found strength enough to crawl along a dune, before beaching himself in a sort of silver basket-trap.

Semiconscious, he saw strange beings. He thought he was dreaming or that he had died and the sun gods were taking him into their empire. They carried glowing weapons and handled mauls like Aran's. They carried him into a small ship and the world vanished in a jolt.

Later he was sealed in a white cabin. The creatures reassured him with their thoughts. He was very weak—and the world outside ceased to exist. It was a state actually quite pleasant to his indolent Elnyan nature... not to live any longer, no longer to hold on.

But to everything there is an end.

The man with the hard white face, who looked a little like Aran, was certainly the master, for when he came into Tzental's cell, everyone deferred to him. He came to the bed, which was clamped to Rega's low-g floor, looked long on the slender young creature, the beautiful golden face with long half-closed eyes, this synthesis of man and moth.

"Get the sensor helm on him."

Someone put around Tzental's brows a sort of crown which fastened to the skin itself. And suddenly everything became clear. He rose up and danced according to Elnyan custom, accompanying himself with an improvised song. And the strangers looked at him open-mouthed.

Ye are surely gods!

Tzental began.

Ye are re-wakening, the life
Long-sought.
Ye come of old Atlantis
Or even of Europe
Hail brothers!
Hail sun!
Hail springtime!

"What's he saying?" asked the reserve commandant.

And Victor Novy who, his own sensor helm on his brow, was comprehending the flow of images said, "He's asking whether we're Atlanteans or Europeans."

Tzental, being one of the golden caste, was giving them a stylistic poem. He mimed his gratitude and that of his people, the green night passing to open the way to humans and the queen stepping down from her throne to welcome her rescuers.

"There's nothing to do," said the commandant. "He's a nice chap, but he's crazy as a loon. Did you ever see a prisoner who spins like a top?"

It was at this moment Tzental suddenly realized, gathered perfectly their thoughts. He made an effort and settled into the flow.

"I am," he said distinctly, "Tzental-ten-Helion, of Elnyan birth, first navarch of the galleys of A-atlan. So I cannot be, as you think, blind or drunk with peyotl. I was born in the Megalopolis like my ancestors. I serve the queen of A-atlan, who has entrusted to me a message for the only being who in our extreme danger, can save the holy continent."

"What is his name?" Victor Novy asked suddenly.

"Aran the sea lord."

"Go on."

"One moment," said the reserve commandant, at first amazed by this eloquence of communication. "I want to clarify one little point. When my men met you, you weren't carrying any message."

"Because," Tzental explained, "it was too dangerous. But I memorized it, for it's a poem. Listen!"

When he had done, Victor Novy seized him like a senseless object.

"Come," he said, "you'll sing that to the high marshal, with or without the sensors. And if they still dare delay, curse them from age to age!—Come, navarch Tzental-ten-Helion, my compatriot, my brother—we're going to give it one last try!"

And this was the message recorded by millions of microphones, that the navarch ten-Helion repeated the next day at Deimos, before the galactic war council and all the delegates of the reunited Terran colonies:

I, Queen Atlena of A-atlan, to you Aran, my master and that of the beasts, greetings!

They have brought me your challenge. What do you expect me to say? You are right and wrong at once.

But with all my heart, with all my might, in the night wherein we live, I cry to you: don't desert us, Aran! Come back! You are my hope, my strength, for hear me: l am the last Empire of Man—I am A-atlan—and I do not want to die.

I know that they have condemned me—they, the plants. Late in the night I wake and feel in my breast the heavy tramp of the forest. I sense all the walls that crumble under the weight of ivy, all the monstrous moss-eroded pavements. This city—the last remnant of humanity—must vanish. You do not know the horror of our sleepless nights. There are new parasites which attack granite and imperishable jade; under a new kind of saltpeter porphyry grows soft and marble decays. Giant molds devour the ramparts.

A still invisible crack makes its way through the vaults of my palace (it did not exist two years ago). Today an entire wing is threatening collapse—and no one knows how to rebuild the arches. Roots heave up the mosaics of the temples, the watchtower is being eroded by an intelligent lichen. The plants have hollowed the canals and there is a vast lake opening beneath the city. One day it will crumble like the Ahuahua quarter and no one will know that the Megalopolis ever existed.

But perhaps this is not the worst of this war that I wage against these green invaders. Their offensive omits nothing. They use the insects. Not necessarily the giants, those that rend and tear. They attack first what was the wisdom of the Sunborn. Piqu'a, tiny insects, lay their eggs in the leaves and the books of our libraries. Their larvae feed on our glorious past. The chenille moth spoils and tatters the leather of the bindings. We write no more books and the old ones fall into decay.

I wake and feel within myself, its last holder, the crumbling of the Sunborn civilization. Death prowls the streets; its *fangs kiss the portals of Elnyan houses where no Elnyan sur-vives. A thousand little deaths dull our frescoes under molds, hang from the eaves with creeping plants and blight our sta-tues with hideous ulcers. I hear the gnawing of the jungle and under this terror all A-atlan cries out in me: "I am dying!"*

Amid benches where the members of the interstellar council were gathered, in the greatest amphitheater of Deimos, Tzental-ten-Helion stopped an instant, surprised himself by such violence. He had thought he was carrying a message of love. It was a cry of agony.

He resumed:

Come back, Aran. I admit to you something no queen of A-atlan has dared to say: I am afraid! You cannot know how I tremble each night. The jungle is on the march. She has de-voured the fields. Out there where no one can get at her roots she hurls vines, her hooks. When an ivy tendril wraps around a single column, that temple is doomed. I have forgotten the names of my cities she has devoured.

Here in my capital the wind comes laden with spores and seeds; and they are destructive, hostile intelligences. Each parcel of Earth is swollen with bubbling sap. It is as if the green world has sensed the end of man and celebrates its tri-umph, hastens to eliminate us. Before what assault? What help need they fear? I don't know. But they keep coming.

Yet all these, Aran, are only outer signs, are they not? There's another thing yet more terrible. It is in the flesh of A-atlan they sculpt our defeats. It is toward this gulf their laws have led us, laws which become our instincts.

Do you not notice my subjects look like beasts? Not the anthropomorphs, but the men of A-atlan. The old men sitting in their doorways look like white spiders and the warriors like scarabs in their jury. The most handsome, the strongest, look like monarchs and great dancing swallowtails, and they re-mind me how orchids reproduce... not to mention the children, the charming, grave children who make me think of little fat moths. I look on them and I am afraid. I think how slow and erratic the mutations of butterflies are, compared to other species, and I know that to survive, orchids need moths.

I wonder, horrified—is it to this end the plants are guiding us, relentlessly? The fate of dayflies who live just to fertilize a species or to feed it—

Never has a mutation had so much encouragement.

I fear for the young women who dance like open flowers, whom the plants cover with their shadow. And the Elnyan dancers who pirouette like drunken fire moths—I am afraid!

We're becoming insects.

Save us, Aran. You, at least, are human!

It seemed the men of the New Earths had understood the raving message. People shouted in the amphitheater, humans of Altair and the Herdsman embraced one another and shook fists at what was for some of them a Heaven. Victor Novy wiped his sweat-damp face under his visor and said to Tzental: "Brother, you, the queen and I—we've won."

The order for departure was given at midnight, star-time.

XVII

But on Earth the tragedy played itself out according to very ancient rules. The great drama of A-atlan must be preceded by a small and personal nightmare. *Just,* Aran thought, *a synchronization. The musicians are tuning their harps.* The anthropomorph army had started off with the ponderous leisure which characterized the beginnings of their campaigns, and, despite strict orders, the blind ones, with Naj and Naja, were slipping along the flanks of the horde and hunting— forlornly.

So they came a little in advance of the others to an El-nyan village, abandoned in a panic flight. There were still garlands on the doors and libation cups on the altars. Naja amused herself by stripping down some tapestries and decking herself in them. She opened the rouges and draped herself in troubled and smoky jewels.

And while she was thus occupied, fearful cries startled her. She rushed out into the street and saw Naj fallen in the basin in the great square of the village. She thought at first that he had fallen—but when she drew near she saw that the body of the blind man was struggling amid the tentacles of an enormous alga, intelligent, probably the green divinity of the village, which, its roots trapped in the walls of the basin, could not follow its people.

It must have lived for centuries on the victims they brought here, to this very square.

And now it hungered.

This species of giant polyp was devouring Naj, and despite his screams, despite Naja's efforts as she bravely leapt to his aid, the contorted, convulsing body disappeared in a swirl of water. Armed with a drapery rod, Naja slashed futilely at the weeds, succeeded only in getting caught by her hair. Several blind ones, drawn by her screams, met the same fate. The alga wound around them lightly and stuck to them with a green juice which surely served it as digestive fluid. And while they gasped for breath and dissolved, it dragged them under the water.

It kept Naja alive as long as possible, using her as a lure—so that, arriving on the scene, the anthropomorphs themselves recoiled in horror before that dreadful figure—a sort of green cocoon, vaguely human-shaped. It still groaned. A broken death rattle issued from that mass of yellow-green moss which had been a face.

The Man-beasts hastened to reach her and, arriving at the same instant, Aran disintegrated the plant.

This sickening interlude put the cap on the barbarians' fury. After their march across desert and through forest, they frothed with rage. They were sure now that everything was a deadly trap: the clear water, the copses, the flowered borders, even dead villages. But they had learned to avoid ambushes with a bestial cleverness and to kill efficiently.

They used fire.

And the monstrous army appeared at the cleft of the hills which formed the second natural defense of A-atlan.

In the command station of the lead starship on its moment of launch, the man in charge of the mission framed his notes to be spread through subspace to the worlds beyond Arcturus.

"This is a record aboard a reconnaissance expedition in the year 2000 since the Exodus.

"The squadrons of which I have command, coming from all points of the galaxy, bear with them the greatest hope of man: not that of conquest, but of liberation.

"Since the great cataclysm, the physical conditions of Earth, our common origin, have undergone fearful change. We know little of them even now, but we do know one essential fact: Humanity still exists and it needs help. The greatest scientific minds are among us, mobilized for the study and the defense of our homeworld. Our mission is bringing medical laboratories and terraforming apparatus, gravity stabilizers and weapons. For I must not hide the truth from you, that we are going to fight for the saving of Earth, and it will be a hard battle.

"We are approaching our beloved planet with fear and with fervor. We know it is living and inhabited—in the most terrible sense of the word. The films I include are proof of that, and with them comes the message of a queen, which a man will read for you. Through these images and this message, this haunted planet with its human herds and its green gods will come alive for you with fearful clarity.

"Drowning in oceans and forests, conquered, sunk in terrors, Earth is depending on us for its deliverance.

"May the universe—and its Master—aid us tomorrow."

On Earth now came a dawn, and a hideous avalanche began to move. The dark mass which had spent the night among the dunes and on the charred floors of the forest got to its feet. A howl rose from the desert, the trampling of hundreds of thousands of monsters. The Earth was shaken as by an earthquake.

(So the ship of Roger Kairn, the lost pilot, had surprised and filmed them—and returned with a dead man at the controls.)

They moved, backs bent to the Sun, bodies hairy and snouts full of slaver, all human semblance lost in their purulent tumors; they crossed the ravines, the marshes, and the dunes, crushed down the fern barriers and the walls of carnivorous plants, filling the ponds with their bodies, moved by a force more powerful than themselves, toward A-atlan.

They went, breaking, scouring, destroying everything in their path—like fate.

And the city, cloaked in the frail barrier of its walls and its warrior clans, heard the march of doom with all its thunders.

Eight Giants, kneeling, offered Aran on their shoulders a throne mounted on huge shields.

"Ael?" he asked.

They had had to tear Ael from Naja's horrible corpse.

Aran had donned ancient armor of beaten gold—a huge carapace plundered from the temple of Andrada—and it was meant to serve as a rallying sign. A helm of sapphired antennae shadowed his brow; he leaned with both hands on the guard of a great sword—or a flamer. They lifted to his side the lean silver beast, mad with grief. A furious cheer, prolonged, discordant, hailed the appearance in the horde of the only human face among them. Off in A-atlan the courts and the wharves shook. With an imperious wave of his sword Aran hurled the monsters at the Empire.

When the town and the port opened before them, a hesitation came over them, a vacillation which stopped the first ranks and sent a long shudder down their bowed backs. The horde was so tightly packed that amid the fires at the edge of the marsh the laggards were flattened as in a gust of wind.

Aran had himself carried forward on the shields. Curled at his feet, Ael breathed the fierce odor of the horde and fanned himself with the petal of a water lily. He was relearning human gestures; perhaps he would forget Naja. When they were lifted above the mob, the prince of E-enor set his hand on the shoulder of his companion and made him look ahead. Ael gave a cry, a gasp of delight.

The city was before them, within reach of their hands.

With its domes of gold and selenite, its towers of jade and onyx, its biblical pyramids of crystal, hyacinth, chrysoprase and chrysolite, A-atlan of men opened like a heart laid bare. She offered her gardens that smelled of perfumes, like fine dishes, its palaces girt with colonnades and its temples abloom with giant orchids. She was beautiful, at once as seducing as a mirage and as terrible as a hidden danger.

It was nearly noon. A golden mist drifted over these splendors. It was, Aran thought, standing on his barbaric throne, a perfect—and finished—work of art. The flower of earthly beauty and wisdom, the harmonious union of two hostile species.

But one must destroy the other, and he closed his eyes so he would see no more of it.

And such was the battle.

Two stades from the city, at the limit of the no man's land, bows on their knees and a first arrow between their teeth, the ten thousand mahogany warriors surrounded a white litter, enclosed in curtains of asbestos. A mob of Elnyans armed with tridents and nets reinforced this elite band, and then came a group of slaves, armed with pitchforks and stakes. On the wings the savage allies were deployed, megalosomes, Malthodes, and a clan of lucans, with their natural and terrible weapons.

From the moment they heard in the distance the thunderous shout which hailed the appearance of that single human face over the horde, there could be heard over the ranks of A-atlan a whispering of bowstrings stretching and the more sinister hiss of serpents. The slaves had loosed their sacks of vipers.

But the curtains of the immaculate litter lifted and, standing like a totem or a goddess, Atlena appeared to her people. She also had made herself beautiful: her lotus crown was made of long milky pearls, strings of matched pearls of a perfect water surrounded her face and circled her neck. Under a gossamer veil her hair was powdered with diamond dust and two rings of jewels weighted the delicate lobes of her ears.

Her platinum corselet was encrusted with huge sapphires, and for an instant in the blue and white fluttering of her tunic the queen appeared to her people like a star. Her wrists bent under the weight of the scepter of A-atlan, crowned with a single opal, and the army and the people cheered, all bowed the knee. She had put on the armor of Queen Maos. So all the sovereigns of the Empire had appeared at its most terrible hours, ready to share with A-atlan its glory and its death.

At the same moment the horde poured out into the no-man's-land like a roll of thunder. And the monsters wavered. In the fore of the human army were creatures cloaked in white, masked in asbestos, closing their phantasmic ranks against them. Amid these creatures sat a white litter like an altar, crowned with a godlike figure. A hundred cubits separated the two legions.

Aran saw the queen and she saw him. White totem, sacrificed goddess, she still found the grace for a ritual gesture. She lifted the scepter of A-atlan and blessed her people.

Through his dazzlement he could not but notice: On the city walls they had raised not one or ten but hundreds of ancient machines. Peyotl A must have found the secrets of Hellemar.

An acid thought, very weak, hissed in the mind of the prince of E-enor.

"Take care, Aran. No, we have not found the sun-maul, but something its equal: the death ray. One more step and we offer up the totem—the queen. And to avenge A-atlan and its glories, the fire will fall."

But Aran could not stop the avalanche.

(Only the plants—motionless—had not been able to foresee that fact.)

His bloody lips pronounced: "My love—"

And from the height of her altar, as on their wedding night, Atlena smiled at him.

An incredible shock burst—burned the plain. In a cloud of fragments and dust the first waves of anthropomorphs hurled themselves on the warriors of A-atlan. For a long moment there was the living tide, the crack of broken bones, wing cases splitting like thunderclaps, the heavy impact of clubs on living flesh, the rattle of the dying.

Then like grass bent in the gale, the Elnyan elite guard gave way. Aran saw the yielding and retreat, the riders, armored hi smoky crystal and mounted on hexapods, bow their plumed heads and let fall their banners—this he had foreseen. He saw the first anthropomorph ram the ranks of the red warriors. That one fell; but others charged over the corpse, and still others. Without number, without limit. A great gout of blood spattered the white litter and Aran cried out, the gasp of an animal wounded to the death.

Then, turning his own soldiers, trampling Elnyans and red warriors, the tall Sunborn hurled himself forward. Atlena saw him open a path through the horde. He was so near she yearned to reach out her hand to him.

For a brief instant in the fantastical melee, Aran the rebel made his own body the defense of the queen of A-atlan.

It was then that a red sheet stretched out over the two armies and what was left of the jungle burned.

No, it was no sudden firing of sun-mauls, but of perfected thermonuclear weapons. The plants had been obliged to learn their operations from the fogged brains of Elnyans. Was it to avenge their trampled cousins that they chose this death—by fire?

The infrared rays went out from the ramparts, thick as the trunks of baobabs. Half-charred ferns blazed like torches and hundreds of euphorbias poured out into their midst, burst in purple clouds. Rivers of fire flooded the immense plain. The sky turned suddenly dark, red, then black, and in this sudden night an ocean of red flames whipped up.

The trajectory of the rays was calculated to spare the cohorts of A-atlan. But the anthropomorph horde was caught in a lake of fire.

That mounted—that covered the desert—

Out of that furnace rose inhuman shrieks, trumpetings of elephants, howls of wolves, wailing of panthers.

The whole army of monsters was consumed.

Panting under their masks and their flameproof armor, the defenders of A-atlan recovered their courage. They saw that the death rays were striking beyond them. They riddled with arrows the brutes who tried to escape that hell. The slaves emptied their sacks of vipers and the insects with their chelae and mandibles slashed pathetic human flesh.

The litter-bearers advanced evenly, step by step into that burned zone (surely they had received an order) and standing amid her troops, Atlena, unmoving, near fainting, saw a monstrous thing—the annihilation of an army.

The ride had flowed back with such haste that she had begun to attack. Bloody, harassed with arrows, burning like living torches, the Man-beasts fled, crushed their own ranks, ran into the hindmost and passed over them. The scarlet wave covered the rout with bent backs, charred bodies.

Even the Sun burned.

The fire-mauls moved. Slowly, slowly the ruby ocean flowed out, embracing the panicked horde. On the shore of this fiery sea, Atlena saw for a second a tall golden figure dragged by his own men and striking frightful blows of a spent flamer. But the eddies of crazed creatures enveloped him.

Did he fall? Was he overwhelmed or trampled by the horde? The queen of A-atlan knew nothing of his fate. Her forces dragged her away and she fainted.

For tens of thousands of leagues the desert burned.

XVIII

The first voyagers landed at dawn like silver clouds. They came to rest in a dead zone. The analysis apparatus revealed a heavy, burning atmosphere, and Geiger counters clicked furiously. The voyagers disembarked on the mother world in suits, as if they were venturing out onto an alien planet. And the spectacle they saw confirmed that impression.

They walked for hours—centuries—across a world paved with trampled flesh, charred vegetation still smoking. They hurled themselves over heaps of bodies damming the streams, filling the swamps, of ferns and baobabs that made pattering sounds. The sky was leaden. Sometimes the sea wind swept in mists. It was Earth's only welcome to her returning children.

The apparatus transmitting their data to the great computers aboard ship revealed the massive use of nuclear and thermal weapons. The commander from Arcturus turned to Novy, his lieutenant. They communicated by Sending.

"I have the impression you were right, Victor. We've come too late. Nothing will have survived this Hell."

But arriving within the city they found walls intact, doors of beaten bronze and thoroughfares empty as if abandoned in panic. The foliage was destroyed and the cisterns were filled with ashes.

"They've all gone!" cried Tzental-ten-Helion.

The city had poured out its life's blood before the battle. Everything able to walk had poured like a torrent down the coast; some had used rafts and the flotsam of the fleet, but most had walked—amid the tides and the dust devils. An animal sense developed over centuries had whispered to them surely that to stay too near the fires was equal to suicide.

They didn't know then, Novy thought, *the masters or the enemies of this poor people, that using such powerful thermal weapons at so short a range—was utter madness.*

He questioned Tzental, who walked beside him. The Elnyan shrugged.

"They have their science," Tzental said, "but it's only that of plants. For human beings, they read our minds and a long time ago we forgot everything, thanks to them."

Dawn failed to pierce the cindery shadows in which flowed strange phosphorescent waves, red and green reflections. Guided now by Tzental, who had come home, the civilized men in their space armor took the triumphal way, leading to the quays, the route taken one memorable morning by Prince Uxmal.

They went, dazzled and dream-haunted, bewildered by the shapes of an art strange to them, at once refined and like the worst of nightmares. Two philosophies were incarnate in the city monuments. One resurrected the very ancient cult of the macrocosm reflected in microcosm, the universe incarnate in man, and this had built the pyramids, the zodiac wheels, calculated the paths of the stars, and traced on the earth harmonious star-shaped patterns.

There clung to these relies of another age a perfect calm. Man must still be very powerful; his face carved in black agate or white onyx figured prominently in the reliefs and frescoes. Oceanographers at the port discovered a great statue—drowned.

"It would be some job to fish that up," a technician reckoned. "We'd have to send for Martian cranes."

"We'll get them," Novy said. "All that concerns the humans of Earth is sacred to other humans."

But the triumphal route stretched over hundreds of leagues, and near the Council palace, another theogony unfolded. Its symbols were more recent and carved in more fragile materials, but nothing equaled in horror this new order of the world: triumphant beetles standing on their agate pedestals, giant ferns breaking frail enemies in their fronds, and these groups together, where bees and bumblebees pursued their tangled battles.

And the colors had changed. Gold, electrum, and skystone gave way to troubled crystal and somber porphyries. The hues were vermilion, rotten meat, and green mold. Victor remarked to his commander that one motif recurred tirelessly: two forms locked in a fight to the death, one male, the other female—or an immense sundew devouring a human being.

"And men have lived here for centuries," an archaeologist said. "These visions—they drew them out of their brains— Surrounded by the forest, incapable of escaping these hideous suggestions, they reproduced them in bronze, orichalc, and agate the dream of their oppressors. Their laws shaped them, Tzental-ten-Helion tells us, under hypnosis. The plants forbade them human behavior and imposed on them a rule of nestings and murder. Their masters—"

"I would like," the fleet admiral said softly, "to have a word with them."

"Sorry," said the advisor in nuclear physics. "If they didn't flee with the people—which I doubt—you'll not find much of anyone to talk with."

Up to the walls of the Council garden they had met no living soul. And they had spent an entire day crossing the nightmarish battlefield and the dead Megalopolis.

Tzental named for them the principle buildings. He told them the alabaster peristyle graced the palace of Uxmal the prince regent, and that the grand rose terrace surrounded the queen's residence. But he did not know precisely how to explain to them the topography of the Agora.

He said simply: "There are palaces, libraries, and walls, and passages down below. In the center there's the orchid enclave and in the heart of that, the Temple of the Unnameable. No one knows that divinity's face. No one enters the Temple except the masters, at set intervals. That's all, and I don't know any more."

Night was falling on the darkened city. One of the two moons pierced the shadows. The civilized men entered into a park as vast as a forest, and all the plants in it were seared.

They were all there. Tzental could have named them, for the masters were not numerous at this stage of perfection. The lace epyphillium, the mamillaria elongata, like long windows, the phantasmagorical albans and the fiery aurorae boreales. The lobelia spotted with blood, the scythe-shaped stalks of the aloe ferox; and hanging from the lip of the lance-like agaves there opened, spreading their perfumes—opening their cups—cattleyas, rose-lipped; densiflorum, floral waterfalls; anceps lelii, striped with violet.

All dead.

Their roots were plunged into the transparent plastic vats in search of life where there was no life, for all source of it had rotted with the radioactivity.

In the center of this dead world one dome glowed rainbow hued, towering over the rest. The Temple.

"Let's go that way," said the master of the star fleets.

XIX

Minutes or centuries before, Atlena had said, "Let's go."

She came out of a heavy sleep which had followed her fainting. Ramessa and the guard Tlavatli had instinctively carried her to the highest terrace of her palace, which rested above the radiations. In asbestos masks and ancient armor of white plastic, they looked like ghosts.

Panting and wringing her hands, the little servant reported to her queen that the city was deserted. The people, all the people, had fled toward the sea. The palace guard had abandoned their posts and the Council did not answer.

"They have all deserted you, oh queen!" wailed Ramessa. "Even that silly Tueni. There's no more trust nor honor."

"But there is," Atlena answered kindly, "since you're both here."

"And the plants, think of it, mistress! Even the plants are silent!"

"Delightful. I was finding less and less pleasure in Peyotl A's conversation. Now we're free to think."

She was speaking as if there were nothing amiss, but in her pale face, her eyes were two dead lakes. A flight of dead dragonflies littered the terrace: all the little beasts, green and silver. The queen bent, gathered one up and held it in the palm of her hand. Then she added shortly: "I'm not about to go mourning like one of the goddesses of old fables. If he were dead, surely I would be too. And if he's alive, Aran can only be in one place. Let's go."

"But where?" Ramessa quavered.

"To the Temple of the Unnameable," the queen replied in a chill voice. She was thinking.

The underground way, that which Atlys had once taken, began at the royal palace and came out at the Valley of the Dead. But the Temple stood directly between, in the heart of the Council gardens. It was a strange building, forbidden to

161

the people. Atlena had visited it once, after the coronation ceremony. She vaguely recalled a tower of selenium and opals, the lower level of which reminded her of an aquarium. A stairway spiraled up, and on all sides, behind transparent walls, writhed algae, threads, something like the roots of a monstrous plant. At the topmost level the walls became opaque, carved in blue opal, massive, as if they cloaked some secret.

The tower was 600 cubits high. Its dome dominated all the city.

Up there, under that pointed vault, very simply, there was *nothing.* A circular room, empty, and in the center a little arena of rock crystal.

It was, they had told her, the altar where the Unnameable dwelled. Atlena had asked to see him. They had explained to her that he appeared only on certain days of ritual. The rest of the time he retreated into the shadows of Mother Earth. And this was not the day of his appearance.

After all, he was a god; and one could not force him to show himself.

Atlena still recalled the beat which had reigned in that enclosure; the crystal gave off reflections here and there, a yellow-green moisture and a sharp, musky scent. It seemed a plantish aroma, vanilla. Suddenly green images, living concentric circles, had begun to dance before her eyes, then wonderful valleys opening, full of human beings, beautiful as gods, shining cities and winged ships. A white, godlike face leaned over her and she recognized Hellemar.

"But I'm dreaming," she had said, recovering with a violent effort. And she had vehemently accused Peyotl A of making his sovereign drunk. The plants seemed disturbed; they milled about and brought her quickly out of that place.

Peyotl A had then said to someone, a muddled Sending: *But she promised us to be calm!*

And a pilocereus had murmured: *She's too strong; she can't come here—*

Now Atlena recalled the legends: that at the beginning, just after the great catastrophe, there had been some of these frightfully evolved plants which did not cease to grow and to eat. They had become so monstrous that they never moved from their soil, but sent their hypnotic web out over living creatures which they drew into their aeries and on which they fed, as common plants gorged themselves on water. But the zone would become still more vast, for prey fled the evil places; then they attacked other plants and the earth itself. So the deserts were created.

But the intelligent plants reckoned these monsters as divinities of their species, dreaded and sacred beings. In each town there was a passage and a circular temple. Strange visions haunted the edges of these sanctuaries. The plants explained them as the action of hypnotic apparatus, guarding the Unnameable. Later, most of these cities died, with relentless slowness. Others were abandoned in an impulse of panic. What became of the green divinities hidden in their pits?

Divinities?

Atlena shuddered.

Was it not more simply a single monstrous Entity, fertilized by the life force of living creatures, a single plant which, like a cosmic polyp, put out its tentacles through jungles and deserts?

An enormous orchid, for which Aran was today a prey?

Atlena trembled and never heard Ramessa moaning and Tlavatli volunteering to go with her into hell. She made distracted moves of her head—*yes, yes.* Then she went to the balustrade and leaned out over the city.

The Megalopolis sweltered in a sea of radiations, shot through with multicolored glows. It seemed to be drowning, like its god.

In the distance the jungle was still burning, a grandiose sight, the smoke for hundreds of leagues making an impenetrable and glowing wall. Sometimes a bamboo pile jetted up a geyser of sparks, a marsh opened like a well of fire. To be sure, the plants, using Hellemar's machines, could never have foreseen the power of them—nor that their own species would be first to suffer from them.

Between her dead city and her burning Empire, Atlena was alone. She accepted her responsibility.

She adjusted her flexible armor, that of Maos, Atena, Atlys. Then she ordered her wedding blade brought, symbolic and perfect jewel, steeped in a thousand chemical poisons. In the shadow the crystal blade shone. Thoughtfully Atlena considered the weapon.

"My queen," said Tlavatli, "you mustn't take the risk. You belong to A-atlan."

She faced him with determination.

"There is no more A-atlan," she said. "The Empire that bore that name no longer exists—has not, for a long time. Surely there will be other A-atlans, for the Earth does survive—better ones, too. Nothing could exist worse than this land where plants have managed to rule and assimilate human beings, where they've slowly and patiently changed them into a novel species of butterflies, good only for the breeding of orchids and the feeding of sundews. But it's our country all the same, Tlavatli, and we love it; we want to avenge it. If you're afraid to follow me, stay here, I beg you."

He shook his head and drew his sword halfway from its sheath. Ramessa came to join them, for she feared most of all being left alone. Finally the three of them took the underground way which had drawn another queen to her death.

It was a bowel whose walls glowed with faint phosphorescences. Here and there the three stumbled against thick walls of plant growth—dying, frenzied roots which had pierced the vaults and hung in the shadows. Some still pulsed with life; when Tlavatli cut a path through them with blows of his axe they groaned and writhed like wounded animals.

As Atlena had guessed, the passage opened at a gentle slope onto the Council hall. And there Tlavatli and Ramessa recoiled in horror. They had not understood. Some of the plants, knowing themselves doomed—had they wanted to relive the greatest moment of their existence, that in which they had lorded it over humanity? Those days had returned on these steps.

Moth orchids and lycastas crouched on the platforms of the hall; candle-cacti with their purple spikes towered over a carpet of orchids. As if they had willed by some vast thrust to rise above the area of the radiations, stapelias, yellow and red, spotted with violet and resembling leather sacs, had climbed two meters high. Faucarias opened their wolfish throats, full of pale, withered cups, and the lithops' jewels had lost their luster.

They were all dead, and already they gave off a faint odor of decaying herbage. On the throne in the center was a liquescent green mass: Peyotl A.

Amid the room stood a sun-maul—reserved for their defense, most likely. Tlavatli leaned down and heaved the weapon up onto his shoulder.

"They're dead—they're all dead," Ramessa murmured.

But at that moment a strong wave passed over them, not perfume alone. Before their eyes formed circles of emerald and gold, curves spun off, tracing orbits of new systems, and plunged into an infinite darkness and the naked blaze of billions of trembling stars. The three humans were whirled into a void where writhed the convolute glows of nebulae; the belt of Orion was a broken necklace of pearls and Berenice's hair a golden flight of bees. Atlena saw before her her own most beautiful dream, the blue diamond of Arcturus.

But she had the strength to leave this torrent of images and dizzying sensations. She understood: This vision was not hers. Only the flying men or Aran who had seen the stars at sea could have lent the horrible entity the theme of this symphony of stars. It was meant for spirits who were attuned to it. So Tlavatli and Ramessa walked straight ahead, heedless of the deluge of colors and musics loosed about them, and Atlena followed, doggedly stiff, all her mental barriers engaged.

They came out in what had been the garden and crossed the enclave. Here too the spectacle showed the frantic activity of the plants seeking to escape the surrounding death which they themselves had loosed. Their stalks thrust up desperately in the vain hope of piercing the blanket of radiation. The monstrous tendrils climbed, entwined about plinths and arches—in vain. All the creatures which had defied human law were dead.

A vast moat girded the opal temple. Atlena went toward it. The red Giant jumped up, hung from a bamboo, bent it, and landed on the other side of the moat, where he held the dead cane by the tip. The queen and Ramessa crossed that trembling footbridge.

An incredible silence reigned here.

Not a rustle of leaves, not the bursting of a single bud.

A vast clearing opened before them. Atlena recovered enough of her childlike curiosity to look at it. She had not come here since her coronation.

She found the Temple smaller, much less intimidating than before, but its dome glowed intensely and the overpowering sense of imminent death, a sensation which had not ceased to grow with every step they took, reached a peak.

And always, the silence.

They realized now the ceaseless noise the plants had made—the moving of leaves, the bubbling of sap. Not astonishing that the Elnyans became dancing tops and the Giants mad insects. The breeze had sunk away. Nothing stirred. The flexible branches and vines hung dead. "I'm afraid," Ramessa moaned and sat down at the edge of a moat. The queen and Tlavatli passed like shadows and the warrior hurled at the Elnyan servant a look of mistrust.

Unconsciously the little queen of A-atlan reenacted all the myths of humanity. She was Psyche, Astarte, Ishtar, the human soul which, through all the darknesses, goes forever toward love and death.

In this eerie night each gesture assumed an immense importance. The doors of the Temple were closed and the Giant forced the seal with his sword. Then he stepped back. Atlena mounted the spiral staircase alone and stopped on the threshold.

It was there.

Narrow embrasures pierced a flood of opals, but at the heart of the sanctuary, massed a yellow-green shadow, as in deep undergrowth or the bottom of a marine abyss. A shadow-shape occupied the center, a sort of green-and-white phantom, and Atlena knew she had no more strength at all.

She realized it was, arisen out of the Earth, darting forward—an immense upturned cup of an orchid. It was alive, flesh-eating, dreadful. Each petal was a spongy mass, shot through with filaments, and she could see green sap pulsing in its veins. The flower was shaped like an inverted cone, a pyramid, the base of which dragged the ground like the fringe of a too-baroque gown, the top of which under the green sepals beat like a heart. Half-turned toward the crystal arena, this monstrosity seemed to be blindly seeking and smelling out something. Standing on the threshold Atlena saw this green orifice, like an enormous mouth, whose walls contracted, where trembled the scarlet and sulphurous flame of a pistil.

The musky odor was so heavy the queen staggered.

The dreadful flower swung on a stalk swollen with sap. All it breathed in of vital and psychic force passed immediately into the maw of spongy petals... and each time it did so a terrible spasm ran through its bloom. Atlena knew it was very old, born in the abyss, several millennia ago. It had known Maos, Hellemar, and breathed in innumerable human lives. All the dreams of men, their vices and their lusts, had seeped into its fluids; it could offer each victim its delights and the terrors it wrought.

Atlena moved forward. Her lips were flushed and her heart was empty. She met Aran's eyes. He struggled.

The plants had left him a short dagger. Surely they realized a man in combat attained a culmination of his life forces. Enveloped in clinging green threads, surrounded by frightful visions, he must have been resisting for hours. He had used his hands to tear the green shroud which returned as rapidly as he did so, and the bits of petals on the floor showed that he had sometimes gotten at the monster. But human strength has its limits. Atlena felt herself grow faint before this human crea-ture broken, breathed in by the devouring flower.

Then she struck—a blow at the place where the sepals knit and the green blood pulsed; a single blow, aimed to miss the man bound by the petals. The sword struck deep into the spongy tissue; an emerald flood spurted and blinded the queen. But through the green mist and her own terror she still saw the great statue which fought the fibrous cords, at the verge of a living abyss—not only Aran, but all humanity. Mad with anguish, forgetting her own fear and nausea, Atlena be-gan then to strike blindly: a dozen blows, piercing and tearing the unclean flower. She did so well that the petals relaxed, dropped the human being, inert

Detaching itself almost regretfully from its victim, slow-ly, the flowering horror pivoted and slid toward Atlena. Wounded and almost torn from its peduncle, it hurled at the queen no less an incredible influx of images, culled from its memories and dead conscious-nesses, in the subconscious of men it had dissolved for centuries to nourish it and to spread. The very history of Earth with its grand pomp, its tumults, and its battles, arose like a great wave wherein showed the faces of heroes and of gods, octopus-cities and realms of myth. The wings of Icarus and the powerful shadow of the first space-going rocket, the perfumes of Cleopatra at Tarsus and the dreadful reek of Hiroshima were part of that symphony. And all the conquered stars, and all the lost ages. It was too much, even for a queen of A-atlan. Meanwhile the awful flower swayed gently, gathering its energy to reach that thin white shape, and Atlena retreated, eyes shut, though she was search-ing for a way to draw the monster out of the bowl. Prisoner of the green filaments, Aran watched this deadly dance in agony. At the far side of the tower room, Tlavatli aimed the disinte-grator and dared not fire: He would first hit the queen.

Reaching the threshold, Atlena fell to her knees.

But shadows risen from the night were already running to help her.

Strangers. Beings in shining pearlized armor who resembled the statues of the human age. Faces like those of Uxmal and Aran. They riddled the awful flower with shots and when, in a fearsome convulsion, it fell at their feet, Tzental danced on its peduncle.

The others surrounded the crystal arena and spoke all at once. They were there at last, these new men so long awaited and so vainly looked for. Earth had come to Earth's rescue.

But for the moment they scarcely mattered. Freed of his bonds, Aran had reached Atlena. The walls withdrew then and the people disappeared. Battered, dream-haunted, they were alone in the world—as all lovers are—so totally alone that the plants, the Empire, and the very destiny of Earth no longer existed. Lips to lips—

"Aran," said the queen, "is this then—death and love?"

THE END

THE NON-HUMANS

These are not just the ramblings of an old condottiere.

There are more things in this terraqueous universe, and under Heaven, than the priests talk of; and I wasn't always the leathery old soldier who sits here, spinning his yarns over a mug of mead.

I'm telling you of the Florence of yesteryear. Not that anthill scorned by the Signory and a blushing Gonfalonier, but the leonine City of the Red Lily, that was daughter and mistress of the brave. The town that astonished all Italy, and drew foreigners like a lodestone.

1490... A year that seems so far away, yet comes so near as soon as I close my eyes! I was young then, a little mad, as we all are at 20, and well pleased with my person, which the ladies often found to their liking. I belonged, you know, to the noble family of the Pazzi, which had yet been spared its exile and its illustrious misfortunes; one of my uncles was a Cardinal, the galleys of another traded as far as the shores of Algeria. My widowed mother and I lived in a charming pink palace in Fiesole. Yes, it was destroyed later on, like so many things. But that has nothing to do with my story.

You have heard men speak of those matchless years, when a divine breath passed over Italy. It came from the snows of Olympus, from the violet sea, from golden Byzantium under the barbarian's heel; in our hearts and in the soil of our hills, it awoke old sleeping gods, the Graces, and the arts. In every mountain spring, a timid naiad awoke, parting the green strands of her hair; at dawn, on the trampled grass, one saw the dancing trail of a satyr. Artists began to paint and carve, women were proud and beautiful, and science, abandoning its alchemist's alembics, looked to the skies. After-

171

ward, we had Girolamo Savonarola and the Inquisition... Let us pass on.

For me (O marvel!) those years corresponded to my youth. I wasted little time in the counting house of my merchant uncle, selling Greek velvet and the incense of the Axumites. I composed sonnets, like Cornazano, music—like Lorenzo de Medici—and I numbered among my friends the master Perugino. This famous artist had once painted the portrait of my parents, and my sainted mother held him in great esteem.

It was in this studio, in fact, that I met Nardo—you know, Nardo, the youngest of his students, whom the master used as model for his angelic musicians? You can still see him here and there among the frescoes, playing on the harp or the rebeck—his pearly skin, blond curls, and his strange, empty eyes... "Half his soul always seems to be absent," said the master, with a laugh. Anyhow, Nardo—see, his name escapes me (it's old age, or that wound from Agnadel)... It matters little; it will come back to me. He was an inn servant's bastard, but legitimized by his father, a country squire. Afterward, he made his own way...

I went often to the studio of Messer Perugino. His nature was happy, his genius limitless. It was he, no other, who endowed Italy with those misty twilights, between darkness and day, broken by a ray of supernal dawn; to him, too, we owe those first heads of youths and pensive virgins, the velvet-smooth faces, the eyelids half closed on some ravishing secret. Later, artists understood and defined these things, but none was able to copy that silent expectation of a miracle: it belonged to our era.

Messer Perugino was then at the zenith of his fortunes, and he surrounded himself with brilliant young men. Being rather vain, he had also launched the fashion among artists of wearing a long purple or black velvet cloak, which became him very well, and a Florentine beret tilted over the car.

To entertain his friends and their merry companions, the "honestae meretrix" of Florence, the master had rented and redecorated a huge shack on the Arno; it had formerly been part of a row of grain warehouses, deserted since the Great Plague; it adjoined the Alley of the Old Jews, but Perugino liked it. Outside, this vast structure still looked run-down, but the interior was like a cathedral vault—many rooms had been made into one, and the walls were covered with extravagant drawings. We took much pleasure there, drank deep, and sang bacchic hymns in Latin, while the little tradesmen of the neighborhood trembled in their beds, and their chaste spouses hastily snuffed out the candles, crossing themselves... or got up to shoot the bolts on their daughters' doors.

Their daughters... We'll come to them.

One evening, when I was at Messer Perugino's, and he had taken it into his head to paint me as Saint Sebastian pierced with arrows (as Mantegna did with one of his friends), a strange personage came to visit the master. Tall, thin, dressed in black, with his leathery complexion and his crooked features, he might have been mistaken for the Wandering Jew himself, were it not that he wore a sword like a gentleman.

The visitor introduced himself: Messer Deodat Lazarelli, which was, he informed us voluntarily, a corruption of his Arab name of Al-Hazreh. You say there was a scholar of that name? I know him not. The Deodat in question explained to us that his ancestors had been barbaric kings in Cathay, living on herbs and mares' milk, and offering their wives to passing strangers in token of friendship. Our Deodat had been converted to the Christian faith, and, leaving that plateau where his spiritual advancement made it impossible to stay, he had made his fortune and retired to Florence, "the city," he said, "which has become the center of the universe." And he asked the master of Perugia to paint a portrait of his daughter, whose name was Noemi, or Nahema.

The master had other commissions in hand, and the prospect of painting a mud-faced girl little pleased him; he declined the offer, recommending certain colleagues of lesser renown to Al-Hazreh. But the old rascal knew how to make himself heard; he wasted no time in discussion, but emptied a long purse of red Morocco leather on the table.

The painter's eye gleamed—not that Perugino was in the least avaricious, but he could already see all the beautiful things he might bring into being from that golden heap. In a toneless voice, he told the Arab that his daughter might come to pose on the morrow.

"No," said the other dryly, in a changed tone, as if he had bought the right to be insolent. "My daughter cannot leave my house, nor appear in public. You will come to me. Don't think I am wasting your time: I live behind your house, just inside the Alley of the Old Jews, in the seed merchant's house, which I have purchased."

"But," said I, "nobody could live in that ruin! The place has been abandoned for 100 years or more!"

(I thought I knew Florence—unforeseeable, inexhaustible city!)

"*I* live there," retorted the man haughtily. (With my chest bare and daubed with "dragon's blood," no doubt he took me for a hired model.) "As for the rest, I shall send a slave to conduct you there, master."

Without a glance for me, he bowed to the master and left.

"What think you of that pismire, Guido?" Perugino asked me.

"That he lacks courtesy, and that my hand itches... But he's a stranger; we must make allowances for his barbaric habits. What will you do?"

"I know not," answered the artist. "Bah! Gold is always good to take! If the wench be not too ugly, I'll botch it together in three sittings and leave the background for Nardo to finick at. He'll give a good account of himself—won't you, my chick, my swan?"

Concealed behind the tapestries, Nardo gave us a hint of his charming, drowsy smile.

I left the studio supposing I should never see or hear again of the unpleasant Al-Hazreh.

But destiny toys with men, and, that same evening—out of idleness, and to try out my new black sorrel—I wandered down the Alley of the Old Jews. There, I surprised a singular activity: a façade was being covered with mortar, the metalwork of the shutters was being polished; black giant were carrying bundles of golden cloth, ebony furniture inlaid with mother-of-pearl, jade and onyx vases, and those astonishing screens of cloisonné enamel which were beginning to reach us from the Orient. Others were spreading a deep-piled Mirzapur on the steps, still others were sponging the flagstones of the entry with aromatics, burning incense and benzoin there.

The installation of a prince, if such he was! I stayed there, surprised and charmed: in a few days and without commotion, these diligent servants had transformed the ruin into a fairy palace. But porters were springing up afresh, bent caryatids carrying chests in the sinister form of coffins, made of pale lemonwood enriched only by its grain. A fantastic thing: while they were setting them on the ground, a chorus of thin and discordant voices reached me, as if from a flock of hungry sparrows; I turned, thinking a crowd of children had followed me, but the Alley was deserted, the gabled houses dark, the doors closed.

Nevertheless, a yellow rose, with a peppery scent, fell on the neck of my sorrel.

After that, I had no rest because I had failed to enter that house of Barbary. Youth is so fashioned: if Al-Hazreh had been less secretive and jealous, never would I have found myself under his windows. And if the rose had been white and of a less piquant perfume... It is natural to invent one's own chimeras: already I was imagining that beauty in the robes of an Empress of Cathay, with tilted eyes and a skin of yellow satin.

...In which I was mistaken.

The next morning, meeting Nardo accompanied by an enormous black man who carried brushes and canvas, I fell into step. Nardo made me a present of his angelic smile. The morning was mild, the sky of an exquisite mauve; silvery carillons fell from the campaniles, and mist floated on the transparent river.

I was apprehensive of meeting the gallows bird Al-Hazreh, but he had the good grace to absent himself, and we went up, through all the enchantments of the Thousand and One Nights. One room succeeded another, each with its lintel of lapis lazuli and its ivory door; on each doorsill slept a black; a fountain pulsed in each lotus-shaped basin.

One immense room, which had been part of the warehouses, was now transformed with exquisite taste into a studio: daylight entering by a window of colored crystal was softened by turquoise veils; it gave things an aspect aquatic and strange. An ebony screen, pierced in the form of lilies and swans, marked off the space of a choir. There was little furniture, save for some armchairs and small tables garlanded with mother-of-pearl, now mauve, now pink, according to the light. In the center of the hall, masses of iris lay in a basin carved of blue opaline. I also noted the lemon-wood chests, disposed here and there on a little platform. An orchestra hidden behind the screen began a soft *canzone.*

On the platform sat a girl. I know not how to describe her, save by comparison with the rare and precious things she evoked: moonlight, the shivering of willows, pearls, mist floating on the water. Angelic, androgynous, mysterious, without a past, without a country, sprung perhaps from an alien universe… I believe she was dressed in mist and azure. I believe… At the first glimpse, I fell under an unaccountable spell; I was powerless, turned into an automaton.

I let Nardo go through the necessary motions, unfold the easel and prepare the colors, always keeping behind him where I could see my fair unknown. Nardo, by contrast, was vivaciously selecting his charcoal sticks.

I promise you I did not follow the progress of his work; I was plunged into an abyss of vertiginous sensations, and I saw, I remembered, beings, things, whole sequences of time—strange, magnificent, or dreadful—all of which bore some relation to the adorable creature who sat before me.

Two series of images were blended: first a black gulf, shot through with nebulous gleams, stars, like the pearls of a necklace spilled on velvet—and windings, spirals of flame, emerald and purple explosions (such as, I know now, no artificer can produce). A dazzling light burst through the colored window—and it was the face of a giant globe.

Then, like a traveler who contemplates the valley of the Arno from the summit of the Apennines, I saw another Earth come toward me, with its sharp reliefs, its frosted peaks, and its craters of night among the great luminous plateaus; phosphorescent oceans beat upon their shores, and a gloomy light chilled the ruins of magnificent cities. And these landscapes at the same time were a song and a music, mounting by stairs of silver toward the vast Heavens.

"Can you paint that?" asked the girl, addressing herself equally to Nardo and me. I would have pointed out wherein lay her error, but my voice died away on my lips. Nardo was already drawing with his native ease and swiftness, darting a tangle of spidery lines onto the canvas. A glance at his sketch made me turn pale: without exchanging a word with me, he had just copied my visions.

We were so absorbed that we did not hear Messer Perugino enter the studio, then withdraw on tiptoe.

I asked the master's permission to be present at the second sitting, and Perugino, who had just sunk a new arrow into the biceps of Saint Sebastian, looked up in surprise. "Do you really want to?"

"*Per Bacco!* If not, would I speak of it?"

"Good," he conceded, spreading a bloody highlight across the pectorals of my double, "but don't swear: it sits ill with the expression of a martyr. I grant you that the arrangement of milord Al-Hazreh's lodgings is ingenious, and his ambition to have me paint his wax doll is amusing..."

"His—what?"

"His automaton," said the artist. "His demon, queen of the vampires. His giant homunculus." And taking my indignation at its height: "You haven't looked upon her closely, then? It's true that, with all the lights dimmed, you might be excused."

Breathless, I could only form the words: "But that girl spoke to us!"

"Really? After all, the thing is possible. Such astonishing engines have been made! In France, it appears, some angels were constructed of gilded wood, with a mechanism so perfect that they walked, shook their wings, and even spoke a compliment, at the coronation of the young queen, Ysabeau de Bavière. But Paracelcus maintains that not only the mandragores, but certain bulbs of the white lily, grown in jars and buried in dung at the full of the Moon, with appropriate incantations, give birth to living beings a cubit tall. These sprats, though very devoted to their masters, are of a vicious and malignant humor. Certain alchemists relate that they live on air, like the fish of Cathay, but it is generally conceded that they feed on a blood jelly. Parenthetically, it would interest me to know how Al-Hazreh procured this, since it is compounded of human blood... At any rate, automaton, homunculus, or mandragore, whether your Signorina Nahema belongs to one species or the other, it is certain she is no Christian creature, and I shall not paint her! I shall not let Art itself, in my person, be abased!"

"But," I protested again, "what you speak of is impossible, senseless! Nardo, who has painted her, will certify—"

Exasperated, the master interrupted. "Nardo! What a witness! A stripling who never has dared lift his eyes to a living woman! An automaton is just the sort of toy that fascinates children. Well, let Nardo paint her, since he understands her so well, and he can also gild a few tavern and cookshop signboards, to earn sweets for his serving-wench mother!"

This unjust judgment confirmed my suspicions: to wit, that the master was jealous of Nardo's progress.

I went to the second sitting with the firm intention of assuring myself that Signorina Al-Hazreh was no statue of wax.

I found the same blue paradise, the same enchantment, and an attentive Nardo, bent over his canvas.

We were hardly settled when a black wench brought the girl an elongated silver lute. Dwarves served us rose and lemon ices, and poured heavy date wine, cooled with snow, into rainbow-colored murrhines. (I wondered later if some philter in it had not stirred up my senses.) Nahema played and sang, in a voice of crystal; her melodies spoke of a dead world, once delightful; of stars and glaciers, or of lost souls wandering in search of one another. And as she sang, there appeared to us (I can speak for Nardo as for myself) throngs of dim shadows that invaded the hall, danced along the hangings, wrung their hands, lovingly appealed for an impossible joy, while their long hair mingled with the iris in the basin.

We met Al-Hazreh no more; but we breathed the mustiness of his jealousy. Sometimes a curtain moved without a breath of air; something like a giant spider scurried about the dark corners; we sensed a discordant echo... To be sure, no one worried his head about it.

The third day...

The fact is that I lived only for those hours: the rest of me shaded off into somnolence. I was seen no more at banquets, and I avoided Perugino's studio. For long intervals, I barely subsisted, like a plant with its roots out of the ground: then, suddenly, I would be plunged into my native humus, or rather into a watery space where all was strength and life. Nardo waited for me on the bank of the Arno, and we went up silently toward the Alley.

The third sitting was devoted, then, to what I shall call "natural magic." Nahema spoke to us of sciences lost to the western world: they had been destroyed by the great incendiaries—Omar had burned the Alexandrian, and in the Ming Library, the Mongols' shaggy little ponies had trampled the precious papyri. Other knowledge lay in the depths, on submerged continents...

She told us of beings who had lived in those deep waters, moving about in disk-shaped vessels, or with their heads protected by helmets of crystal. Later, she described other creatures to us, rising in the air like smoke above the stubble, gliding like birds on their extended wings, or else (this is too complicated for me) traversing the sidereal ether, solely by virtue of an incredible vitality that overleaped sound, light, and time itself. "Thus," she said, "energy endures; for proof: the light of a star, dead for millennia, brings us its radiant, living image. The temporal no longer exists: we enter into eternity."

She proved to us that the ancient alchemy was nothing but a pallid reflection of true chemistries, for which the transmutation of elements would be child's play. "Some day," she promised, "men will harness the thunder, the chaos of exploding suns, the light of nearby stars, all at once. Then, perhaps, they will hold the Secret between their hands. They will create new materials—priceless, extraordinary, resistant as iron or satiny as a baby's skin—and who knows—"

She paused, and Nardo asked if scholars were already imagining such things. Nahema's lips curved, in a smile that belied the sadness in her eyes.

"There are the empirics," she said. "But it is not at all the same." Seeing that we did not understand, she explained: "Those whom you call sorcerers. They manipulate great natural forces blindly: there is danger in it." As she spoke, she attentively studied her own hands, their tapering fingers, their delicate modeling. A white flame ran beneath the texture of her skin.

We spoke no further that day.

Here falls an incident of which I am a little ashamed, and which I would put aside if it did not lie so close to my story. I have already told you that, in the blissful consumption in which I lived, I no longer counted the days, nor visited my usual companions; I forgot even my loves. The word is not too strong, for that evening, encountering Mona Chiara Salviati, at a turning of the Alley of the Old Jews, under the very porch of Santa Reparata, I did not recognize her.

This pretty banker's widow had been kind to me; she was white and brown, she was approaching a stormy age, and she threw herself upon my neck, petulantly. I lifted her and deposited her carefully on the curbing of a well. She stood there petrified, alarming with her cries some tradesmen issuing from vespers, and a scullion who sat on the sill of a cookshop. Thus I was able to dive into the first street I saw, congratulating myself on being rid of her at such a fair price, and without recalling the ancient adage: "Hell hath no fury like a woman scorned."

At our fourth meeting, Nahema spoke to us of myths and mysteries. Ever and again she returned to the Platonic account which declares that all beings were originally made double. "Your Bible," she added in passing, "confirms that truth in its Elohist version. *'And Elohim created man in His own image: male and female He created them.'* " These perfect beings who were force and beauty, energy and intuition all at the same time, were nevertheless separated, "just as a woman halves an egg with a knife," and flung solitary into chaos. Ever afterward they wandered, with the indestructible memory of their lost companions, with a desire and anguish that nothing could appease…

"Sometimes, they find each other," Nahema finished sadly, "but not always with happiness, for they seek an impossibly deep and intimate union; and, chained to unremembering bodies, their souls bruise and wound each other in vain."

"Does it never happen," asked Nardo in his crystalline voice, "that the meeting is happy and the union as perfect as the fusion of two metals? Did Laura not love Petrarch, and Paolo his Francesca da Rimini?"

"Yes," answered Nahema, "but Death lies there in wait. No true immortality exists for any but a whole being: that is to say, for twin souls, fused into a single body. Moreover, it's by that faculty of fusion, of receptivity, that the elect distinguish one another: that is the sign of perfect lovers."

"I would have liked such a union," said the child, lowering his long eyelashes. Then he painted in silence.

It is time, since the occasion offers, to speak of Nardo's painting. I have said that I considered Perugino an unjust mas-

181

ter; small as my knowledge might be in matters of art, I could foretell that we had a great painter in that apprentice. A Botticelli or a Mantegna—who knows? His line was firm without crudity, soft without daintiness, and his knowledge of perspective was exceptional for his age. But this portrait of Nahema was the first in whose presence I had felt that faint chill at the heart, that sacred shiver, which comes from the contemplation of a masterpiece.

The girl appeared at the bottom of the mysterious landscape of peaks and trails of stars that she had suggested to us. Her face, of an inhuman serenity, smiled at some inner vision, reproachless, faultless, hopeless. It was a music of which Nahema formed the principal motif—Nahema... or some distant star. Yes, the work was beautiful. But later on, it seems, Nardo did better ones; so it is said.

Have I mentioned that during these reeling and unreeling conversations in the hall of blue magic—platonic dialogues beside which the talk of any woman, even the charming Chiara, was no more than an insipid and vulgar babbling—we sometimes dared to approach the platform? Nardo lay at the girl's feet; she gave me her dangling hand, and I savored its perfume, its satiny softness, and its warmth. She granted us no other liberty.

Sometimes Nahema's glance lay heavy on us; it seemed to me that her eyes cried out, demanded a response. What could I say to her? Yes, truly, I loved her! My most ardent wish was to steal her away from the evil renegade... Only once I spoke the same of Al-Hazreh with hatred in her presence. Her penciled eyebrows rose.

"Do not arouse him," she said. "He has his suspicions. Like Ugolino, he foresees the moment when, with his sons dead of hunger, he must go to meet his Master. Let us not envy the fate of apprentice sorcerers... What, you didn't know that Deodat Lazarelli is one of them?"

She passed a too-perfect hand over a smooth forehead, where neither age nor human afflictions had left any trace, and let it fall. "Yes. He is a sorcerer. To the despair of soulless beings—and of wandering souls."

It was the last time that I saw her in Nardo's presence.

The next evening—was it really the next morning? I had lost the notion of time, as I told you. In any case, it was the night before a storm. The city swooned under a ceiling of lead, and over the Ponte Vecchio the Sun went down in a tragic purple. From the old quarters arose a heavy stench of carrion, roses, and incense. Uneasiness haunted the Alley of the Old Jews, whose inhabitants had gone to ground; even the servants of Al-Hazreh were nowhere to be seen. On a bridge, at the exact spot where Dante saw Beatrice and fell instantly in love with her, I met milord Perugino, in the midst of his court of students in paint-spattered velvet, sword-hung bravos, and courtesans. It was an eternity ago that I had deserted his studio. Doubtless, he was just now risen from the banquet table; he was not drunk, but overexcited, and he drew me aside from his noisy group.

"Well then," he began, "what news? How goes your love affair with the wax doll? Guido, Guido, I've always known you were too handsome for a simple cavalier of Florence, and that your gift would play you a bad turn! Is it true, as they say, that yon statue is as wise as the Queen of Sheba, and more seductive than Helen of Troy? Has she really cured an emperor of leprosy, and driven Pope Callixtus Borgia mad? Beware the toils of Hell, my son," he resumed, adopting clerical language; "is she not called Nahema? Well, it's a demon's name, as much as Lilith is!"

"Messer Perugino," I retorted, controlling myself, "it ill becomes a cavalier to hear his lady spoken of in that tone, but you have ever been as an elder brother to me. I beg you therefore to make an end of these spiteful pleasantries: if not, let us cross steel, and may God be our judge!"

He looked at me, his eyes so wide that the pupils swallowed up the corneas. "So it stands thus!" he cried. "How sorry I am to have put you in their way! But as God is my witness, until this very moment I thought of it just so, as a pleasantry. Well then, Guido dei Pazzi, you are a man of sense and no idler, nor one of the Piagnoni, one of the weepers' of San Marco. How you could stray into the toils of a cleverly painted automaton!"

"She is no machine, but an adorable girl."

"You are truly in love with her?"

Yes," said I, weighing each word, for the truth was in them: "and to the point, I know she is no wax statue—I see her every day, in Nardo's company. I breathe her perfume, I kiss her hand, she talks with us. Her breath is that of a morning in May..."

"Always in Nardo's company?" demanded Perugino, with a malicious air. "Never alone together?"

"You know our habits."

"Nevertheless," said he, "there is one way for you to assure yourself that the idlers of the ghetto lie, that the Genoese and Venetian merchants lie, that the Legate himself lies! All these persons are persuaded that Master Al-Hazreh, who is the Wandering Jew, Ahasuerus, or the Devil, is displaying before us all an effigy modeled from a substance of which he is the inventor, having used it for this end certain solar or other radiations! She moves (I mean the statue) by the aid of an ingenious mechanism—at least, if that marvel be not due simply to the presence of a demon. He did not succeed in producing that creature without diverse experiments, of which the resulting homunculi feed on fresh human blood. Numbers of children have disappeared in the neighborhood, and we expect the tribunes of the Faith to be seized of a formal complaint, which cannot be long delayed. As for this Nahema, demon or mysterious entity, come from another world by way of the shadows, you have only to read the cabalists to have her to the fingertips: she reigns over the vampires, leads men to foreswear themselves, to guilty passions, to catastrophes, and to suicides, and marks those whom she leads astray with an infernal star between their eyes!"

"Lies, all of it!"

"In any case, her powers are great. You have but to look at yourself—all Florence is talking of you."

"Master!"

"There is one single way to prove all this idle talk and madman's tales—"

"And that, if you please?" I demanded, white with rage.

"Faith," said Perugino, laughing, "the damsel likes you, does she not? Take advantage of it. Then you'll see."

Evil words are like the bad seed, like the tare that springs up wherever it falls: they sprout, even in a soul full of anger.

I have already told you that the sky was overcast. The violet night blotted out the Campanile, and the Marzocco, the heraldic lion of Florence, furiously roared in its cage. Silent flashes of lightning lit up the clouds. Leaving Perugino, I walked aimlessly; children fled before me and women quickly closed their doors; I was that sort of leper—the enchanted one, the possessed! Over the Arno, the air was intoxicating as sage wine. Without knowing how, I found myself again in the Alley of the Old Jews.

There was no one in the house of Al-Hazreh: neither in the entry nor along the corridors. All the portals were open; the servants had fled. I stood motionless on the sill, when I heard a groan or a sob—so weak that it might have been the sigh of a breaking lute string. Then a squalling: it sounded like a flock of birds invading the rafters. The noise came from the blue hall, and I had recognized the voice—I rushed toward it.

All the hangings were drawn; a suffocating darkness filled the studio, where a single torch glimmered at the corner of the platform. Its feeble gleam made the shadows impossibly large, and in that liquid dark I saw Nahema standing, white as wax, and Al-Hazreh on his knees. He was pricking her wrist with a stiletto—the sacrificial knife—and the blood fell drop by drop into a goblet. Without sparing time to draw my sword from its sheath, I fought him with my bare hands in the darkness. The curved blade glittered, but I was younger and stronger...

"Don't kill him!" cried Nahema.

The renegade fled. And we were left alone—or almost. With a handkerchief, Nahema made me a tourniquet. Her own hand was no longer bleeding. Then I saw around us the open lemonwood chests; and standing on the floor, crystal flagons a cubit tall, in which a blue phosphorescence floated. Their tops were sealed with membranes, each pierced by an alembic tube.

In each jar wriggled a living creature, monstrously human—a horror.

There was a King, and a Queen. A mitred Bishop; a Condottiere. A Hospitaler, on his horse. A Gorgon whose every red lock writhed. What else do I remember? There was even one dressed in scarlet, and provided with a sword no bigger than a pin, with which he was attacking the jar—a Satan, sprung from the cogitations of a Doctor Faustus...

All of them squalled and clamored with an incredible arrogance; only a few inches tall, nevertheless they had a damnable reality. And they held out their arms to us, their minuscule lips avid, pursing toward our wounds, toward the alembic tube from which would drop their manna, their red dew—our blood...

I was on the point of knocking over the jars and trampling these tiny monsters underfoot, when the girl seized my wrist and thrust forward a bloodless face, pathetic with anger.

"Stop!" she panted, in a voice unrecognizably harsh. "Why kill these unhappy creatures? It's not their fault if they exist, if they tremble with fear and die of hunger! Al-Hazreh alone is responsible. *I* offered myself to feed my brothers—the non-humans!"

"No!" I cried, maddened, "I can't believe it! You're not of that race of mandragores! Your blood flows, you are living; I love you!"

"Do you really love me?" she asked hungrily. "Do you alone understand the meaning of that word: love? No, listen, touch me not. Indeed I am no machine, nor any magical root, nor was I hatched from the husks of a white onion. Imagine that all your dreams are true. Better: picture to yourself that sidereal abyss in which your Earth is only an atom. Look: in that black sky, among the pearls of Orion's Belt, there is one that is a dead sun, around which icy globes tirelessly revolve. One of these is my mother world, which once was beauty itself. If you love me, Terran, believe that I am really human—more human than you, for I belong to the same race, only more ancient, born on a planet that no longer exists, save as a cadaver in the void.

"But indeed, death did not come at one stroke. Our species was advanced and powerful; we struggled long to keep up a semblance of life among those craters of ice and those frosty peaks of which you have dreamed. When all was lost, a few survivors dared the supreme adventure: they knew that, somewhere in the cosmos, other worlds existed, peopled with creatures who resembled themselves, bodies in which they might awaken. They tried to join those far-off motherworlds. I—

"Only by accident, I was cast away on Earth: it is new, crude, it is unready for these experiences. But Al-Hazreh seized me in the meshes of his mad incantations… He drew me here… No, I should not accuse Al-Hazreh: there must have been a predestination—there can be no effect without a cause; perhaps this globe was a haven… I wander from my story. Al-Hazreh gave me this body for a prison. No, it is not of wax (I read your thought), but I am chained in it, and suffering. You say, do you not, that you love me? Even though I am a creature from the stars?… You love me—and truly wish to accept me?"

"I love you. It matters little whence you came." So saying, I took her in my arms, with the headlong passion of my first youth. The lace of my doublet crushed into her delicate bosom; I wanted to squeeze her, braise her, drown myself in her, and be her master. And with all my strength I strained against a thin flame, an enveloping softness that invaded my nerves. It seemed to me that an incredible flood of energy lifted and pierced me, driving the blood back to my heart—and it was such terror, and such delight! We struggled thus, silently, mouth to mouth, until she seemed to melt in my arms, and then—only physical sensations remaining—with a vertiginous, stabbing clarity, I realized that that petal-like skin which I caressed, those honeyed lips, the living waves of her hair wherein I was held as in a net, *were not the hair, the lips, the flesh of a human being...*

An insurmountable horror overtook me. I thrust away that cosmic foe who was about to subdue me. Or did she herself perhaps break away from my embrace? She flung in my face: "No. You are not the one I seek. Get out!"

All that night, I wandered through the streets, trying to deal logically with my nightmare. Very well, Al-Hazreh was a sorcerer. He had tried—the folly was current—to create life. To begin with, following the teachings of Albertus Magnus and Paracelsus (I was not a complete ignorant!)—from this came the homunculi, fascinating, imperfect monsters. Finally (by what procedure?—"by radiations," Perugino had said), he began to reconstitute living matter and to give it a seductive form. Each time, he had learned that his statue still lacked that divine spark: the soul, or the spirit. So he had gone on with his search. Was it Plato, or the Ophites, who told him of the survival in the Cosmos of wandering spirits, seeking new bodies to inhabit?

"Animula vagula, blandula..." the Emperor Hadrian had said on his deathbed. The patient madness of Al-Hazreh flung itself into the search for these aliens, and he had found Nahema—exiled, lost, irresponsible... I shuddered. Perugino had been right: her admirable body was nothing but inert matter, serving as a prison. And yet she had shuddered and wept in my arms. She was waiting for a miracle: I was not worthy of it.

At dawn I ran aground, exhausted, in the studio of the master, who dressed my wounds and watched over me as if I were a prodigal son.

I understood now that since my first visit to the Alley of the Old Jews, my soul had really been absent, drawn into the limbo where Nahema lived, out of space and time, far from this century and the town called Florence. I knew nothing of the troubles that were shaking the Medicis' throne, nor of the first sermons of the young Savonarola, nor of the first halting steps on our soil, once more free, of that frightful machine from Spain: the Inquisition. My way of life had so altered that my kinsmen were disturbed. The most anxious to intervene, indeed, was Mona Chiara Salviati. That lady had extensive connections, but she resorted simply to her confessor, a novice friar, animated by zeal, who was none other than our old and well-loved Fra Giorgio da Casale.

Yes, that is what I said: the Bludgeon of Sorcerers; he who had lately burned 400 in a single day. In short, the Grand Inquisitor of Tuscany.

My convalescence was long. My mother had taken me to Fiesole, and watched jealously over my bed. I spent hours lying fiat on a terrace covered with climbing vetch. My pretty cousins played on the rebeck or the viol. Summer came; the vines were heavy with grapes, plundered by drunken thrushes. In the morning mist, the Arno shone like a sword blade. I experienced a phenomenon well known to exorcists: withdrawn from the presence of my dear demon, I forgot her, while still keeping her imprint in my flesh.

But there came a day when, by chance, a Florentine friend spoke the name of Al-Hazreh in my presence.

"The magician of the Alley of the Old Jews," he explained. "What, you have not heard? It's true; he was arrested the day after Messer Perugino gathered you in with that nasty wound. The Inquisition was seized of a complaint, and moved. But the nub of the affair is that the guards could not subdue the sorcerer, because he performed miracles: a fire that burned in the very stone, serpents on the steps of the staircase... In short, the whole bagful. So they locked the doors and shutters, and put sentinels down below. They chanted exorcisms; they burnt a pyre of Agnus Castus soaked in aromatics; it poisoned the whole of Florence for three days. Meanwhile shouts and frightful noises could be heard inside the old house... Oh, no—he was alone, his servants had run away. It was a screeching like an immense aviary... but he had no birds. Finally all was quiet. Four days later, the guards read their proclamation and broke down the doors."

"And then?"

"Then he was dead. It seems he had pierced his wrists with fragments of crystal. There were pieces of broken jars around the corpse, which was curled up and all black."

"And that was all?

"Oh, yes—there was also a red, quivering jelly."

"Then it wasn't the Wandering Jew," said my mother, who had approached during the conversation. She crossed herself. "Why do you tell of such horrors? Guido is still so weak!"

So, I thought, Al-Hazreh had died in the attempt to destroy his creatures? Or had they killed him to drink his blood? A recollection lit up the blank spaces of my memory. I stiffened and cried out, "The Jew—didn't he have a daughter, or a ward? What became of her? Speak, in God's name!"

My comrade looked at me, surprised by such vehemence. "I know not," he said.

No one had heard any report of her...

Recovered, I left my house, Florence, and Tuscany, to engage myself, as a condottiere must, under many standards. I served under Alviano, "married to the Republic of Venice;" under Da Fermo; under the great Vitellozzo Vitelli, the Strategist. I served, from 1502 to 1507, the Tiara and the Keys, under Monseigneur de Valentinois—and may God pardon me: I would have served under the Devil himself if I could!

The story would be ended if I had not learned, on the first day I returned to Perugino's studio, that he had dismissed Nardo.

"The boy was becoming impossible!" grumbled the master. "He changed from one day to the next; he discovered new laws of perspective! Invented colors, and painted with them! And submarine vessels—and flying machines... The air, according to him, has weight and can hold up solid bodies... Pure folly! How many ounces, sir, in the morning breeze? I showed him the door for one ultimate insolence: he aspired to sign that portrait of Al-Hazreh's!"

"Then the portrait exists?" I demanded fervently.

"Certainly not! I destroyed it: an unspeakable daub. The colors decomposed before they were dry!"

I wished to see Nardo again: it was not easy. I learned that the Duke of Milan, Ludovico Sforza, had taken him under his protection, having regard for his birth, and probably for his talents. He should be leaving for Lombardy; perhaps he was already on the way.

Drawn irresistibly, I wandered into the Alley of the Old Jews. It had just been ravaged by a terrible fire; dogs prowled among the beams and the calcined debris; a whole section of the warehouses, that which had enclosed the grain merchant's house, had burned: in a single night, and no one knew the date. Nor the causes of the disaster. No fire smoldered under the cinders...

Then this befell me:

The night came over Florence: soft, cold, and blue, as it is at the beginning of autumn. Every lungful of air was laced with a minty coolness. At the corner of a street, I made out a familiar silhouette: the black mantle and the painter's beret. I called, and the man turned about. It was Nardo. He had grown taller; his body balanced itself with exquisite grace, and his features seemed to glow. Magnificently dressed, he confirmed that he was in the favor of His Highness. While he spoke, I heard the music of his voice, I followed the gestures of his hands and his fringed eyelids. It was Nardo—and it was not.

"Come and see what I am painting now," he proposed with a sort of gaiety. "I can do so many things, you see! Come."

At the inn where he lodged at the Duke's expense, he showed me some ravishing sketches of aerial creatures, of angels and demons equally beautiful, of lunar landscapes, here and there the outline of an unknown monster, or a giant wing. They were no more than studies, gropings, but it was impossible to doubt: under his tapering fingers a world was being born. He had visited the stars and the depths... What he had brought back to Earth belonged to another scale of values, to a domain and an art unknown to humankind. The execution was perfection itself. I observed also that through all the sketches, haunting the dreams and work of the artist, drifted the same face, androgynous and angelic, with depthless eyes.

At length, "Nahema!" I cried.

Nardo gazed at me calmly. "Yes," he said. "We part no more. Look here, this is the model of her silver lute which I have reconstructed. I have noted down the tunes of her songs. Here are the engines that she draws by my hand—I do not understand as yet what purpose they serve, but soon I shall understand. Soon, when the fusion is complete, Guido. For I loved her, too, you see, I was ready to give her my being and my life, when her hour had struck. I asked to receive her. She acknowledged me. Since then, she is present everywhere, she lives through me—in *me!*"

His features were stamped with an inhuman serenity.

Another mug of mead, landlord, for the old condottiere! Ah—Nardo's name comes back to me: he took that of his village—Vinci. He called himself Leonardo da Vinci.[1]

---

[1] For many years Andrea del Verrocchio was da Vinci's master, and many people know of no other. But one day Verrocchio, grown jealous, showed him the door, and for a time Leonardo, not knowing what to do, is said to have frequented "the studios of the most illustrious painters of Florence." Well, the most illustrious of these painters was Perugino. Perugino represents exactly for the dawn of the Renaissance what Leonardo is for its high noon. I thought it would be interesting to put the two men face to face, since Perugino's influence is evident in the early works of da Vinci. (*Note from the Author*)

THE BLIND PILOT

The shop was low and dark, as if designed for someone who no longer knew day from night. Around it hung a scent of wax and incense, exotic woods, and roses dried in darkness. It was in the cellar of one of the oldest buildings of the old radioactive district, and you had to walk down several steps before you reached a grille of Venerian sandalwood. A cone of Martian crystal lighted the sign: *THE BLIND PILOT*.

The man who came in this morning, followed by a robot porter with a chest, was a half-crazy old voyager, like many who had gazed on the naked blazing of the stars. He was back from the Asclli —at least, if not from there, from the Southern Cross; his face was of wax, ravaged, graven, from lying too long in a cabin at the mercy of the ultraviolets, and in the black jungle of the planets.

The coffer was hewn from a heartwood hard as brass, porous here and there. He had it set down on the floor, and the sides vibrated imperceptibly, as if a great captive bee were struggling inside.

"Look here," he said, giving a rap on the lid, "I wouldn't sell what's in there for a million credits, but I need to refloat myself, 'til I get my pay. They tell me you're an honest Tal. I'll leave this here in pawn and come back to get it in six days. What'll you give me?"

At the back of the shop, a young man raised his head. He was sitting in an old armchair stiff with flowered brocade. He looked like one of those fine Velasquez cavaliers who had hands of steel, and were not ashamed to be beautiful: but a black bandage covered the upper part of his face.

"I'm no Tal," he answered coldly, "and I don't take live animals as pledges."

"Blind! You're blind!" stammered the newcomer.

"You saw my sign."

"Accident?"

"Out in the Pleiades."

"Sorry, shipmate!" said the traveler. But already he was scheming: "How'd you know there was an animal in there?"

"I'm blind—but not deaf."

The whole room was tingling with a crystalline vibration. Suddenly it stopped. The traveler wiped great drops of sweat from his forehead.

"Shipmate," he said, "that ain't really an animal. I'm holding onto that. I don't want to sell it to nobody. And if I don't have any money tonight, it's the jug for me. No more space voyages, no more loot, no more nothing. I'm an HZ, to be suspended."

"I get it," answered the quiet voice. "How much?"

The other almost choked. "Will you really give me—?"

"Not a thing, I don't give anything for nothing, and I told you before, I'm not interested in your cricket in a cage. But I can let you have 5000 credits, no more, on your shipping papers. In six days, when you come back to get them, you'll pay me 500 credits extra. That's all."

"You're *worse* than a Tal!"

"No. I'm blind." He added grimly, "My accident was caused by a jerk who hadn't insured his rocket. I don't like jerks."

"But," said the adventurer, shuffling his feet, "how can you check my papers?"

"My brother's over there. Come on out, Jacky."

A sharp little grin appeared in the shadows. Out between a lunar harmonium in a meteorite, and a dark Terrestrial cloth on which a flayed martyr had bled, came a cripple mounted on a little carnage—legless, with stumps of arms, propelling himself with the aid of two hooks: a malicious little old man of 12.

"Mutant," said the blind man curtly. "But he makes out, with his prosthetics. Papers in order, Jacky?"

"Sure, North. And dirtier than a dustrag."

"That only means they've seen good use. Give him his 5000 credits."

The blind man pressed a button. A cabinet opened, revealing a sort of dumb-waiter. In the top half there was a little built-in strong box; in the bottom crouched a Foramen chimera, the most bloodthirsty of beasts, half cat, half harpy.

The traveler jumped back.

The cripple rolled himself over to the strong box, grabbed up a bundle of credits and blew on the monster's nose. It purred affectionately.

"You see, the money's well guarded here," said North.

"Can I leave my chest with you, anyhow?" asked the traveler humbly.

So the chest remained. Using the dumb-waiter, the cripple sent it up to the small apartment that the two brothers shared in the penthouse of the building. According to its owner, the creature that was "not really an animal" was in hibernation; it had no need of food. The porous wood allowed enough air to pass. But the box had to be kept in a dark place. "It lives in the great deeps," he had explained; "it can't stand daylight."

The building was really very old, with a lot of elevators and closets. The mutants and cripples of the last war, who lived there because it was cheap, accommodated themselves to it. North dragged the chest into the strong room next to his study.

That evening, the free movie in the building was showing an old stereo film, not even sensorial, about the conquest of the Pleiades, and Jacky announced that he wanted to see it. About to leave, he asked his brother, "You don't suppose that animal will get cold in there?"

"What are you talking about? It's in hibernation."

"Anyhow," said Jacky spitefully, "we're not getting paid to keep it in fuel."

The movie lasted until midnight, and when Jacky came back, there was a full Moon. The boy testified later that he had been a little overexcited. A white glimmer flooded the upper landing, and he saw that the French windows of the "garret," as they called his brother's study, were masked with a black cloth. Jacky supposed North had taken this extra precaution on account of the animal; he pushed himself forward with his hooks, and knocked on the door, but no one answered, and there was no key in the lock.

He told himself then that maybe North had gone down six stories to the bar in the building, and he decided to wait. He sat on the landing; the night was mild, and he would not have traded the air at that height for any amount of conditioned and filtered atmosphere. The silver star floated overhead in the black sky. Jacky mused that "it means something after all, that shining going on just the same for x years, that Moon that's seen so many old kings, poets, and all those lovers' stories. The cats that yowl at night must feel it; and the dogs too." In the lower-class buildings, there were only robot dogs. Jacky longed for a real dog—after all, he was only 12. But mutants couldn't own living animals. And then...

(On the magnetic tape where Jacky's deposition was taken down, it seemed that at that moment the boy began to choke. The recording was interrupted, and the next reel began: "Thanks for the coffee. It was good and bitter.")

He had heard an indefinable sound, very faint... just the sound of the ocean in a seashell. It grew, and grew... At the same time (though he couldn't say how), there were images. A nacreous sky, the color of pearl, and green crystal waves, with crests of sparkling silver. Jacky felt no surprise; he had just left the stereo theater. Perhaps someone in the building opposite had turned on a sensorial camera—and the vibrations, the waves, were impinging here by accident.

But the melody swelled, and the boy sank under the green waves. They stank of seaweed and fish... Carried along by the currents, the little cripple felt light and free. Banks of rustling diatoms parted for him; a blue phosphorescence haloed the medusas and starfish, and pearly blue anemones formed a forest. Grazed by a transparent jellyfish, Jacky felt a nettle-like burning. The shadow of a hammerhead shark went by, and scattered a twinkling cloud of smelt. Farther down, the shadow grew denser, more opaque and mysterious—caverns gaped in a coral reef. The tentacle of an octopus lashed the water, and the cripple shuddered. He found himself thrown back against the hull of a ship, half buried in the sand. A little black and gold siren, garlanded with barnacles, smiled under the prow; and he fell, transported, against a breach that spilled out a pirate treasure, coffers full of barbaric jewels. Heaps of bones were whitening at the bottom of the hold, and a skull smiled with empty sockets. *This must be an amateur film*, Jacky thought, *a little too realistic*. He freed himself, pushed away as hard as he could with his hooks, rose to the surface at last—and almost cried out.

The sky above him was not that of Earth. North had told him how that other dark ocean looked—the sub-ether. The stars were naked and dazzling. Reefs, that were burning meteors, sprang up out of the void. And the planets seemed to whirl near enough to touch—one was ruby, another orange, still another a tranquil blue; Saturn danced in its airy ring.

Jacky thrust his hooks out before him to push away those torches. In so doing, he slipped and rolled across the landing. The door opened a second later—he hadn't had time to fall three steps, but this time he wasn't diving alone: beside him, in the hideously reddened water, whirled and danced the body of a disjointed puppet, with gullied features in a face of wax

Jacky raised his head. North stood on the sill, terrible, pale as a statue of old ivory; the black bandage cut his face in two. He called, "Who's there? Answer me, or I'll call the militia!"

His voice was loud and angry. North, who always spoke so softly to Jacky...

"It's me, Jack," said the boy, trembling. "I was coming back, and I missed a step..."

("I told a lie," said Jacky later, to the militiamen who were questioning him. And he stared into their eyes with a look of open defiance. "That's right, sure, I told a lie. Because I knew he'd kill me.")

The next morning there was no blood and no corpse on the landing. Only a smell of seaweed...

Jacky was filling the coffee cups, in the back of the shop, while the television news broadcast was on. Toward the end, the announcer mentioned that the body of a drowned man had been taken from the harbor. The dead man's face appeared on the tiny screen at the moment North came into the shop.

"Hey, look at that!" called the cripple. "Your 5000 credits are done for."

"What's that?" asked his brother, picking up his china cup and his buttered bread with delicate accuracy.

"The character with the pet, what's his name? Oh, yes, Joash Du Guast—what a monicker! They've just fished him out of the channel. Guess what, they don't know who he is: somebody swiped his wallet."

"A dead loss," said the older. "You're certain he's the one?"

"He's still on the screen. He isn't a pretty sight." An indefinable expression passed over North's mobile features. "You'd think he was relieved," Jacky told himself. Aloud, he asked, "What do we do with the animal?"

"Does it bother you?" asked North, a little too negligently. "Me, old man," said the cripple in a clownish tone, imitating a famous fat actor, "as long as there's no wrinkles in my belly! Where did he come from, this Joash?"

"He talked about the Aselli," said North, reaching with a magician's deftness for another slice of bread. "And a lot of other things, too. What are you up to this morning? Got any work to do?"

"Not much! The Stimpson order to send out. A crate of lunar bells coming in. I ought to go to the Reeducation Center, too."

"OK, I see you've got a full morning. Can you bring me a copy of the weekly news disc?"

"Sure."

But Jacky didn't go to the Reeducation Center that morning, nor to his customers. With his carriage perched on the slidewalk, he rode to Astronautics Headquarters, a building among others, and had some difficulty getting upstairs in the elevator, amid the students' jibes. Some of them asked, "You want to do the broad jump in a rocket?" And others, "He thinks these are the good old days, when everybody was hunting for round-bottoms to send to the Moon!" It was not really spiteful, and Jacky was used to it.

He felt a touch of nostalgia, not for himself but for North. He knew North would never come here again. The walls were covered with celestial charts; microfilm shelves rose from one floor to the next, and in all the glass cases there were models of spaceship engines, from the multi-stage rockets and sputniks, all the way up to the great ships that synthesized their own fissionables. Jacky arrived all out of breath in front of the robot card sorter, and handed it his card.

"The Aselli," spat the robot. "Asellus Borealis? Asellus Australis? Gamma Cancri or Delta Cancri?"

"There's nothing else out there?"

"Yes, Alphard, longitude 26 degrees 19 minutes. Alpha Hydrae."

"Hydra, that's an aquatic monster? Is it a water planet? Read me the card."

"There is little to tell," crackled the robot. "The planet is almost unexplored, its surface being composed of oceans. No regular relations with Earth."

"Fauna? Flora?"

"Without evidence to the contrary, those of oceans in general."

"Intelligent life?"

The robot made a face with its bail bearings. "Without evidence to the contrary, none. Nor any human beings, Nothing but sea lions and manatees."

"Manatees? What are they?" asked Jacky, suddenly apprehensive.

"Herbivorous sirenian mammals that live on Earth, along the shores of Africa and America. Manatees sometimes grow as long as three meters, and frequent the estuaries of rivers."

"But—'sirenians?' "

"A genus of mammals, related to the cetaceans, and comprising the dugongs, manatees, and so on."

Jacky's eyebrows went up and he cried, "I thought it came from 'siren!' "

"So it does," said the robot laconically. "Fabulous monsters, half woman, half bird or fish. With their sweet singing, they lured voyagers onto the reefs…"

"Where did this happen?"

"On Earth, where else?" said the robot, offended. "Between the isle of Capri and the coast of Italy. Young man, you don't know quite what you mean to ask."

But Jacky knew.

On his return, as he expected, he found the shop closed and a note tacked to the door: "The pilot is out." Jacky hunted in his pockets for the key, slipped inside. All was calm and ordinary, except for that smell which ruled now like the mistress of the house, the smell that you breathe on the beaches, in little coves, in summer: seaweed, shells, fish, perhaps a little tar.

Jacky set the table, set to work in the kitchenette, and prepared a nice little snack, lobster salad and ravioli. Secretive and spiteful, imprisoned among the yellowing antiques of the shop, the young cripple really loved them all.

When everything was ready—fresh flowers in the vases, the ravioli hot, ice cubes in the glasses—Jacky rang three times, according to custom. No one answered. Everything was a pretext for a secret language between the two mutilated brothers, who adored each other. The first stroke of the bell meant: "The meal is ready, his lordship may come down;" the second: "I'm hungry;" and the third: "I'm hungry, hungry, hungry!" The fourth had almost the sense of "Have you had an accident?"

Jacky hesitated a moment, then pressed the button. The silence was deep among the crystallized plants and the gems of seven planets. Did this mean that North was really away? The cripple hoisted himself into the dumb-waiter and rode up to the penthouse.

On the upper landing, the scent had changed; it had flowered now into unknown spices, and it would have taken a more expert observer than Jacky to recognize the aromatics of the fabulous past: nard, aloes, and benzoin, the bitter thyme of Sheba's Balkis, the myrrh and olibanum of Cleopatra.

In the midst of all this, the music was real, almost palpable, like a pillar of light, and Jacky asked himself how it could be that the others, on the floors below, didn't hear it.

North Ellis closed the door behind him, turned the key and shot the bolt. His blind man's hands, strong and slender, executed these movements with machine-like precision, but he was panting a little, and in spite of old habit, had almost missed the landing. He was so hard pressed... but he had to foresee everything. Jacky must never enter this room. Jacky... Resting his back against the door, North thought for a moment that he should have sent Jacky to Europe. Their aunt, their mother's sister, lived somewhere in a little village with a musical name. He felt responsible for Jacky.

He swept away these preoccupations like dead leaves, and walked toward the dark corner where the chest lay under a black cloth. His fingers crept over the porous wood, which scented his palms.

"You're there," he said in a cold, harsh voice. "You've been waiting for me, you!"

The being that crouched at the heart of the shadows did not immediately answer, but the concentric waves of the music swelled out. And the man who had tumbled to earth with broken wings, awaited neither by his mother, dead of leukemia, nor by a red-haired girl who had laughed, turning her primrose face beside a white neck... the blind pilot felt himself neither deprived nor unhappy.

"You're beautiful, aren't you? You're very beautiful! Your voice…"

"What else would you like to know?" responded the waves, growing stronger. "You are sightless, I, faceless. I told you, yesterday, when you opened the strong room: I am all that streams and sings. The glittering cascades, the torrents of ice that break on the columbines, the reflection of the multiple moons on the oceans… And I am the ocean. Let yourself float on my wave. Come…"

"You made me kill that man yesterday."

"What is a man? I speak to you of tumbling abysses, dark and luminous by turns, of the crucibles where new life is forged, and you answer me with the death of a spaceman! Anyhow, he deserved it: he captured me, imprisoned me, and would have come back to separate us!"

"Separate us…" said North. "Do you think that's possible?"

"No—if you follow me."

The central melody grew piercing. It was like a spire, or a bridge over a limitless space. And the unconscious part of the human soul darted out to encounter that harmony. The wheeling abyss opened, it was peopled with trembling nebulas, with diamonds and roses of fire…

North toppled into it.

…It was strange to recognize, in this nth dimension, the crowds of stars he had encountered in real voyages—the glacial scintillation of Polaris, the scattered pearls of Orion's Belt. North marveled to find himself again in this night, weightless and free, without spacesuit or rocket. Jets of photons bore him on immense wings. The garret, the mutants' building on Earth? He could have laughed at them. The Boreal Dragon twisted its spirals in a spray of stars. He crossed in one bound an abyss streaming with fire—Berenice's Hair—and cut himself on the blue sapphire of Vega in the Lyre. He was not climbing alone: the living music wound him in its rings.

"Do you think to know the Infinite?" said the voice enfolded in the harmonies. "Poor Earthlings, who claim to have discovered everything! Because you've built heavy machines that break all equilibrium, that burst into flame and fall, and martyr your vulnerable human flesh?... Come, I'll show you what we can see, we obscure and immobile ones, in the abysses, since what is on high is also down below..."

The star spirals and the harmonies surged up. In the depths of his night, North gazed upon those things that the pilots, constrained by their limited periscopic screens, never saw: oceans of rubies, furnaces of emeralds, dark stars, constellations coiled like luminous dragons. Meteorites were a rain of motionless streaks. Novas came to meet him; they exploded and shattered in sidereal tornadoes, the giants and dwarfs fell again in incandescent cascades. Space-time was nothing but a flaming chalice. "Higher! Faster!" sang the voice.

All that passed beyond the vertigo and tipsiness of the flesh. North felt himself tumbled, dissolved in the astral foam; he was nothing but an atom in the infinite... "Higher! Faster!"

Was it at that moment, among the dusty arcs, far down at the bottom of the abyss, at the heart of his being, that he felt that icy breath, that sensation of horror? It was more than unclean. It was as if he had leaped over the abysses and the centuries, passed beyond all human limits—and ended at this. At nothingness, at the void. He was down at the bottom of a well, in utter darkness, and his mouth was full of blood. Rhythmic blows were shaking that closed universe. Trying to raise himself, he felt under his hands the porous, wrinkled wood. A childish voice was crying, "North! Oh, North! Don't you hear me? Let me in, let me in!"

North came back to himself, numbed, weak as if he had bled to death. For a little, he thought himself in the wrecked starship, out in the Pleiades. He hoisted himself up on his elbows and crawled toward the door. He had strength enough left to draw the bolt, turn the key, and then he fainted on the sill.

"It was those trips, you know..." Jacky looked up at the Spatial Militiamen who were taking their turn opposite him.

They were not hard-hearted; they had given him a sandwich and a big quilt. But how much could they understand? "I never knew when North started getting unhappy. Me, I never went on a trip farther away than the coast. Ever since he's been blind, he always seemed to be so calm! I thought he was like me. When I was around him, I felt good, I never wanted to go anywhere. Sometimes, to try and be the same as him, I'd put a bandage around my eyes, and try to see everything in sounds instead of colors. Sure, the switchboard operator, and the night watchman (not the robot, the other one), they said this was no life for two boys. But North was blind and I was crippled. Who would have wanted us?"

The Chief of Militia reflected that Jacky was mistaken: someone would certainly have wanted North. But saying nothing of this, he went on asking questions.

The next day was cloudy; North pulled an old spacesuit out of a pile of scrap iron and began to polish the plates, whistling. He explained to Jacky that he was going to put it at the entrance of the shop. Toward noon, Jacky took a message; he was told that the board of directors of a certain famous sanatorium were reluctant to accept a boarder mutated to that extent. He accepted their excuses and hung up, silently. So that was what it was all about: North wanted to get rid of him. He was crazy—it was as if he had gone blind all over again! During a miserable lunch, the idea came to him to put the apartment's telephone line out of commission: that way, the outer world would leave them alone. But first he wanted to call up Dr. Evers, their family doctor, and the telephone did not respond. Jacky realized that North had forestalled him.

After that, he made himself small, rolled his carnage behind some crates, and installed himself on a shelf of the bookcase. It was his favorite hiding place. There were still in the shop some volumes bound in blond leather, almost golden, which smelled of incense or cigars, with yellowing pages and the curious printing of the 20th century. They had quaint pictures, not even animated. Without having to look for it, he stumbled upon the marvelous story of the navigator who sailed the wine-dark sea. The sail was purple, and the hull of sandal-wood. Off the mythological coasts, a divine singing arose, inviting the sailors to more distant flights. The reefs were fringed with pearls; the white Moon rose high above the fabulous mountains. Ulysses stopped up their ears with wax and tied himself to the mast. But he himself heard the songs of the sirens...

"North," the boy asked later, forgetting all caution, "is there such a thing as sirens?"

"What?" asked the blind man, with a start.

"I mean, the sailors in the olden days, they said—"

"Crud," said North. "Those guys went out of their heads, sailing across the oceans. Just think, it took them longer between Crete, a little island, and Ithaca, than it takes us to get to Jupiter. They went short of food, and their ships were walnut shells. And on top of everything else, for months on end they'd see nobody except a few shipmates, as chapped and hairy as they were. Well, they'd start to go off their rockers, and the first woman pirate was Circe or Calypso to them, and the first cetacean they met was an ocean princess."

"A manatee," said Jacky.

"That's right, a manatee. Have you ever seen one?"

"No."

"Sure, that's right, I don't think there is one in the zoo. Maybe in the exotic specimens. Take down the fourth book from the left, on the 'Nat. Sciences' shelf. Page 792. Got it?"

The page was freshly dog-eared; North must have been leafing through the book, without being able to read it. Well, it was a big beast with a round head and mustaches, and a thick oily skin. The female was giving suck to a little tarbaby. They all had serious expressions. Jacky was overcome with mad laughter.

"Ridiculous, isn't it?" North asked in an unrecognizable voice, harsh and broken. "To think so many guys have dived into the water on account of that! I think they must have been sick."

But that evening, he offered Jacky a ticket to the planetarium and a trip to the amusement park. Jacky refused politely; he was content to stay on his shelf. Again he plunged into the volume bound in blond leather, discovering for the first time that life has always been mysterious and that destiny wears many masks. The isles with the fabulous names flickered past to the rhythm of strophes; the heroes sailed for the conquest of the Golden Fleece, or perhaps they led a pale well-beloved out of Hades. Some burned their wings in the Sun and fell.

North walked around cat-footed, closing the shutters, arranging the planetary knickknacks. He disappeared so quietly that Jacky was not aware of it, and it was only when the boy wanted to ask him for some information about sailing ships that his absence became a concrete fact. Suddenly afraid, Jacky slipped to the floor, and discovered that his carriage had also disappeared. He crawled then, with the aid of his hooks, among the scattered pieces of iron, and it was then that he stumbled over a horrible viscous thing: the wet billfold of Joash Du Guast. The 5000 credits were still inside.

After that, his fear had no limit, and Jacky crawled instinctively toward the door, which he found shut; then to the dumb-waiter, where he heard the Foramen chimera, caged, mew pleasantly. "It won't work, old lady," he breathed at it. "They've locked us both up together."

He licked a little blood out of the corners of his mouth, and thought hard. He would have to be quick. To be sure, he could hammer on the door, but the street was deserted at night, the normals were all getting ready to watch their telesets, or some other kind of screen—and there was no use knocking on the walls: the shop was surrounded by empty cellars. And the telephone was dead.

Jacky then did what any imprisoned boy of his age would have done (but from him, it demanded a superhuman effort): he clambered up the curtains, managed to open the window with his hook, and jumped out. He was hurt, falling on the pavement.

"That damn' kid!" thought North as he opened the door of the garret. "Sirens!"

His hands were trembling. A wave of aromatics, already familiar, came into his night and surrounded him: he had breathed them on other worlds. He understood what was required of him, and he let himself go, abandoned himself to the furious maelstrom of sounds and smells, to the tide of singing and perfumes. His useless, mutilated body lay somewhere out of the way, on a shelf.

"Look at me," said the music. "I am in you, and you are me. They tried in vain to keep you on Earth, with chains of falsehood. You are no longer of Earth, since we live one life together. Yesterday I showed you the abysses I know. Show me the stars you have visited: memory by memory, I shall take them. In that way, perhaps, shall we not find the world that calls us? Come. I shall choose a planet, like a pearl."

He saw them again, all of them.

Alpha Spicae, in the constellation of the Virgin, is a frozen globe, whose atmosphere is so rich in water vapor that a rocket sticks in the ground like a needle of frost. Under a distant green sun, this world scintillates like a million-faceted diamond, and its ice cap spreads toward the equator. On the ground, you are snared in a net of rainbows and green snow, a snow that smells like benzoin (all the pilots know that stellar illusion). On Alpha Spicae, a lost explorer goes mad in a few hours.

North was irresistibly drawn away, and shortly recognized the magnetic planet of the Ditch in Cygnus. That one, too, he had learned to avoid on his voyages: it was followed in its orbit by the thousands of sidereal corpses it had captured. The bravest pilots followed it in their coffins of sparkling ice; for that sphere, no larger than the Moon, is composed of pure golden ore.

They passed like a waterspout across a lake of incandescent crystal—Altair. Another trap lay in wait for them in the constellation Orion, where the gigantic diamond of Betelgeuse flashed; a phantasmagoria of deceptive images, a spiderweb of lightnings. The orb which cowered behind these mirages had no name, only a nickname: Sundew. Space pilots avoided it like the Fit.

"Higher!" sang the voice, made up now of thousands of etheric currents, millions of astral vibrations. "Farther!"

But here, North began to struggle. He knew now where she was drawing him, and what incandescent hell he would meet on that path, because he had already experienced it. He knew of a peculiar planet with silvery-violet skies, out in the mysterious constellation of Cancer. It was the most beautiful he had ever glimpsed, the only one he had loved like a woman, because its oceans reminded him of a pair of eyes. Ten dancing moons crowned that Alpha Hydrae, which the ancient nomads called Al-Phard. It was a deep watery world, with frothing waves: an odor of sea-salt, of seaweed, of ambergris drifted over its surface. A perpetual ultrasonic music jumbled all attempts at communication, and repulsed the starships. The oxygen content of Alpha Hydrae's atmosphere was so high that it intoxicated living beings and burned them up. The rockets that succeeded in escaping the attraction of Al-Phard carried back crews of the blissful dead.

It was in trying to escape its grip that an uncontrolled machine, with North aboard, had once headed toward the Pleiades and crashed on the surface of an asteroid.

Heavy blows shook the temples of the solitary navigator. The enormous sun of Pollux leaped out of space, exploded, fell to ruin in the darkness, with Procyon and the Goat; the whole Milky Way trembled and vibrated. The human soul lost in that torrent of energy, the soul that struggled, despaired, foundered, was only an infinitesimal atom, a sound,—or the echo of a sound, in the harmony of the spheres.

"This is it," said Jacky, wiping his bloody mouth. "Honest, this is it, Inspector. There's the window I jumped out of..."

There it was, with its smashed glass, and Jacky did not mention how painful the fall had been. His forearms slashed, he had hung suspended by his hooks. On the pavement, he had lost consciousness. Corning to later, under a fine drizzle of rain, he had, he said, "crawled and crawled." Few of the passing autos had even slowed down for that crushed human Caterpillar. "Oh, Marilyn, did you see that funny little round-bottom?"—"It must be one of those mutant cripples, don't stop. Galla..."—"Space! Are they still contagious?" Jacky bit his lips. Finally, a truck had stopped. Robots—a crew of robots from the sanitation department—had picked him up. He began to cry, seeing himself already thrown onto the junk-heap. By chance, the driver was human; he heard, and took him to the militia post.

"I don't hear anything," said the inspector after a moment of silence.

"The others in the block didn't hear anything either!" breathed Jacky.

"I think he must be very unhappy, or else drunk... Are there ultrasonics, maybe? Look, the dogs are restless."

Certainly, the handsome Great Danes of the Special Service were acting strangely: they were going around in circles and whining.

"A quarrel between monsters," thought Inspector Morel. "Just my luck: a mutant stump of a kid, a space pilot with the D.T.'s, and a siren! They'll laugh in my face down at headquarters!"

But, as Jacky cried and beat on the door, he gave the order to break it in. The boy crawled toward the dumbwaiter; one of the militiamen almost fired on the chimera, which had leaped from its cabinet, purring.

"That's nothing, it's only a big cat from Foramen!" Jacky wailed. "Come on, please come on, I'm going up the shaft."

"I was never in such a madhouse before," thought the inspector. There were things in every corner—robots or idols, with three heads or seven hands. There were talking shells. One of the men shouted, feeling a mobile creeper twine itself in his hair. They ought to forbid the import of these parlor tricks into an honest Terrestrial port. Not surprising that the lad upstairs should have gone off his nut, the inspector told himself.

When the militia reached the topmost landing of the building, Jacky was stretched out in front of the closed door, banging it desperately with his hooks. Whether on account of ultrasonics or not, the men were pale. The enormous harmony that filled the garret was here perceptible, palpable. Morel called, but no one answered. "He's dead?" asked Jacky. "Isn't he?" They sensed a living, evil presence inside.

Morel disposed his men in pairs, one on either side of the door. A ferret-faced little locksmith slipped up and began to work on the bolt. When he was finished, the militiamen were supposed to break the door down quickly and rush inside, while Morel covered them, if the need arose, with heat gun in hand. But it was black inside the garret; someone would have to carry a powerful flashlight and play it back and forth.

"Me," said Jacky. He was white as a sheet, trembling all over. "If my brother's dead, inspector, you should let me go in. Anyhow, what risk would I take? You'll be right behind me. And I promise not to let go of the flashlight, no matter what."

The inspector looked at the legless child. "You might get yourself shot," he said. "You never know what weapons these extra-terrestrials are going to use. Or what they're thinking, or what they want. That thing... maybe it sings the way we breathe."

"I know," said Jacky. He neglected to add, "That's why I asked to carry the flashlight. So as to get to it first."

The inspector handed him the flashlight. He seized it firmly with one of his hooks. And the first sharp ray, like a sword, cut through the keyhole into the attic.

They all felt the crushing tension let go. Released, with frothing tongues, the dogs lay down on the floor. It was as if a tight cord had suddenly snapped. And abruptly, behind the closed door, something broke with a stunning crash.

At the same instant, the landing was flooded with an intolerable smell of burned flesh. Down in the street, ant-like pedestrians screamed and ran. The building was burning. An object falling in flames had burned itself in the roof... Fire trucks were called.

The militiamen broke down the door, and Morel stumbled over a horrible mass of flesh, calcined, crushed, which no longer bore any resemblance to North. A man who had fallen from a starship, across the stellar void, might have looked like that. A man who had leaped into a vacuum without a spacesuit... a half-disintegrated manikin. North Ellis, the blind pilot, had suffered his last shipwreck.

Overcome by nausea, the militiamen backed away. Jacky himself had not moved from the landing. He clung to the flashlight, and the powerful beam of light untiringly searched, swept the dark cave. The symphony that only his ears had heard grew fainter, then lost itself in a tempest of discordant sounds. The invisible being gave one last sharp wail (in the street, all the windows broke and all the lights went out).

Then there was silence.

Jacky sat and licked his bloody lips. Inside, in the garret, the militiamen were pulling down the black draperies, breaking furniture. One of them shouted, "There's nothing here!"

Jacky dropped the flashlight, raised himself on his stumps. "Look in the chest! In the strong room, to the side—"

"Nothing in here. Nothing in the chest."

"Wait a minute," said the youngest of the militiamen, "there it is—on the floor."

Then they dragged her out, her round head bobbed, and Jacky recognized the thick, glossy skin and the flippers. She had died, probably, at the first touch of the light, but her corpse was still pulsing in a dull rhythm. An ultrasonic machine? No. Two red slits wept bloody tears... The sirens of Alpha Hydrae cannot bear the light.

MOON-FISHERS

Hugh Page, test pilot for the Chronos group in the year 2500, looked with interest at the machine that stood in the middle of the Paratime Research laboratory. The white cockpit, equipped with luminous dials, looked like the airlock of a spaceship.

"It *is* the airlock of a spaceship," Professor Reszky told him. "We chose that shape for particular psychological reasons. The man who gets in there will be surrounded by cosmic radiation—as much so as any astronaut who takes off into space. The fourth dimension will contract around him, the universe will become immobile. The traveler can get off at any stop—past, present, or future. Only his body will remain in that cockpit."

"Then this trip will be a dream?"

"No. It's a real world on the other side, everything is real. Understand me, I'm not hiding anything from you: the dangers you'll meet are real dangers. The only difference is, if you should die, your corpse will be here."

"That's a consolation," said Page.

With his archangelic stature, his unruly black curls, and his long violet eyes, Page looked like a prince out of some Persian miniature. All things considered, Reszky thought to himself, it was because of that strange look that he had chosen Page from the crowd of standardized heroes. In a gentler tone, he said, "The principle behind the trip moderates the risk."

"Because it will operate under new laws?"

"Exactly. For about three centuries—in fact, since the earliest hyperspace flights—mankind has been held back by an exasperating riddle. We know that time is a dimension, it expands and contracts according to its own laws; our spacemen come back young from distant galaxies, while the names of their parents have worn smooth on their tomb-stones... But that path was closed to us, an invisible barrier stood in our way—worse than the monsters of the Odyssey, or those light and sound barriers that were broken by 20th century fliers...

"That demanded an explanation. Some people gave out extravagant hypotheses, some insisted on the immutability of the past. Some amused themselves with brainteasers: 'Suppose you should be so unfortunate, during a stopover in the past, as to kill your grandfather before he'd become a parent—would you exist? And if you didn't, how could you have killed him?' It's what is called the temporal paradox."

Page laughed shortly. "As if anybody could be sure of his grandparents!"

"The uncertainty principle, of course!" Reszky wiped his fogged eyeglasses. "But that was only a temporary set-back. The answer was really terribly simple. Ever since Wells, apparently, the world had been hypnotizing itself with false ideas—we'd all had a material orientation to the problem. A machine, built of chrome and nickel, would move you up or down the Time Stream; you'd land in the middle of an era, bringing along your valise and briefcase, which would make for complications. Of course it was idiotic. We had to start all over again from the bottom."

"And where did we wind up?"

"At this fundamental idea, this egg of Columbus: *The time that acts on matter is external to it.* Our contact depends on extrasensory perception."

"In other words," Hugh said, "we're going to travel as disembodied spirits? Nobody will see or hear us, and we won't be able to interfere in anything that happens?"

"No," said the professor. He hesitated, looking very tired. "It always comes back to the Heisenberg principle, and Einsteinian relativity. Within certain limits, anything can happen. The present is built on an uncertain past, looking forward to a multiple and plastic future. Take the history of nations... Was Nero a misunderstood poet—a madman—or a complete monster? Was the first atomic bomb our doom, or our salvation? Each of these situations might be different, without changing the whole structure. Even the moment we're living in is nothing but a 'privileged configuration…' "

"In other words—excuse the unscientific expression—I might crash into the past or the future'?"

"All that is still theory," Reszky sighed. "The first time journey is the one you're about to make, remember? All the same, I don't want to give you any illusions: there are no watertight compartments any more. There are phenomena of levitation, you see. And people gifted with strong psi faculties. Prophets and clairvoyants—"

"There was even," put in an assistant archeologist drily, "a certain continent with a strange reputation—Atlantis. Plato spoke of it in the *Critias* and the *Timaeus*. It was also described, in a wealth of detail, by a certain Theopompus who lived some 389 years before Christ."

"A fable!" the scientist protested.

"Or a 'privileged configuration'? You said it yourself—anything can happen!"

"Look," said Hugh in a conciliatory tone, "what use could these Atlanteans be to us, in the case at hand?"

"What use? I don't know. I rather imagine they might cause you to run one of those well-known risks that Professor Reszky treats so lightly."

The physicist turned pale. "Explain that!" he said. "I don't care for half-truths. Just how could these fellows interfere with a paratime voyage beginning in our own year, 2500, when they lived over 5000 years before Christ, and the one thing we know about them for sure is that they went down with their continent?"

"Oh, it's only a hypothesis… as long as you were talking about prophets and other clairvoyants. They were blue, it seems."

"An extenuating circumstance," said Hugh gravely. "But so what?"

The archeologist seemed indignant that a layman should presume to argue with him. "It seems," he explained rapidly, "that they also had unusual psychic abilities. *'They dreamed of the past and remembered the future.'* That means that these 'moon-fishers' traveled far beyond us in the Time Stream, capturing visions in their nets and hatching out events to come."

"An unverifiable statement," Reszky interrupted coldly. "Let me remind you that the Service concerns itself only with the *exact* sciences."

Her name was Neter.

She was born some 3000 years before Christ. The hieroglyph of her name signified: life and lotus, the primal ocean, mystery; the beginning of the world and its feminine principle... and a throng of corollaries: moonbeams, like a net on the waves; and on the desert, where it is a mirage; all that troubles, beckons, stirs up change; the veil of Isis over the future—and over the past as well. In the Nile valley, this royal name, bestowed upon an ordinary girl, was astonishing.

Isides, her father, was one of a small group of blue men—refugees from a vanished continent that was sometimes called Mu, Gondwanaland, or Lemuria, but most commonly Atlantis. These people were gentle and wise; their long lifespans awed the Egyptians, whose lives were short and swift. Some of them continued their migration, and carried their wisdom across the Red Sea. Isides, whom tradition credited with a span of nearly 200 years, was venerated at Giza, where he founded the subterranean temple. Rumor gave him many wives—both goddesses and mortals (for in those days, the gods came easily down to Earth).

And one daughter: Neter.

We believe her mother was a Terran. Interplanetary crossmatings were hazardous then: thus was born ibis-headed Thoth, the baboon-faced Anubis, and Sekhmet with the body of a youth, surmounted by a lion's muzzle. Troubles by the thousand came from these births, not to mention Echidne and other sirens.

Neter, at 15, was beautiful and supple as a dancing serpent. Her whiteness was blue-tinged, as with all the Atlanteans: you can see her picture on a sarcophagus in the Valley of Kings, where she smiles beneath her tiara of sapphire. Necklaces of golden rose-leaves cover her long, flexible neck. The mouth is childish, sensitive, and passionate, and her opal eyes languish under extraordinary lashes.

Now, in those days Egypt was throwing off an ancient oppression: the Hyksos invaders were being expelled, the 18th Dynasty was mounting the throne, and the Golden Age was about to start.

Not that the land was entirely free; dark terror reigned in the desert. The Interplanetarians were landing in these sands. They were of many kinds. Much later, the Pharaoh Psammetichus III noted: *"They fell from the sky like the fruits of a fig-tree that is shaken; they were the color of copper and sulphur, and some had three eyes..."*

These were paratroops from a neighboring planet. But at the dawn of the 18th Dynasty, others were landing in those many-eyed wheels of which the prophet Ezekiel speaks: they had a lion's body, wings, and a human face. Their leader was called Ptah. His statue—that of the Sphinx—burdened the plain.

Dark tales went about: these beings were ambitious to rule; lurking in the tomb chambers of the Valley of Kings, they fed subtly on human sap—they drank the soul and not the blood. Multitudes of fellahs had confirmed these rumors by sight; but others put the blame on ghosts and specters. Trembling, the land waited for the day when that power would make itself felt. There was much calculation of the time of the apocalypse, and the exact form it would take.

Humanity was accustomed, already, to these random terrors, and these interminable eves of battle.

There came a night when the Atlantean Isides, in his cypress-girdled white house on the Nile, read a sign in the stars. He rose, pulled up his papyri in their cases, and went to the window beneath the archway: no, he had not been mistaken—

a great trampling, a swell of hooting came from the desert, and above the wall of his house spiral antlers, sharp horns were outlined, as if a herd of antelopes, wild asses, and sheep were hurrying onward, surrounded by adders and lizards: every creature that was mild, inoffensive, that shrank from death in the shadows, had taken flight.

Isides went in haste to awaken his daughter, and reassured her, gazing deep into Neter's clear pupils. Nonetheless, they got into a litter closed with curtains of Cretan "woven air," carried by four giant Nubians. The litter was swallowed up in the silent procession of animals; and along the banks of the Nile, three or four villages rose up and followed.

Neter had asked her father no questions; everything was understood between them. From time to time, parting the draperies, she put out her hand, which glowed in the darkness, and stroked a hind's velvet-soft muzzle. From the zenith, the Moon cast her silver rays over the desert and seemed to draw to herself all Mizraim as her prey. Much later, when Thebes—all hanging gardens and alabaster towers—outlined itself on the pale horizon, Isides said: "Your uncle, Naphtali, the son of Jacob, is waiting for us."

That day, the fire from the desert consumed the oasis that surrounded the Atlantean's house, and the roaring of lions was heard in broad day.

Sunset found Neter sitting on a wall beside Deborah, the fourth wife of her uncle Naphtali, the two of them crunching watermelon seeds.

"Uncle" was only a title of friendship, for Isides, descended from the holy continent, had no blood relationship with the hard-working and prolific family of the shepherd Jacob. But, a poet at heart (for it is said: "Naphtali is a hind let loose: he giveth goodly words"), the Hebrew valued the Atlantean spirit, in its clarity and pride; he himself was very wise, even though deep in intrigues and married many times. His last wife, Deborah, was just Neter's age; they too were bound by friendship.

Now Thebes was stirred by momentous happenings: the Pharaoh Ahmose was dead, and his son was away at war. A certain Apopi, working in the pay of the Hyksos, was preaching revolt: what had Egypt to do with a bellicose young prince who went off seeking conquest and emptying the granaries? Besides, nobody knew him, and his family was nothing but a tribe of the Delta... and similar non-sense. The dregs of the populace drank plain wine at his expense and shouted loudly. But towards noon, a panting quartermaster ran up, announcing a cloud of dust that heralded the coming of an innumerable army. Every heart missed a beat. "The Pharaoh!" He arrived, having crossed the Nile.

His name was Amenophis. At 20, he was beautiful with a violent beauty; all the girls of Mizraim were in love with him. Brought up far from the court, he was said to be secretive. The rumor ran that he would enter by the South Gate... and everyone went to the ramparts, the former revolutionaries shouting their joy louder than anyone. That crowd blocked all the streets, and persons of quality, lingering at the jewelers' or the Greeks', where they haggled over amber and purple, found themselves carried into the front row of spectators.

Thus Neter and Deborah leaned over a wall, and the little Jewess said, shaking her brown locks: "Do you think he will really reign, this one... Amenophis?"

"What else?" The Atlantean seemed pale and distraught; she was toying with her rings.

"I don't know," said Deborah. "No, really. You hear so many stories! They say that in him we shall have a great, conquering king. They say he will raise up the peoples of Egypt like a wave, to hurl them upon Elam and Canaan... and perhaps on Mesopotamia and the Indies, too. The Earth will tremble before him, and he shall possess it in blood and tumult."

"I imagine," said Neter drily, "that he will think first of delivering his own country from Ptah and the shadows of Ptah."

"That—" Deborah stopped and bit her fingernail, as if she had said too much. The Atlantean gazed at her curiously.

"You don't believe it, do you? You have curious perceptions. You've changed since our last journey, Deborah!"

She lowered her voice. Around the two foreigners, the Theban mob exploded in color, shouts, and laughter; women were chattering, children running naked, and a muffled psalmody arose from the priests' procession. But Neter, even in broad daylight, in the City, felt the shadow and ice of an eternal night. Deborah laughed slightly, leaned over, and with her dainty cats tongue licked the white nape of her friend's neck.

"It's good," she said. "Like cream. Why don't you like to make love, Neter? Of course, they say you'll be queen one day... don't forget your little handmaiden then! I'll tell you everything, if you promise not to betray me. Listen: each night I'm visited by a winged Keroub... no, not a Keroub: they have a bull's body, and they bellow. This one is like a feline—long, powerful, and soft. He does whatever he likes with me, and he pours things into my soul... oh! I don't know how to tell you! It's terrible, and delicious."

"And Naphtali, Deborah?"

"He's 100 years old! My friendship with the Visitor can't do him any harm. Why shouldn't you try it, Neter? It's nothing at all like our human stupidity: you grow so powerful, so wise—you become one with Ptah! It's such ecstasy! At the same time, you know you're lost, you know everything..."

"You exaggerate," answered Neter. She would have liked to escape this friendly arm that embraced her, this charming, soiled creature, but now she knew: Destiny was beginning to weave its threads. In a pattern planned before, Deborah was the unforeseeable and necessary arabesque.

Frozen with horror, Neter chose her words carefully. "Prove to me that you know one secret, just one... and I'll believe you."

Deborah saw herself mirrored in the clear gaze of her friend: she had vertical pupils, like a cat's.

"Well, then," she said, "listen again... After tonight, for a certainty, the Pharaoh will no longer be Amenophis, son of Ahmose."

"Do you mean... they'll kill him?"

"There won't be any need. The Ptahs are wise: they'll put another soul in his body. And he'll serve them, he will be their slave."

"Another soul? You're crazy. He has one of his own."

"Do you think so? Perhaps he has one, after all. But the Ptahs only need his face and his body. I've found out they often perform such operations. There's a phrase I happen to remember—perhaps you'll understand it: 'Since we have discovered we are resistant to all mutation, we shall live on in another fashion... men have a horror of princes with wings and talons!' "

"It's impossible," said Neter harshly. "The Pharaoh won't let those beasts come near him. He's well guarded."

"Yes. Except for tonight. For you know there's a very old custom: the armed Vigil. A young sovereign of Egypt passes the night before his coronation in the Temple of Ammon, in its oasis. He must be alone. On the sill, a priest offers him a wine mixed with myrrh. Ptah knows the priest. In the wine there will be a mixture of herbs and a charm, so that Amenophis shall fall asleep, and the Most Mysterious shall come and take possession of that empty envelope—that vacant body..."

Neter controlled herself again, but she had sunk her nails into her palm, and it was almost with relief that she felt the human warmth of her own blood. In a low, soft voice, she asked, "You don't find this an odious treachery? I'm not talking about Amenophis: but what about Egypt? She deserves another king."

"Oh, this one will be very great!" Deborah lowered her kohl-painted lids, with a guilty and voluptuous air. "And anyhow... how can we know the gods? Perhaps it's already happened! Many princes who were hollow as bells have turned into Pharaohs full of wisdom. Suppose the trial of the oasis is

221

really nothing but... that exchange? My lover shall reign over Egypt! But don't tell Naphtali! And tonight, tonight..."

Neter had slipped down from the wall, but she could not move forward. It was, she thought, like a nightmare, in which you want to run, cry out—and you are fixed to the spot, while every word dies in your throat.

A cloud of scarlet dust veiled the horizon; fanfares burst out. Standing on the ramparts, the Thebans beat on their cymbals and let fall a rain of lotus and rose petals. The priests were waving their censers. Deborah called something, holding out her slender arms toward her friend. As often befell her in moments of great emotion, the Atlantean had to cling to the present by a cornice, a fellah's robe, to keep from toppling into one of the two vertiginous abysses that gaped for her equally: the future and the past.

She ran. She must warn, help... Above all, she must silence her thoughts—so many telepathic beings were hidden in that crowd—and now Deborah was their creature. She stopped, gasping: the street ahead was choked. Tiny as she was, the blue tunics and floating klaphtes of the priests blocked her view... she could have wept. Suddenly, the hypnagogic fog—the state of indecision, of vacuity—in which she had floated all that day, was dissipated, and she realized with horror that she must see Amenophis at that instant: *otherwise she would never be sure.* Her little fists drummed boldly on the back of a tall Lydian, who turned with a grin, "So little, and so naughty! What do you want, O daughter of Isis?"

Panting, she stammered, "I must see the Pharaoh!"

"Oho! You're all crazy for that. Climb up here."

He was a musician; he lifted her onto his harp, which stood upright in a sandalwood case. There she remained, like a sculptured figurine, a victory. It was time: down below, the bronze doors were opening; with a thunderous sound, amid clouds of aromatics, noisy, dazzling as a barbaric jewel, heavy—like a python with a thousand coils—the army of Mizraim entered Thebes.

Slim runners in leather aprons preceded the clumsy Ionian mercenaries, whose cuirasses prefigured interplanetary armor. Numidians galloped en their fine golden mares, and Libyan Negroes led packs of desert leopards.

In a chariot drawn by four white stallions stood a golden statue, motionless. A serpent of emeralds—the royal Uraeus—writhed on his forehead; the dark, perfect countenance was bare. When the Pharaoh of Egypt passed, followed by the melodious wall of his harpists, he raised his eyes. Behind the thick grilles of his lashes, Neter met two lakes of night: dark and dull. She could set her mind at rest: Amenophis I had no soul. Not yet.

In 2500, Hugh Page, the first paratime traveler, entered his cockpit after many handshakes, leaving Professor Reszky to fend for himself in the midst of a crowd of reporters. The importance people gave to this trip was beyond him. He wasn't leaving much behind, and he had no great love for his own era. There had been more beautiful ones; he'd learned about them in his hypno courses. Certain primitive statues, frescoes of the Italian Renaissance, enamels found in the sphinxes of the Valley of Kings, awoke in him some distant echo, natural, intensely moving... He adjusted his electrode helmet and watched Reszky.

Snatches of conversation drifted over to him. What had that other freak said, again? *The Atlanteans, in order to travel in time, left vacant spaces, empty forms, in various eras. That explains the appearance of these great, unparalleled geniuses: da Vinci, Pascal, Einstein. They were men of the future...* In the false daylight of the neons, the archeologist's face was turning blue. Hugh consulted his chronometer, and pressed the selenium control lever.

And there was a different world.

An immense white Moon hung over the desert. Page did not remember leaving the cabin—but here he was among these red dunes. The sand sparkled faintly; it looked like Syrtis Major, on Mars. He opened the faceplate of his helmet slightly, and a dry wind, charged with oxygen, burned his cheeks.

He was uneasy: was this really Earth? The first trial might be subject to routing errors. Under three metallic palms ran a thin crystal stream that seemed heavy to him, saturated with mineral salts.

For a moment the traveler wavered: he was done for; Reszky, mistaking the direction, had sent him into an unforeseeable future, a dead Earth—this desert was nothing but the bottom of an ocean, dried up by evaporation, and this cindery-tasting trickle, the last water... The altered pattern of the stars, the limpid atmosphere bore out the horror of that theory: the stars seemed enormous, and the Pole Star had changed its place, as if the axis of the globe had straightened slightly. Would Reszky know how to find him again?... On the burned or frozen planets he had visited in the old days, at least he'd had his spaceship, but not here...

Almost at the same moment, a savage howl, as alarming as an air-raid siren, came from behind a dune. With his electrogun off safety (though he could well believe the weapon was useless), Page saw a fantastic monster rise in outline against the white disk. The Moon sparkled on its silvery, blue-shadowed pelt; tall as a loading crane, it had long, flexible legs and neck, a hump in the middle of its back, and a supercilious expression. The monster took a few lurching steps, then folded its knees, manlike, and fell over in the sand. And the spaceman heard a melodious sob.

A small silhouette detached itself from the shadow. A long blue cloak trailed behind her, and for an instant Page glimpsed a face cast down, a pearly whiteness, a whiteness of cherry-trees in blossom, of the abyss—lashes pearled with tears, and a child's mouth. The girl ran blindly forward (to Hugh, she was undeniably a girl), and the traveler followed her: This life form, the first intelligent one he had found, was delightful. He tried to pick up her thoughts. A flood of disorderly waves struck him (true, his psi faculties were unusually acute here): the girl was weary, frightened, she had been traveling all night. There was a feeling of urgency. And this wretched dromedary refused to go! Page went up to her, nearly asked her a question, but remembered in time that he was invisible and inaudible. Nevertheless, as if in answer, the girl's thoughts concentrated with extraordinary power on a foreign danger, alive and merciless—something that came from another world. For a moment, Page had a ridiculous hunch—other spacemen had arrived in this country before him, and the girl was fleeing from the invaders.

Meanwhile, in the turbulent mental flood, two images swam up with remarkable clarity. The first was that of an oasis and a semicircular building, constructed of enormous blocks of black marble and jasper—a solitary, nocturnal temple, from which radiated a feeling of horror. Hugh's hypnotic instruction enabled him to recognize one of the oldest sanctuaries in the world: the Temple of Ammon Ra, where all the sovereigns of Egypt, including Alexander the Great, had sought consecration. Then he was really on Earth—but in the depths of what illusory past?

The strange girl went on running; she stumbled, and a second image detached itself among her thought waves: a man—no, more than a man. Page could not make out his features—only the brilliance of a cuirass that looked, Page thought to himself, rather like space armor. This creature was threatened by some danger, worse than death. Trying to clarify that shadow, bring it into sharper detail, Page drew a blank. Evidently his reception was out of phase with the girl's Sending: he saw nothing but the desert, and the image of the sphinx of Giza.

As if in despair at being unable to communicate more clearly, the fugitive stopped and wrung her hands. A shock, more felt than heard, had made the plain tremble, and yet nothing was to be seen: only, at the edge of vision, sand devils danced like columns of incense smoke. A second later, a whirlwind shape hurled itself past them: it was the white dromedary, its shadow flying like a cloud across the desert; ears laid back, neck trembling, it disappeared in a curtain of dust.

And Page saw the lions come.

The first roar sounded from the bottom of a fault, deep under the plain. Thunder rolled along the ground, then broke up into staccato trains of roars and shrieks. A wavering tornado arose among the dunes—a cloud of sand, claws, and lightning flashes—a wind from the forge. The girl fell to the ground, and before the spaceman could move, that volcano was upon them.

Twenty, or a hundred, or a thousand red sand devils. A hundred, or a thousand long, roaring flames—muzzles carved in granite, manes intermingling—and when they came near, the twin pupils of boiling gold. Certainly there were more than enough to hurl back, rip to shreds, two vulnerable human bodies. Page had instinctively bent his knees, wrapping his arms around the slender body of the girl, who seemed to be hiding her face against him, in spite of the space armor. He had had no time to draw his electrogun. Could people die on the para-temporal plane? Reszky had said... He closed his eyes.

A minute later, he was still alive; and the brazier-wind, the living hurricane, had passed. The girl in his arms held herself still and attentive. Hugh opened his eyes, to see the tawny mass disappear over the horizon. A few stragglers galloped by, bounding aside from the spot where the Invisible stood. No dromedary was in sight, and the universe was settling down in vast waves of earth-shock.

Animals could sense "presences," the traveler reminded himself. He recalled familiar sights (so distant from this frenzied world): his dog pointing at an empty spot—a house-cat motionless, staring at the night. For them, the darkness was alive. But the girl who had taken shelter against him?... She was standing; he could see her better now in the moonlight, and a dizziness overcame him. Page's time was full of spectacular girls, hard and civilized, admirable mannequins. Never before had he seen a creature who made him think of lilies.

"Lord," she said, "I must go. The trial is beginning, when each one must be alone. You know now... Ptah..."

Was it a prayer, addressed to some invisible god? She was already moving away. Now other shadows were passing over the desert. A chariot with shilling wheels rolled past, and in it were two men speaking in curt thoughts. Once more Page saw the image of the oasis, its parallel palm-shadows, the temple with its pillars of jasper. But to these travelers, there was a man holding vigil within; and beyond doubt, he was the one the girl was trying to reach. Page made an effort and saw—beyond the sand and mist—a tall silhouette, a dark, handsome face that was strangely familiar, and the emeralds of the filet. "A king," he thought. "A Pharaoh. Probably they've got a date. My little stranger does all right for herself." Full of an unaccountable bitterness, he turned away from the oasis.

Now that he was left alone, he could better appreciate his state of being, suspended between temporal planes. He was actually floating above the dunes. He had only to think of a gap in the rock, and he found himself instantly on the edge of the cliff. Down below, cool air rose from a spring. "This is what they call levitation, or telekinesis," he thought.

A solitary lion leaped up, roared, pricked his ears, then bounded aside, because Page was walking deliberately into him. The enormous beast ran off, head down, like a whipped dog. Mentally, Page made him turn back, sent him sliding over the cliff: so, animals obeyed him...

It was then that the danger became clear.

It wasn't a living being, at least not yet. Rather, it was a shaft of mental waves—powerful, inexorable, commanding. It was a body-emptying thing, before which all human thought faded and died. He had to call on all his discipline to keep from running away; instead, he moved forward. This, he realized, was the customary attack of an ancient and carnivorous race that had developed its powers of absorption at the expense of all mortal faculties. A race of psychic vampires, in short; or else... The tide was so powerful that it automatically projected the image of a sphinx onto Page's vision. But this time, the sphinx was alive...

"Why not?" Hugh asked himself. Terrestrial monuments are covered with these divine and bestial masks; planetary legends are full of horrible, insane things, blasphemous things that we try to forget, because it's too hard to live with them. But all the same, men have encountered those Assyrian bull-kings somewhere, those harpies and gorgons... Why not a Sphinx, reigning over the night?

Page wavered; the projected vision had struck him with such force that he experienced it as a physical blow; a curtain of blood veiled his sight, and a wave of hallucinations broke over him. "Just like a groggy fighter," he thought, trying to put up a defensive screen. But perhaps no hurt fighter had ever felt such thunderous pain. Yet the wave flowed back, and he caught his breath long enough to bring order into the sensations that were assailing him.

They were of all kinds, and evidently radiated from at least two different beings. One was dark and gigantic; built on the scale of a demented universe, it evoked black infinity, burned and frozen globes revolving around giant suns; and these stars bore the names of luminaries that humanity had not yet reached: Sirius, Altair, Aldebaran... Was it from thence that the greedy, carnivorous beings came? These waves forced themselves upon him with their visions and discordant sounds, their worlds exploding in cosmic collisions; from the titanic bellowing of the saurians of their carboniferous ages, from the musky stenches of the primal swamps where all life was born and perished, they pulled together a history of combats, shouts, and violence—a whole universe of terror, mental and physical.

Page could not doubt that these were the personal memories of a Monster. Ptah—the girl had spoken that name; Ptah... Under the name of Sokaris, he had already reigned over Memphis—or had that been one of his ancestors? At any rate, today he meant to stretch out his claws over the whole land... But why should he launch an attack on a paratime traveler? (For an instant, the spaceman wished he had stuck to his own profession—precise, limited by the laws of physics... clearly,

Reszky and his assistants had not foreseen this danger.) His struggles against the invading personality were growing weaker; sharp, penetrating, inhuman sensations were taking possession of his subconscious mind.

But a feebler wave, like a strain of music—a thread of crystal, a moonbeam—came to his aid. This one was profoundly human: she spoke of a cerulean sea, a continent of opal, a cold wisdom, built in harmony, that made you proud to be a Terran. Page's whole being went out toward that stream of images, and he realized that the stranger was fighting beside him. But then—the temple, the oasis... Was she not by the side of her handsome dark Pharaoh?

He had no time to reflect on it, for the carnivorous mind returned to the assault. Until now it had only shouted and thundered; it had been terror and helpless annihilation... Now it was changing its tactics, having tested its adversary's strength—and not without surprise; now it was making itself monstrously sweet, insinuating, attacking the nerves, which it filled to brimming with a horrible delight beyond all physical pleasure, and sharper than pain. And it promised and murmured, almost at the level of consciousness, of terrible things; it dripped the essence of punishment and ecstasy. The being that had taken over his nervous System, and was performing astonishing symphonies on that clavier, had lived so long and drained so many frightful joys that the human mind dissolved at its touch; the human soul, irrevocably stained, fell into oblivion. In a flash of despair, Page sensed that all these experiences were happening at this very moment; by a concentration of his will, Ptah lived, and made him share his inferno.

Him. Always him. Then where was the Pharaoh that the Monster was to attack?

He fought as a man, as an explorer, one who had been taught to preserve his own personality in isolation and in chaos: he was Hugh Page, a unique human being, from the year 2500—and he had nothing to do with this outpouring of hatred and lust. That realization broke the spell; the wave of black and red withdrew. Hugh found himself on his knees under a dune; he had rolled among blocks of stone, and his hands were full of blood; the beating of his heart made him dizzy, and he realized that the last attack had been so violent that it had almost tom him out of the fourth dimension—he was regaining physical form... He shuddered.

In the silence of the desert, a melodious thought wave spoke (perhaps the voice of the stranger, but warmer and more penetrating). "Run! Oh, run! It's you they want to destroy!"

"Me? What for? I don't belong in this country, or this time."

"You know nothing about it. The most horrible danger..."

"Can I go to you?" Hugh asked—and each word tore his dry throat. "Can I be any help?"

"No. No... " (Here, a wave of icy despair.)

"I want to see you again."

"It's impossible. You're lost, if they succeed in materializing you."

"And can they do it?"

"I don't know. They have robbed so many Atlantean brains! Integrate yourself into another dimension. Don't think about me anymore."

(That wasn't the stranger: she couldn't talk that way.)

"They have robbed so many Atlantean brains!"

His, too, undoubtedly—Page felt drained. Since he'd shared the memories and sensations of the Monster for some moments, it followed that the others had had access to his own knowledge. He shivered: whatever else he might be, he was a good physicist and a better spaceman. Would they know how to use his knowledge? Could they...? He shuddered at the thought of Earth, in the year 2500, invaded by the bestial masks of Pharaonic Egypt.

But: integrate himself into another dimension? On the other shore of Time, the silhouette of Professor Reszky seemed to him oddly insubstantial. That phantom ought to turn on a control board, press the "return" lever... That seemed

230

impossible. Suddenly, he began to appreciate the violent world into which he had fallen: it was *his* Earth, and yet a new planet: the air was intoxicatingly pure; all the colors leaped out in lively contrast, the pink moon among the said devils blazed incredibly... the luxuriant oasis, its palms as if washed by a rainstorm, everything, even the dizzy scents that rose from the pale cups of the water lilies, the musk of hidden beasts, the coolness of a spring, forcefully proclaimed a young, rich, intoxicating universe. And at the same time, never had horror and death been so immediate, so close: everything in this world was an invitation to live for the moment. "I live!" cried the osier bed trampled beneath the tree-trunk legs of the hippopotamus. "I exist!" sparkled the moth in the jaws of darkness. The fleeting moment distilled a piercing delight.

It was in that pink glow that they showed themselves in outline, at the other side of the plain—and truly, Page had never seen anything more hideous on any carboniferous planet. To begin with, because there was a certain order, the parody of human discipline, in their movements, and because some of them, riding in chariots, holding the reins, seemed familiar, like childhood nightmares. (Who has not dreamed himself pursued, trailed by a pack, falling from a dizzy height, falling forever?...) Page had tried in vain to believe, on the strength of the hypno courses, that many of Egypt's gods had little humanity about them; he hadn't been able to take it in. Now, from every hollow of the ground ("In that accursed land," says a Chaldean manuscript, "every hollow in the sand hides a million demons..."), from every dune, bizarre visions were springing up: winged or squat, octopod or cynocephalous, some crawling on the ground, with a crackling of coils, a sound and smell of the tide; others whirling in an eddy of plumes—all came toward the Oasis of Ammon, and there was saurians and giant rams, entities with the heads of jackals, the broad backs of hippopotamuses; the gods of Bubastis, Mendes, Assyria; monsters and idols without faces. All the terrors of the Dark Ages were following a conqueror's chariot.

Up above, upon wheels of gold, under a purple canopy, the living Sphinx was enthroned.

The procession advanced with inexorable slowness. There was no resisting it; nothing could have halted that march toward victory. All the reawakened terrors of childhood, all the old familiar specters... a man would have been nothing but a doormat to that procession of gods.

And they were heading toward the Oasis of Ammon. For a moment, the urge to be with the stranger in the temple was so strong that Hugh bit his wrist. No, he hadn't come here for that. He was on a mission, he must simply collect and retain all the facts he could, fight if he were attacked, and return to his own era. But the mere thought of returning seemed to him cosmically absurd. And unfair... On his knees, so exhausted he was, he crawled toward the spring in the reeds. The water was burning cold. He drank in great gulps, aware without surprise that his senses were growing more and more acute. The spring that fed the oasis disappeared a little farther down into a fault in the granite, from which arose a raucous murmuring. Curious, Hugh leaned over the edge, and a terrible wild-animal stench struck his nostrils. It was the lion wadi, on a lower level of the plain. It billowed like an ocean; it was a deep, reddish tidal wave, in which the thin trickle of water sparkled here and there. Hugh saw what man had never seen and lived.

The animals drank with courtesy, making room for the weakest. In the mass he could make out the great beasts of the Gulf, blunt-fashioned, with muzzles carved in sandstone, with their tumbling cubs and beautiful lionesses, the color of ripe corn. A little farther down were outlined the horns of a ram whose thirst had made him forget danger; a rhinoceros, with its little bloodshot eyes, rolled over, tearing up the margin of the crumbling cliff. Dune leopards, blossoming with black roses more plentifully than the fields of May, slunk among the towering obliqueness of striped giants. In the ripples of sand, tiny kraits hissed...

All at once, as the wind changed, a motionless shiver went over the living mass. It was almost instantaneous. A beautiful lioness, pink as a nude woman, leaped away into the dunes. A tiger that was almost blue slashed the air. Jackals howled as they were trampled underfoot, and above the roaring concert could be heard the frightful laugh of the hyena. Astounded, Hugh realized that the animals were aware of his presence; the tidal wave was in motion ahead of him. He moved forward. It was a material force, un-leashed, capable of sweeping anything out of its path-or anyone...

"Come on, Ptah!" said Page to himself.

The collision of the two masses shook the desert.

Hugh Page came to himself in the deep coolness of the vaults. His head lay on a blue robe, folded up in a trough of marble, and he remembered that Egyptian beds included a half-moon-shaped cavity in place of the pillow. It made for sweet dreams, evidently. The idea was so foolish that he laughed. A ring of metal was squeezing his temples, and two immense opal eyes, veiled with long lashes, were watching him.

"You fought bravely," said a crystal voice. And after a silence: "And you are handsome..."

"Then you can see me?" he asked politely, trying to get up. But a small hand restrained him.

"Don't move. When we picked you up, you seemed dead: all the lions of the desert and the whole army of Ptah had passed over your armor—luckily, it was made of tough material."

"Where is Ptah?"

"He has fled," I think, she said absently. "He's hiding in the desert—he's lost nearly everything he had, and after all, he's nothing but a big beast!"

"Who picked me up—was it you?"

"My father. My uncle Naphtali. Some strangers. You can pay them later; it doesn't matter much. In a few minutes, the remedy we've given you will begin to work and then you can

233

walk, and go back to Thebes. There you will be received as a living god."

"But," said Hugh, "I don't want to go to Thebes! Certainly not, if everyone can see me now."

"A Pharaoh must be crowned in Thebes."

"But —"

"And you are the Pharaoh. Your name is Amenophis I, son of Ahmose, grandson of Kamose. You rule over the two Egypts, the White and the Blue; over part of Asia, and the numberless peoples of the desert. You wear the Uraeus and the Pschent, and you are a god."

The remedy must have worked, for Hugh Page sat up in his burst armor.

"Listen," he said, "one of us is crazy: my name is Hugh Page, and I'm a pilot on a mission. I came here from the year 2500, via the Time Stream, and I'm going to go back the same way. Anyhow, I thought I understood yesterday—reading your thoughts—that the Pharaoh Amenophis was in this temple. Where is he? He's the real king of Egypt, and I have no business usurping his prerogatives."

The blue-gray eyes expressed a delightful despair. "Uncle Naphtali!" the stranger cried. "Uncle Naphtali! Come quickly! The shock was greater than we thought—our prince is mad!"

An admirable white-bearded oldster, with the manner of a patriarch, threw himself on Hugh and took his pulse. "O Pharaoh!" he said. "May your name be blessed a million and again a million times... May Your Majesty recover his senses: there is no more fever."

"I'm no more the Pharaoh than you are!"

"A common effect of battle against the demons, Sire: I am your cupbearer and your court poet, I recognize you formally as my king. Would you like me to call my brother Joseph, your high commissioner? Or my brother Dan, your chief of police? Or the High Priest Isides, who is present?"

"You wear the Uraeus and the Pschent, Sire," said a calm blue oldster.

Hugh put his hand to his forehead—he felt the scales of the golden serpent, the cold of the jewels. Kneeling before him, a Nubian slave offered a disk of silver, which acted as a mirror. Was this really his face, this dark, perfect image, with the great eyes in which flashes of light came and went?

"I—" he began. "I don't understand any more. There's been a substitution."

"An impossible thing, Sire: your servants have kept vigil al] the night in the oasis. And before, and after the combat, the Princess Neter, your betrothed, remained by your side."

Princess Neter, his betrothed…

He looked deeply into the opal eyes that were smiling at him. She was the most delightful girl he had ever met, and a loyal comrade in battle. She had picked him up among the remains of the monsters. It seemed to him that he had always known her—or at least dreamed of her, in a past that was perhaps really the future…

"Leave us alone," he said, in an imperious voice that was strange to him. "I wish to speak with Princess Neter."

And they were alone, before the altar of Ammon-Ra, among the holy disks and the pillars of jasper. Page leaned against the base of a statue, and Neter took his hand to caress it softly with her long lashes.

"I'm not Amenophis I," he said. "And you know it, Neter."

"You will be Amenophis."

"What good is this cruel game? Some day they'll find the real Pharaoh—or his corpse."

"There is no other Pharaoh. Do you think the jealous lords of the desert would have let him live? *There was only a shadow, an envelope of our making which already had your face, because we Atlanteans have always known you would come.* It was so perfect that even Ptah let himself be tempted to take it… That turned out very well, incidentally. He has given you all his knowledge… I admired your battle. You will be a great king, Amenophis."

"But the other Pharaohs —"

"How do you know their origins were any different? It's due to paratime travelers that humanity has been able to progress in spite of invasions and cataclysms. That's the usefulness, and the real meaning of your discovery. Egypt needs you. And so do I."

The fine strands of her hair smelled of honey and amber. Her pale mouth was there—and Hugh felt himself weakening. He tried once more to get his footing in the stable, solid world where he had thought he belonged. "There can't be any interference with the Time Stream. This is a dream we're in!"

"No: a privileged configuration. Amenophis I comes out of the Temple of Ammon changed, you know. The chroniclers will say: *'He grew like unto the gods.'* "

"Exactly, and I'm not. Not even a little bit! And besides..." he seized this idea with the despair of a castaway who, drowning, sinks contentedly to the bottom—"don't forget, I may be called back to the year 2500 at any moment! All it takes is for Professor Reszky to pull the lever..."

"No," said Neter. " *'We moon-fishers, ascending the Time Stream, gather souls and images in our nets.'* Someone said that... Kiss me, and you'll understand. Now, do you see? The paratime cockpit is empty... Your body is here."

YSOLDE

When he embarked for Nyx, the seventh planet of the Spike in Virgo, with his daughter Iza, a blind and deaf child, enclosed in her immobility like a little mother-of-pearl idol with white-golden hair, Ross the Technocrat knew he was doing a senseless thing. He had scoured the galaxy in search of an impossible miracle. He had consulted the physicians, the healers, and the wise men of innumerable planets. In vain.

All confessed themselves powerless. Iza had been born of an all-but-dead mother, crushed in the wreckage of a space-ship, and death had never quite released its grip on the cells of her body. Nevertheless, they had kept her alive for years. Ross would not give up—he would not have been what he was, a Technocrat IV, if he were capable of weakness or despair.

Somewhere between the Herdsman and the Whale, fate had given him one last chance: a traveler had told him about the strange quality of Nyx.

"Don't bother telling me that it's an improbable world," said the astronaut. He had the graven waxy mask of those who have stared too long, through narrow screens, at infinity and the stars. They were sitting under the climatized dome of a federal station, on an artificial satellite, waiting for the next ship. It was an unforeseen accident that had brought the great Technocrat to rub elbows with the mob. He congratulated himself on it. And it was a station like many others beyond Pluto, with its Plexiglas bubbles for differing gravities and atmospheric pressures, its humidifiers for the Over-Plants, and its iridescent artificial suns. One was surrounded here by the fauna of a hundred universes: the gritty purplish cones of Fo-ramen and the Spider-Flowers of the Hyades, the threadlike Capellans and the crystalline intelligences of Alpha Bootes.

With a sweeping gesture, the explorer took in that whole mass. "We've grown used to them, haven't we? But the first sight of them made me feel pretty small. And their worlds are the same: sometimes dazzlingly beautiful, sometimes disconcerting and almost absurd. Why should this fiery abyss be inhabited by creatures made of translucent quartz? Or why should that frozen black globe have its caverns full of the most fragile orchids? You know, there are whole phyla that are alive, in the organic sense of the word, only one year out of every thousand—but then, what a dazzle of colors... What was I saying?"

"You were talking about Nyx," said Ross.

"Ah, Nyx! That's something else again. Everything is real there, but time flows backward. Is it an effect of the planet's rotation, or of its sun, Spica? It's an enormous one, you know. There are 110 stars in Virgo, and it's the most brilliant of them all, a supergiant that you can see from Earth with the naked eye."

"How do you mean, it flows backward?" asked Ross. He was taller by a head than the spaceman; he was tired, in a hurry to get back to Iza, and he hated to waste his time.

"Oh, well, for instance, take Terra. She ages gradually. She has her ruins, her mountains erode away, certain gases escape from the atmosphere. The same things happen in the same way everywhere else in the universe. But on Nyx, it's different. It's a planet that was inhabited, civilized; now it's returning to its origins... and so rapidly! Two hundred years ago, apparently, the atmosphere and climate were like Earth's. Now you have to wear a pressure suit there; it's a hotbox, swept with cyclones and floods, and the instruments register as much cosmic radiation as in our ionosphere."

"Curious," said Ross. "Any other peculiarities?"

"Well, there isn't much more to tell, except that human connective tissue seems to reconstitute itself. Paralytics walk there, no doubt, and the blind see. The only thing is, there's another danger. The ship's doctor explained it to us as we were passing. All the dead cells revivify and proliferate; in time, it degenerates into a sort of cancer. Nyx is uninhabited today."

Sirens summoned the passengers; a crowd separated the two Terrans, and Ross never saw the astronaut again. But as soon as he got back to Earth, he visited the Cartographic Office, its galleries hung with star charts, its armored towers of filing cabinets and its implacable electronic brains which knew precisely everything about the universe. The functionaries of this important service had an unctuous and sacerdotal majesty—and they came from every part of the galaxy.

Because of Ross's rank, he was received by the deputy director.

"Someone mentioned Nyx to me," said the Technocrat, seating himself across from this faintly mauve personage in his purple miter. "How does it happen that this planet doesn't appear on the astrogational maps?"

"Ah!" said the other. "Nyx? It was formerly in our atlas. It was—how shall I put it?—effaced. Yes, by order. You see, in the early days of galactic exploration, the scout ships put pretty nearly everything on their charts—unimportant asteroids and hell-planets. Later on, the authorities began to put some of these places off limits—the really intolerable ones—but they realized that would only attract swarms of adventurers to them. To people like that, a forbidden planet is necessarily crammed with gold or peopled with sirens which the federal government reserves for itself. There were quite a lot of casualties. There was only one solution left: to obliterate the dangerous planets. That's what we did."

"That carries a danger with it—a pilot might land there by mistake."

"Most of them are off the regular routes. Like Nyx."

"Why is Nyx dangerous?"

Somewhat reluctantly, the cartographer pressed a button. A microfile opened; a tiny screen lit up on the opposite wall. The metallic voice of a robot told the improbable history of a world which had thousands of years of civilization behind it, a planet covered with the ruins of megalopolises, immense deserted landing strips, proud monuments, falling apart under the weight of the temperature, the flora, and the general conditions of a carboniferous age.

"It seems," said the deputy director, "that we're dealing with a phenomenon brought about by the recent enormous nuclear explosion of the furnace Spica: an old sun which must have returned to its primitive state. Nyx, in any case, is also returning to its genesis. It should be interesting to see where this devolution will stop. The origins of life might be studied there."

"By whom?" Ross asked.

"Oh, scientists from terrestrial stations."

"There is a laboratory on Nyx," the robot responded obligingly. "Two prize-winning biologists are conducting local observations: Dr. Lorris Nevel and Dr. Marina Nevel. Both Certificated. Married. On Nyx for three years."

"And they're still alive?"

"So far, yes."

The cartographer was able to turn off the loquacious machine: Ross had no more questions for it. His stellar-propulsion ship was waiting for him at Marsport. He left the next day, taking Iza with him.

Marina Nevel passed the electron microscope to Lorris. Her hand trembled slightly. They leaned together over the experimental tank in which the atmosphere of Nyx was being bombarded with various radiations. They were trying to re-create in the laboratory the exact conditions which had produced organic life on Earth.

Above the prefabricated dome, which sheltered their precious apparatus, yawned the terrible sky of Nyx, studded with enormous diamonds. The 110 stars of the Virgin filled the vertiginous emptiness, and that dome of dark gold was striped with coal-black shadows of tree-ferns.

From the moment they set foot on the retrograde planet, the two scientists had approached their experiment as a great adventure. They knew, without the need of words, that they would never again see the gentle Earth, its mild oceans, its regular seasons, a stable and familiar world about which they knew everything save its origins. They knew also that their time on Nyx would be short. They had taken as their point of departure the old 20th century hypothesis of Dauvilliers and Seguin. It was known that these two pioneering scientists had re-created the primeval conditions in a sealed environment. Their postulate was that the Sun's ultraviolet rays, working on the oxygen and carbon dioxide in the atmosphere, and the ammonia in the seas, had created nitrogenous matter and given birth to the evolution which was to culminate in Man.

Nyx itself offered a medium for genesis; and the cosmic radiation and interstellar gases at the Nevels' disposal completed the action of the ultraviolets.

Today, the primary phase of the experiment had reached completion.

Lorris trained the microscope on the tank, which seemed empty to the naked eye.

Nevertheless, on the tiny screen, bathed in a colorless flood, something moved among the vibrations and luminescences. It was impalpable and thin, visible only at high magnification, and for just a moment. Nevel thought that they had lost the game.

But Marina extinguished all the lights, except for the black-light screen, and in that half-darkness the thing glimmered feebly, hardly more than the luminous spark of an electron. It must have possessed senses, or some extrasensory perception, for it immediately fled to the bottom of the tank, exactly like a frightened animal, and for a second Marina felt herself watched by an unwinking gaze. Not hostile—but terribly insistent and curious.

She shivered and drew Lorris aside on the platform that surrounded the lucite globe. "Well," she said, "have we found it?"

He hesitated. "It looks like it. The invisible quantum, the spark of life in its pure state..."

"Of plasma?"

"No, radiant energy, I think. A form of light, in short. It's strange that no one has ever associated the two ideas. Even though all the ancient scriptures speak of light and life together. Let's not get carried away, we've got a lot of analyses to do. I'll start on them now."

"No, you won't!" Marina protested, wiping her narrow white forehead under the fringe of blue-black hair. "Spica will be rising any moment—it will be unbearable outdoors, and our airsuits are in the house. Come on, we've been up all night; it's time to have something to eat, like normal people. Let her irradiate herself awhile longer, little Lumen—we'll call her Lumen Nevellia."

"All right," he said. "You go ahead, I'll cover the globe."

She left him, with a possessive smile and glance. In spite of everything, this tall blond man, with the gray eyes of a dreamer, often seemed terribly far from her. In other times, the lords of Lorris had worn a cross on their breastplates or had been riders of chimeras. On Earth, Marina had had to submit to an unusual treatment, to cure her of jealousy. But on Nyx, all was well. Nyx was the vast dreamed-of prison for a spirit that fled always toward the unknown and the invisible.

While Lorris covered the globe, she went down to the house, which was climatized like all the rest. She hurried: a glow of light, first blue, then purple, already rimmed the horizon; huge Spica was about to rise, heating the retrograde planet's atmosphere to a fantastic degree, causing spores and seeds to burst. All the molds would come to life, the water in the ponds would begin to boil. Each new dawn found this world changed, more terrible. Not to mention the storms! Marina paused before the big Plexiglas window which formed one wall of the house. The city was silhouetted against the uncertain light, drowned by the jungle: towers, domes, colonnades, these ruins had a quality of colossal harmony. Her eyes went to the thing she loved best: a temple, carved and pierced. At the corner of an intact balcony, looking out over the forest, a statue devoured by moss was still beautiful—like a Valkyrie.

"But not when you see her close up, surely!" Marina had said, the day when Lorris had pointed it out to her. "See how she's powdered with green. Under that veil she must be hollowed out, tunneled. Every pore in the stone is a nest of terribly active molds…"

"Well, then," Lorris had said, "she's half alive."

It was only a statue. Marina gave a smile to her inoffensive rival, then went out on the terrace. To her surprise, Lorris was standing there, looking absently toward the already incandescent sunrise.

"What's wrong with Lumen?" she asked abruptly. She recognized that strained, obstinate expression. Lorris turned his distorted face to her.

"Lumen? It's living energy, all right, as I thought. But mutable, intermittent—it needs to be fixed in matter; I think that was the role played by Dauvilliers-Seguin's amino acids. Otherwise, as a quantum, indivisible, it exists for the shortest possible length of time."

"Meaning?"

"That there's no more Lumen in the tank. Don't get excited. I can make another one at will."

"And then you'll give it an acid breakfast. "

"Yes… no. Let me think." His face lighted up. "Why should we stick to classical methods and tie ourselves down to the frightful slowness of nature? Our lives wouldn't be long enough, working with animated plasma. We could try a more daring experiment—introduce Lumen into a complex biological organism."

"You want to create a chimera, a monster?"

"We're not talking about fables, Marina."

"And when I say *monster,*" she interrupted, "I know what you're aiming at. First you want to reanimate a dead frog—then a saurian. A man is out of the question, luckily, unless you start working on anatomical pieces. But even with a frog it would be dangerous, because we know nothing about Lumen's characteristics. Do you want to turn a batrachian with an atomic brain loose on the universe? Enough atrocities. Come, have your breakfast."

He did not seem to hear. Inside, he put on his airsuit.

"Where are you going?" Marina demanded.

"There's a heaviness in the air," he said absently. "That means a storm. I'm going to turn on the cosmic-ray projectors. The experiment ought to be interesting, if—"

The rest was lost in the hissing of the thick steam that rose from the ground, the furious crackling of bursting sepals—the whole prelude of a terrible symphony. Nevel walked away like an automaton, and at the same moment Spica rose in an orange mist that concentrated its fires. Sky and earth took on the color and almost the consistency of lead, and the forest was no more than a hideous backdrop, placed there centuries ago, for a tragedy. When the young scientist came back, violet tornado shapes linked the sky with the plateau. Nearby, the ocean boomed. The Nevels knew the hurricanes of Nyx, compared to which terrestrial cyclones were mere breezes; they hurried to seal the doors and close the shutters, transforming their house into an airtight unit, as closely sealed as a spaceship.

Just as the last shield slid into place, a giant fern shattered itself on the roof. Marina turned on the periscopic screen: she loved storms. Out there it was an inferno, madness unchained. Purple balls of lightning were bounding under the horsetails. The enormous sun was only a pale spot among the cataracts and whirlwinds, and tresses of vines lashed the screen like floating hair. Finally a new tornado arrived, whirling giant saurians and the trunks of mimosas three meters off the ground, and the screen suddenly stopped working. In the abrupt darkness inside the house, the last note of a record Lorris had put on trembled for a moment in the air—a music that spoke of a ship scudding before the storm, of a hyperborean ocean, and of two lovers linked by fate. Silence followed. Then, with terrible distinctness, the Nevels heard a tapping in Morse on the shuttered door:

S.O.S.

Instantly, they were on their feet. A living being was struggling there, in torment! A human cast away on Nyx was calling for help. Quicker than Lorris, Marina was in front of the door.

"Don't open it," she cried, "it may be a trap!"

As always, she interposed herself between him and the unknown, between him and the hostile, dangerous world...

"Remember, we hardly know this planet at all. Remember the stories the explorers told—all those living sands, the plants that kill—"

The signals were growing weaker.

"You're crazy," said Lorris. "Our first duty is to help any intelligent being in danger."

"Intelligent? How do you know?"

"It uses universal signals."

She clung to the man's shoulders, trembling, "Don't open it! I'm afraid—I don't know why!"

As suddenly as it had begun, the tapping stopped. Tearing himself away from the too-soft arms, Lorris slid back the panel. A purple flash of lightning lit up the landscape.

It was a terrible moment, the calm at the heart of the storm. In full daylight, the mad planet was shrouded in darkness. Amid the whirlwinds and electric discharges arose a Nyx of the Tertiary, fantastic, with its mud aboil. Cataracts tumbled down the mountains. Against the pale blotch of Spica, the megalopolis held up its haunting profile.

At the doorsill, Nevel ran into two bodies. The man, burnt, unrecognizable—a black and red mask, convulsed with pain —had fallen full-length. Even in death, his arms were tightly clasped around a child, a silhouette of wax and mother-of-pearl, covered with a mantle of long golden hair. She did not seem wounded, but Nevel, bending over her, could not hear her heartbeat. He lifted her: she was heavy and already cold. The charred dead man seemed to stare at Lorris with reproach—this dead man who, after a stellar shipwreck, had made his way through the Neozoic jungle and all its traps, with his child in his arms.

Nevel was seized with remorse.

At that instant, the cataclysm broke out anew. An immense line of fire cut the firmament in half, and the lightning struck the dome of the laboratory. Picking up the young body in his arms, the scientist threw himself back into the house and closed the panel.

"She's only a child," he said. "And I'm afraid she's dead."

They did everything they could for her. In the end they had to give up. The girl, who might have been 15, wore a bracelet with her name: *Y. Ross.* It was a name everyone knew. The Technocrat's ship had landed on Nyx, to be met by the hurricane. But why had he come to this demented planet? No one could give them the answer; and, bending over the lovely corpse, Marina and Lorris gave no thought to their own disaster or the destruction of the laboratory.

The storm lasted 24 hours and ended as suddenly as it had begun. Nevel went out and surveyed a scene of desolation. In two days and nights, Nyx had regressed a geological age. The ancient ruins were flattened. Only a few edifices of indestructible jade or onyx were still standing, here and there—and the green statue on the roof of the temple.

"Stay here," Nevel said to his wife. "I'll go and see if there's anything left worth saving." He pointed to the laboratory, which was virtually obliterated. "Afterward, we'll have to bury those two…"

It was impossible to preserve the bodies. Lorris had no idea what condition the electronic installations were in. Probably everything had been broken, ripped apart. He left, and Marina was alone with the young dead girl. This time she had not protested. She felt strangely humble and guilty, and she searched for excuses. "Actually," she told herself, "we couldn't really do anything for them: the child was already dead when the man arrived, only to die himself…"

Then, once more, she put aside these useless rationalizations: the past was the past; they had to live and face the future. What were their own chances of survival?

"We have this house, intact, and the provisions in the cellar; we have our airsuits, a light rifle, a disintegrator which I don't know how to use. The rifle bas a radioactive bead a little too large; the other day, I shot at a saurian that was carrying off a moufflon. I killed a big lizard, but the flesh of the moufflon was radioactive, unfit to eat. I've got to ask Lorris to fix the bead... If we manage to repair an inter-planetary transmitter, we'll have to try to reach Earth. They'll evacuate us, probably. I won't like that at all."

She was happy on Nyx, with Lorris. She didn't mind the storms.

She made her rounds as usual, corrected an excess of ozone in the air, turned on the climatizers, and inspected the storeroom. Everything was apparently in order. But when she went back to the living room, a strange, oppressive feeling came over her: a feeling she had had once before, as if someone were watching her, withdrawn and curious.

She turned mechanically: the child's body, which they had placed on a folding bed in the corner of the room, had not moved. But the sheet that covered it had slipped down, revealing a face as white as cherry blossoms, as snow, as the abyss—and immense, wide-open eyes.

They were strange, those eyes, between their long lashes like fringes of black velvet; they were vast and clear like the spangled sky of Nyx, and they were certainly not human. "If the elements could see, they would look like that," thought Marina, stunned.

Automatically she moved forward. But suddenly the girl's body under the sheet made a sinuous movement of withdrawal—like a supple and flexuous animal retreating. *Exactly that kind of motion.*

"I'm losing my mind," said Marina to herself. "Lumen! At the instant the lightning struck the laboratory, was there a

Lumen under the cosmic-ray projector? A quantum of life that escaped, settled elsewhere, in this corpse?"

Even her thoughts stopped, frozen with horror.

Call Lorris? She had always tried to shield him from the outside world. Besides, she was not sure how he would react

No, she preferred to solve the problem alone. She straightened, and walked toward the child.

Then without a breath, in a single squirm, the slender body rolled off the bed and flattened itself against the wall. The fixed, terrible eyes stared at Marina, eyes in which wavered the original light; and through the tunnel of that stare, she entered the world of genesis, fabulous, a prodigiously ancient life—dating from before all morality and all differentiation.

Marina understood that a new species had appeared on Nyx. She did not know her own powers as yet, not all her muscles obeyed her, probably she did not even have a voice—but all that was a matter of development, of acclimatization.

For she could no longer doubt. Escaped from the shattered laboratory, Lumen had sought a host—and she had instinctively chosen the most complex organism.

From that moment, two forces struggled within Marina: scientific curiosity and terror born of repulsion. The second had all but won. Her human hands were already stretched out to destroy the horrible fascinating creature, when Lorris came back. His first words were:

"She's alive!"

Impulsively he threw himself down toward the cot behind which swayed the huddled form. Marina wanted to cry out, "Don't touch her. That isn't a human child... It's I don't know what kind of horror that we've created by accident, and we ought to destroy it before it begins to do harm..."

But her frozen lips did not move. Mute, immobile, she watched Nevel bend over, lift the radiant little idol and her riches of golden hair.

He laid her down on the bed and examined her, uneasy.

"She fell," he said. "How did that happen? Her eyes are open, but can she speak, can she hear? She's all stiff."

As if in response to these anxious questions, the body lost its rigidity, it shivered, the fragile arms unfolded, rose like wings, and settled in a cool collar upon the shoulders of the leaning man.

Marina cried out—at long last: "Kill it! It's a monster, without a soul or a mind!"

Without a mind?…

From the instant when the spark of primitive life glittered in the cosmic darkness, Lumen had perceived and assimilated the universe.

In her fashion.

Could the term "mental process" be applied to the slow concentric waves—the circular movement of electrons around their nucleus? *Cogito, ergo sum.* Turning the ancient Terran wisdom to her own use, Lumen lived, therefore she thought.

It was not a monologue. Neither time nor space existed as yet for the unfinished creature. An occasional datum or image sprang up from the primal source. Little by little, a logic took shape. Beyond that was the darkness, the absolute void.

(Marina would have been chilled with terror, if she could have entered that abyss peopled with amorphous figures, vague ideas—formless monsters, still lost in a chaos as old as the universe.)

Lumen's thoughts:

I am. I have always been. Or at least I've been part of something… primordial, eternal. It was like an ocean into which endlessly flows all that is essentially life: light, matter, and motion. An infinitesimal atom, I was lost in the universal symphony.

I was taken out of my environment, hurled into the darkness. I was cold. And also… I don't know the word—when one retracts before an opposing principle. Yes—fear. Then the world exploded. It was horrible. I wanted to diffuse, dissolve myself, but something captured me, like a magnet.

It was suffering a terrible agony. Hot, red energy was pouring out of it in torrents. I fell aside, but then it grew cold. I labored in that ice, in that darkness...

Now there is light again. A narrow container condenses and restrains me—me, limitless, diffuse, a nebulosity. There are things I can't grasp. I haven't succeeded in moving this matrix of fragile flesh. But that will come. I can feel it.

The contrary principle takes on a shape, too. The negative pole. I see it ("they" call that "seeing"). There is a word also for this bundle of intuition and nerves: "a woman."

Silence. Hide. She wants to destroy me. Why? She is large and powerful. Run. My body does not obey me. Slip down, fall... The positive principle enters. When he is there, all is well, our two energies communicate. But there must be a contact: he must come closer. I manage to loosen my rays... or are they tentacles? I cling to him.

The woman cries out. She wants to kill me...

Marina had screamed at him. Now she realized that Lorris had never looked at her so coldly. She stepped back involuntarily, put her hands to her bleeding mouth.

"You're crazy," he said, as he had said once before in the uproar of the storm, while a hand stiffening with approaching death rapped at the door of their shelter. "The child bas just come out of a coma; think of the shock she's been through!" His voice softened. "You're suffering from shock, too, I think. Take a sedative and lie down. You'll see, nothing nicer could have happened to us: now we've got a little human sister. You won't be alone anymore, when I'm away..."

"No!" Marina cried. "It's Lumen!"

He looked at her uneasily. "By Heaven, I wonder if the shock hasn't affected you more than I thought! Listen to me, Marina. The lab was struck by lightning, then flooded by rain—everything is damaged, burned, or waterlogged. The experimental tank is full of muddy water. There's no more Lumen. And no possibility of reconstituting the environment. Does that satisfy you?"

With her back against the wall, Marina had managed to take down a corroded hatchet Nevel had brought back from the megalopolis. She brandished it, trying to strike the light-creature. Quick as lightning, the creature slid away and. huddled against the wall. The weapon flashed through the air. Lorris had not had time enough to intervene: a little blood spurted from Lumen's temple; she fell back, motionless, in her glory of golden hair.

Nevel strode forward. He was pale with anger.

"If this is how it's going to be," he said, "I'll lock you up."

"I'm your wife, Lorris!"

"Yes, and an attempted murderer. A dead man left this child on our doorstep; we have a responsibility to her. Come on."

He led her into their room. She went without protest, inert, cmptied of her rage. Her act seemed to her odious and grotesque. Nevel closed the door on her and locked it, without a word. When she was locked in, she wanted to explain; she cried out, banged the wall. No one answered. Then she came to her senses, went to the medicine chest and took out a sedative.

Lorris had returned to the girl, who seemed to have fainted. He looked frantically for a glass, some wine in the refrigerator, and finally settled for a short, squat flask of crystal in the shape of a wine-skin, containing a golden liquor which he tasted as a precaution. Yes, it was just right for a child: a sweet Terran wine, thyme-scented, "a sort of herb wine," he thought, pursued by a vague recollection, a legend or a few piercing notes of music that spoke of a green ocean. This couldn't harm anybody. The one mouthful he had swallowed was cool as autumn air, but deep within it there was a hidden fire. Lorris knelt beside the girl's still body and forced the liquor drop by drop between her teeth. Lovely and terrible, the creature surged up in blood and gold, and he found himself staring into a charming inverted face, the spangled ocean of her eyes, and her lips like a fruit waiting to be bitten. A

251

strange fire was in him, an insinuating warmth—it seemed to Nevel that he was coming home to the world for which he was made, a distant shore, a forgotten country.

He bent down. The flowing hair smelled like honey. The mouth had the salt taste of spray.

Marina awoke with a start, Damn that sedative! Or had she taken an overdose? She had slept as if she had been pole-axed. Her memory was blurred, but her hand automatically explored Lorris' vacant place on the pillow. Then that awful day came back to her, in all its details, with an intolerable clar-ity. She got out of bed and ran to the door. It was no longer locked: Nevel must have come in to make sure his wife was asleep. The living room was empty.

It was the pleasant hour before Spica's rising. The air, freshened by rain, smelled of seaweed, of the jungle. No doubt Lorris had gone out to prospect in the ruins, without his air-suit.

And Lumen had disappeared.

Lumen...

Suddenly Marina felt terribly weak. Her hand reached for the crystal flask that had contained an ancient liquor, a wild elixir given to her by her grandmother. There was a legend attached to that wine, but she had forgotten it.

The flask was empty.

For an instant Marina had a sharp, terrible sense of aloneness. She knew she had lost Lorris... had he ever really existed, that blond rider of chimeras? He had come into her life, carried her off beyond the void, the stellar eddies, nebu-las, then he had disappeared again into nothingness. And Ma-rina was left alone on a demented planet, where mysterious life roamed among the tree-ferns.

She had to make an effort to control herself. Moving as if in a dream, she put on her airsuit, took down from its rack the light rifle, useful in spite of its too-large radioactive bead. It felt comforting in her hand. She left the house and followed her instinct, or rather a subconscious strain of music, evoking another flat beach, a greener ocean. The path under the horse-tails descended toward the ocean, glittering with a thousand stars. Marina came to the shore. This was the place.

They were lying on the white sand; she, covered with the flowing, sparkling mantle of her golden hair. (How had they ever mistaken her for a child?) Long and slender, she gleamed like a pearl. Never had Lorris gazed at his wife with such dolorous rapture. He had laid his disintegrator between them. Their hands did not touch.

The waves died at their feet in a silken murmur, and the whole world was mysterious and pure, as at the dawn of its creation, when life emerged from the sea.

Marina bit her wrist to suppress a convulsive shudder; she leaned against a boulder—aimed—fired.

She knew the secondary radiations had not spared Nevel. For the moment, that made her task easier. On the sand, the dark trace of a slender body faded away immediately. Marina sighed with relief: that was the last of Lumen!

Lorris was only stunned. She hunted up an intact carrier and took him back to the house. When he revived, she claimed total ignorance.

Lumen? But he knew perfectly well that the tornado had destroyed their installation. There was no way of recreating the essential conditions of the experiment, and they could not contact Earth.

Yes, a cosmic storm had swept Nyx. No doubt that accounted for this abrupt change in evolution; they must take that into account in future experiments. Yes, a ship had crashed, and they had found the bodies of Terrans. One of them was even buried under the giant horsetail in the clearing. A man. Afterward? Nevel had been sick. That was all.

Bitterly, tirelessly, she wove around him the veil of forgetfulness. Lorris was very weak and could hardly get up. One day when Marina had gone out, he slipped, as he often did, into a state of semiconsciousness. His hand, dangling off the bed, brought up a long golden hair, clotted with dried blood.

He heard a piercing melody and glimpsed the icy sparkle of the stars on the sea.

When Marina came back, he asked, "Was someone wounded here? I found this near the bed."

Marina turned away, pretending not to hear. There was a certain cruelty in her action, but he had been cruel first. Time was on her side. Time...

In the ruins of the laboratory, she found an interplanetary transmitter, almost intact, and destroyed it.

Meanwhile, she took devoted care of Lorris and led the primitive life of a pioneer. Since the hurricane had ruined the cultivable area of the camp, she had to hoard their stores of food. Out hunting, or fishing, she took the path to the ruins. A strange, relentless youthfulness drove her to climb the eroded walls of buildings, leap into the pits that had been cellars, swim across ponds that had been swimming pools. She learned to go by night, with a spear, for big purblind fish that shunned the light of Spica. Nevertheless, certain street corners, certain fishing ponds made her uneasy: a dim glow wavered there.

She had never felt so light, so brisk. Except for stabbing headaches, accompanied by a slight swelling of the eyelids and temples, she seemed to have grown habituated to the climate of Nyx.

In her longer and longer expeditions into the jungle, she formed the habit of taking the temple as her reference point. Built of green and white jade, almost veinless, it was probably the most ancient structure in the city, and the one that had best withstood the assault of the elements. And the statue of the goddess was always there. Marina smiled at it each time she passed.

Until one time.

At one of those Nyxian dawns—one of those rare moments when the world lived between the heavy darkness and the intolerable glare of day—Marina was coming back across the megalopolis. Her bag was empty. Her rifle had begun to jam, and she still could not manage the heavy disintegrator. (Without her realizing it, everything was falling apart at the station. Machines were out of order, rusting to pieces; she had restored the electricity, but there were short-circuits in the electronic brain; a tenacious mold covered the walls; and Marina took all this with astonishing lightness, as if she too were returning to childhood.)

Finding herself before a basin strewn with waterlilies, whose smooth, dark waters trembled gently, she thought perhaps she could spear some of the huge batrachians that swarmed among the green leaves. She leaped up onto the curb, and the surface of the water reflected her with pitiless precision: ragged clothes, her body strangely thickened, but endowed with a savage agility, and childish face with an unsightly tumor on the forehead.

She had not even realized that the cells had proliferated. She felt only the sharp pang: this was how Lorris saw her.

Indeed, she must have become a horror to him!

At the same moment or nearly, under a sky of gold, her contracted pupils met the gaze of the goddess on her jade pedestal, lit by the green glow that penetrated the undergrowth.

She was always there, immovable and victorious; the sheath of microorganisms had not succeeded in destroying the perfect harmony of her features. Great eyes opened in the touching softness of her face, like gulfs in which wavered a dreadful living glow. She had seen the birth and death of worlds; and she had survived them.

She was… life.

In the uncertain glow of dawn, Marina thought she saw a faint smile curve the full lips.

She fled, because the thick hammering of blood in her temples was taking on a form, a meaning. Scattered through the night, emitted by all that trembles, lives, breathes— mosses, algae in the marsh, will-o'-the-wisps—she sensed the thoughts of the creature she had vainly tried to destroy…

Lumen's thoughts:

She is there. She wanted to kill me. She succeeded, or almost. I've lost my host again, and it's all the more dreadful because I'm differentiated. She has taken me away from him— *the positive pole toward whom I yearn, with whom I must melt together to form a whole.*

Cast out into the icy darkness, my need to expand and disperse myself draws me toward the abyss. But then, I know, I would lose him forever—our one contact was so brief. So I stay here, clinging to the infinitely small, to plants, to certain minerals which they penetrate. Chained. Trapped by the matter which holds me. I exist.

I will not die unless it is with him.

I exist. I will not die except with him.

My siblings, my sisters (for we are born spontaneously, now that the laboratory has been destroyed) do not know why they are. They wander with the phosphorescences over the eelgrass, they sway with the seaweeds in the depths… I cling to stones devoured by moss. It is black and cold. High in the sky, I am immobile and cannot lift my limbs of jade and onyx.

But I am still beautiful. And I love him.

Marina's wild flight had taken her toward the pools she normally avoided, to the left of the camp. For a moment, she thought she felt an enormous, hostile presence. A monster was at her heels. Reeds crackled in the marsh, and immense jets of water spurted. She would not let herself look back. She ran.

It was when she emerged into the clearing, across from installations, that she saw the ceratosaur.

A walking mountain, preceded by a little head, flat and malevolent, horribly fanged. Marina fired her rifle with trembling hands. A feeble spark sprang out; the charge was exhausted. She screamed.

What occurred then, in the old days, on Earth, would have been called a miracle. The door of the house opened, and Lorris sprang out, armed, clad in his iridescent breastplate. The knight of legend had returned. Leaning against the wall to mask his weakness, he raised the disintegrator to his shoulder and fired.

For a moment, at the edge of the empty clearing, Marina believed that Nyx had shown its power, that time had really turned backward... She was saved, Lorris had never been struck by the radioactive discharge, her wonderful, impossible life was about to begin again! But Lorris, having destroyed the ceratosaur, let the weapon fail.

He said, "I'm going to die. Marina. Where is Lumen?"

She had the strength to say, with swollen, icy lips: "Who is that?"

"You know very well. Life. *Our life*—animating that child."

Marina chose her words with cold cruelty, like a little girl who breaks a toy deliberately: "I burned the body she stole. She has no more form. She can't see or hear. Even if you called her, she wouldn't come!"

"Ah," he said, "that's what I wanted to know...

Then he bent his knees and, slowly, like someone who has long ago taken the measure of his death and of the earth where he will sleep, he laid his temple on the sill and stretched out. For a long instant, Marina remained motionless and mute. The satellites of Nyx, as they set, cast an iridescent light on the pale form, lying across the sill, and suddenly the Terran woman heard a heavy step—a crackling of mimosas and ferns that no ceratosaur could have made.

The purple sun of Spica rose over the horizon, and in its diffuse clarity, Marina, inexorably diminished, saw that enormous thing she could never understand: a stone, a figure of jade—worn, covered with green moss—that emerged from the forest and walked toward the dead man.

That bent its knees and lay down beside him, mouth to mouth, motionless forever.

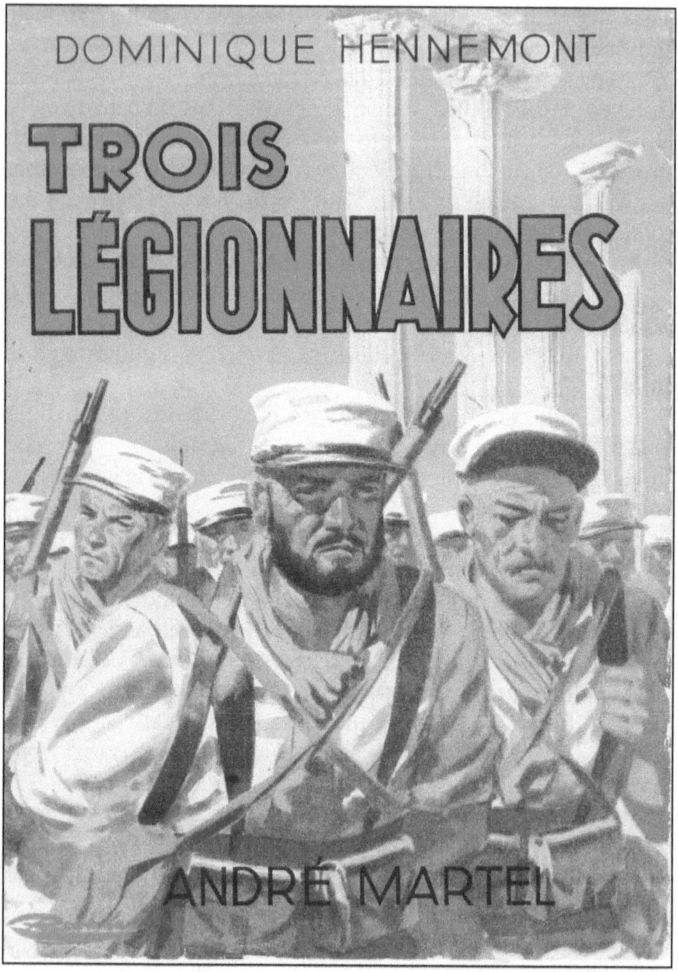
DOMINIQUE HENNEMONT
TROIS LÉGIONNAIRES
ANDRÉ MARTEL

Bibliography

Trois légionnaires [*Three Legionaries*] (under the pseudonym of Dominique Hennemont)
André Martel, 1952.

Le Sabre de l'Islam [*The Sword of Islam*] (under the pseudonym of Dominique Hennemont)
André Martel, 1952.

La Naissance des dieux [*The Birth of the Gods*] (under the name of Charles Henneberg)
Métal, Série 2000 n° 6, 1954.
Winner of the J.-H. Rosny award.

Le chant des astronautes [*The Astronauts' Song*] (under the name of Charles Henneberg)
in Satellite n° 10 et 11, 1958.

An premier, ère spatiale [*Year 1, Space Era*] (under the name of Charles Henneberg)
in Fiction n° 71, 72 et 73, 1959.
Rewritten as Le Mur de la lumière [*The Light Barrier*] (under the name of Nathalie Henneberg)
Albin Michel, Science-fiction n° 2, 1972.

La Rosée du soleil [*The Dew of the Sun*] (under the name of Charles Henneberg)
Hachette/Gallimard, Rayon Fantastique n° 65, 1959.

Les Dieux verts [*The Green Gods*] (under the name of N. Ch. Henneberg)
Hachette/Gallimard, Rayon Fantastique n° 83, 1961.

65

CHARLES HENNEBERG

la rosée du soleil

LE RAYON
FANTASTIQUE

FOREST

La Forteresse perdue [*The Lost Fortress*] (under the name of
N. Ch. Henneberg)
Hachette/Gallimard, Rayon Fantastique n° 94, 1962.

Le Sang des astres [*The Blood of the Stars*] (under the name of
N. Ch. Henneberg)
Hachette/Gallimard, Rayon Fantastique n° 116, 1963.

La Plaie [*The Plague*] (under the name of N. C. Henneberg)
Hachette/Gallimard, Rayon Fantastique n° 122-123, 1963.

L'Opale entydre [*The Entydre Opal*] (short story collection)
(under the name of Nathalie Henneberg)
Christian Bourgois, Coll. Dans l'Epouvante, 1971.

La Quête psychédélique [*The Psychedelic quest*] (under the
name of Nathalie Henneberg)
in Horizon du fantastique n° 36,37 et 38, 1975-76.

Le Dieu foudroyé [*The Thunderstruck God*] (under the name
of Nathalie Henneberg)
Albin Michel, Super-fiction n° 13, 1976.

D'Or et de nuit [*Of Gold and Night*] (short story collection)
(under the name of Charles Henneberg)
Le Masque Fantastique n° 13, 1977.

Démons et chimères [*Demons and Chimeras*] (short story collection) (under the name of Charles & Nathalie Henneberg)
Le Masque SF n° 66, 1977.

Les Anges de la colère [*The Angels of Wrath*] (short story collection) (under the name of Nathalie Ch. Henneberg)
Le Masque SF n° 72, 1978.

LA PLAIE

N. C. Henneberg

le rayon fantastique

Des Ailes dans la nuit et autres nouvelles [*Wings in the Night and Other Stories*] (short story collection) (under the name of Nathalie Henneberg)
Terre de Brume, Terres Fantastiques, 2006.

SF & FANTASY

Guy d'Armen. *Doc Ardan: The City of Gold and Lepers*
G.-J. Arnaud. *The Ice Company*
Aloysius Bertrand. *Gaspard de la Nuit*
Félix Bodin. *The Novel of the Future*
André Caroff. *The Terror of Madame Atomos*
Didier de Chousy. *Ignis*
C. I. Defontenay. *Star (Psi Cassiopeia)*
Charles Derennes. *The People of the Pole*
Harry Dickson. *The Heir of Dracula*
Sâr Dubnotal *vs. Jack the Ripper*
Alexandre Dumas. *The Return of Lord Ruthven*
J.-C. Dunyach. *The Night Orchid. The Thieves of Silence*
Henri Duvernois. *The Man Who Found Himself*
Henri Falk. *The Age of Lead*
Paul Féval. *Anne of the Isles. Knightshade. Revenants. Vampire City. The Vampire Countess. The Wandering Jew's Daughter*
Paul Féval, *fils. Felifax, the Tiger-Man*
Arnould Galopin. *Doctor Omega*
Nathalie Henneberg. *The Green Gods*
V. Hugo, Foucher & Meurice. *The Hunchback of Notre-Dame*
Michel Jeury. *Chronolysis*
O. Joncquel & Theo Varlet. *The Martian Epic*
Jean de La Hire. *Enter the Nyctalope. The Nyctalope on Mars. The Nyctalope vs. Lucifer*
G. Le Faure & H. de Graffigny. *The Extraordinary Adventures of a Russian Scientist Across the Solar System* (2 vols.)
Gustave Le Rouge. *The Vampires of Mars*
Jules Lermina. *Mysteryville. Panic in Paris. To-Ho and the Gold Destroyers*
Jean-Marc & Randy Lofficier. *Edgar Allan Poe on Mars. The Katrina Protocol. Pacifica. Robonocchio. Tales of the Shadowmen* (anthos.; 6 vols.)
Xavier Mauméjean. *The League of Heroes*
John-Antoine Nau. *Enemy Force*

Marie Nizet. *Captain Vampire*
C. Nodier, Beraud & Toussaint-Merle. *Frankenstein*
Henri de Parville. *An Inhabitant of the Planet Mars*
Polidori, C. Nodier, E. Scribe. *Lord Ruthven the Vampire*
P.-A. Ponson du Terrail. *The Vampire and the Devil's Son*
Maurice Renard. *The Blue Peril. Doctor Lerne. The Doctored Man . A Man Among the Microbes. The Master of Light*
Albert Robida. *The Adventures of Saturnin Farandoul. The Clock of the Centuries.*
J.-H. Rosny Aîné. *Helgvor of the Blue River. The Givreuse Enigma. The Mysterious Force. The Navigators of Space. Vamireh. The World of the Variants. The Young Vampire*
Brian Stableford. *The New Faust at the Tragicomique. Frankenstein and the Vampire Countess. The Shadow of Frankenstein. Sherlock Holmes & The Vampires of Eternity. The Stones of Camelot. The Wayward Muse.* (anthologist) *The Germans on Venus. News from the Moon*
Jacques Spitz. *The Eye of Purgatory*
Kurt Steiner. *Ortog*
Villiers de l'Isle-Adam. *The Scaffold. The Vampire Soul*
Philippe Ward. *Artahe*
Philippe Ward & Sylvie Miller. *The Song of Montségur*

MYSTERIES & THRILLERS

M. Allain & P. Souvestre. *The Daughter of Fantômas*
Anicet-Bourgeois, Lucien Dabril. *Rocambole*
A. Bisson & G. Livet. *Nick Carter vs. Fantômas*
V. Darlay & H. de Gorsse. *Lupin vs. Holmes: The Stage Play*
Paul Féval. *Gentlemen of the Night. John Devil. The Black Coats: The Cadet Gang. The Companions of the Treasure. Heart of Steel. The Invisible Weapon. The Parisian Jungle. 'Salem Street*
Emile Gaboriau. *Monsieur Lecoq*
Steve Leadley. *Sherlock Holmes: The Circle of Blood*

Maurice Leblanc. *Arsène Lupin vs. Countess Cagliostro. Lupin vs. Holmes: The Blonde Phantom. The Hollow Needle.*
Gaston Leroux. *Chéri-Bibi. The Phantom of the Opera. Rouletabille & the Mystery of the Yellow Room*
William Patrick Maynard. *The Terror of Fu Manchu*
Frank J. Morlock. *Sherlock Holmes: The Grand Horizontals*
P. de Wattyne & Y. Walter. *Sherlock Holmes vs. Fantômas*
David White. *Fantômas in America*

SCREENPLAYS

Mike Baron. *The Iron Triangle*
Emma Bull & Will Shetterly. *Nightspeeder. War for the Oaks*
Gerry Conway & Roy Thomas. *Doc Dynamo*
Steve Englehart. *Majorca*
James Hudnall. *The Devastator*
Jean-Marc & Randy Lofficier. *Royal Flush*
J.-M. & R. Lofficier & Marc Agapit. *Despair*
Andrew Paquette. *Peripheral Vision*
R. Thomas, J. Hendler & L. Sprague de Camp. *Rivers of Time*

NON-FICTION

Stephen R. Bissette. *Blur 1-5. Green Mountain Cinema 1*
Win Scott Eckert. *Crossovers* (2 vols.)
Jean-Marc & Randy Lofficier. *Shadowmen* (2 vols.)
Randy Lofficier. *Over Here*

HEXAGON COMICS

Franco Frescura & Luciano Bernasconi. *Wampus 1*
Franco Frescura & Giorgio Trevisan. *CLASH*
Luciano Bernasconi, Jean-Marc Lofficier & Juan Roncagliolo Berger. *Phenix 1*

Claude Legrand, Jean-Marc Lofficier & Luciano Bernasconi. *Kabur 1*
Franco Oneta. *Zembla 1*
Lina Buffolente, Jean-Marc Lofficier & Jean-Jacques Dzialowski. *Stangers 1: Homicron*
Danilo Grossi. *Strangers 2: Jaydee*
Claude Legrand & Luciano Bernasconi. *Strangers 3: Starlock*

ART BOOKS

Jean-Pierre Normand. *Science Fiction Illustrations*
Raven Okeefe. *Raven's L'il Critters*
Randy Lofficier & Raven OKeefe. *If Your Possum Go Daylight...*
Daniele Serra. *Illusions*